"I loved reading this book! Just as captivating as the earlier novels in the trilogy, Thrive *completes the story over two decades, providing a rare glimpse into how families, friends, and institutions cope long-term with the traumatic, painful consequences of a dating violence homicide. Reflecting Susan's own journey from surviving to thriving after her niece's death, the scenes are so real you can't make this up!"*

— **Adrienne Doughty, MA, Energy Healer, Reiki Master**

*"*Thrive *is a great read as it explores the varied but, in essence, similar responses each character experiences in the wake of a disastrous loss of someone they knew and loved. While this story is focused on the impact of relationship violence, its overall message is that one can live beyond a tragedy, move past the pain, and find hope, healing, and most of all, forgiveness as thrivers!"*

— **Joal Lentz,** *My Avenging Angel Workshops*™ **participant**

"Reading Susan's book Thrive *has kept me turning the pages, hungry for more of the likable characters she has created who make me feel as if I'm in the story with them. Inspired by true events in a mix of drama, unconditional love, and everyday struggles as well a bit of magic, Susan wraps up her trilogy with a warm, heartfelt message of hope to all who read it—living well is the best revenge!"*

— **Pamela Pestretto, MA, Early Childhood Educator**

What People Are Saying About Susan's Earlier Books In *The Best Revenge Series*™

Awaken

"The life of an abused woman can be seen from many different perspectives. Susan presents a captivating story that leaves you begging to discover what happens next as a variety of events and characters come together creating a sense of home, togetherness and possibility."

—**Dorothy A. Martin-Neville, PhD, Author,** *Dreams Are Only the Beginning* **and** *Your Soul Sings—Your Body Dances*

Emerge

"Emerge is a good read and a great opportunity to learn. With Susan's unique insights into the impact of violence and abuse on women's lives from her personal and professional experience with victims and offenders alike, the characters come alive for the reader. They also learn how stigmatizing trauma can be for its victims."

— Linda McMurray, LCSW, Domestic Violence Counselor

What People are Saying about Susan's Books in *The Thriver Zone Series*™

Entering the Thriver Zone

"This workbook offers faith, courage and dignity to women who have survived the destructive and selfish actions of abusive men. Susan's message is 'Don't settle for anything less than a life that is better than ever.' She knows that women can do it and by the time a woman has worked her way through this excellent guidebook for healing, she will believe it, too."

— Lundy Bancroft, author, *Why Does He Do That?: Inside the Minds of Angry and Controlling Men and Daily Wisdom for Why Does He Do That?*

Staying in the Thriver Zone

"Susan has a gift of giving women who have been battered and beaten new hope and a way forward. This workbook is her best work yet, forging a clear path to a life of power and purpose for women who want to thrive in peace, love, and joy!"

— Alyce LaViolette, MS, MFT, author, *It Could Happen to Anyone: Why Battered Women Stay*

Living in the Thriver Zone

"Since the murder of her niece Maggie, Susan has been an agent of positive change for survivors and offenders alike, strengthening those hurt and converting those who harm. Words can hurt but also transform and Susan's work in the Thriver Zone shows you how."

— Charlene Smith, a South African multi-award-winning journalist, authorized biographer of Nelson Mandela, author of *Proud of Me: Speaking Out Against Sexual Violence and HIV*

Thrive

The Journey of the Human Soul
to Discover a Life of Purpose

Inspired by a True Event

by Susan M. Omilian JD

Butterfly Bliss Productions LLC
West Hartford, CT

Butterfly Bliss Productions LLC
P.O. Box 330482, West Hartford, CT 06133
ButterflyBlissProductions.com
ThriverZone.com
SusanOmilian.com

This is a work of fiction. Names, characters, places, and incidents are the products of the author's imagination or are used fictitiously. Any resemblance to actual events, locales, or persons, living or dead, is entirely coincidental.

ISBN #978-0-9985746-3-9 print book
ISBN #978-0-9985746-5-3 e-book

Author photo by Cynthia Lang Photography
Cover and interior design by Anita Jones, Another Jones Graphics | AnotherJones.com

This book is available at quantity discounts for bulk purchase. Contact the publisher.

A portion of the proceeds of this book will be donated to services for women and children who have experienced abuse and violence.

Names: Omilian, Susan M., author.

Title: Thrive : the journey of the human soul to discover a life of purpose / by Susan M. Omilian JD.

Description: West Hartford, CT : Butterfly Bliss Productions LLC, [2022] | Series: The best revenge series ; [3] | "Inspired by a True Event."

Identifiers: ISBN: 978-0-9985746-3-9 (print book) | 978-0-9985746-5-3 (ebook)

Subjects: LCSH: Abused women--Psychology--Fiction. | Dating violence--Psychological aspects-- Fiction. | Murder--Psychological aspects--Fiction. | Psychic trauma--Fiction. | Self-realization in women--Fiction. | Belonging (Social psychology)--Fiction. | Courage--Fiction. | BISAC: FICTION / Women. | FAMILY & RELATIONSHIPS / Abuse / General.

Classification: LCC: PS3615.M55 T47 2022 | DDC: 813/.6--dc23

Printed in the United States of America

For

Maggie

1980–1999

This is not your story.
But I hope this is the way you
would want this story told.

May the reading of this story be a healing journey
for those who have been
most devastated by your loss.
You were so loved!

Cautious, careful people, always casting about to preserve
their reputation and social standing, never can bring about a reform.
Those who are really in earnest must be willing to be anything or nothing
in the world's estimation, and publicly and privately in season and out,
avow their sympathies with despised and persecuted ideas
and their advocates and bear the consequences.

—Susan B. Anthony
Suffragist and Women's Rights Advocate
1820–1906

ACKNOWLEDGMENTS

Thanks to all those who have helped me tell this story and put it on the page so it can be of benefit to others.

On the publication of this final book in the trilogy of *The Best Revenge Series™*, I hope that these three books together portray for you the journey from victim to survivor to thriver that each of us will undertake in this lifetime. No matter what struggles we encounter in our lives, we do have the resiliency and strength to move beyond them and find a life of power and purpose.

Thanks in particular to "my readers," those who have devoured the books in this series enthusiastically, giving me praise as well as great feedback, including many of their "reader's questions" about the characters and happenings in *Awaken* and *Emerge*, books one and two of the series. Your curiosity has inspired the story here in *Thrive*, book three. I hope I've answered all—or most of—your questions!

Thank you to Claudia Volkman for editing these books, and Anita Jones of Another Jones Graphics for the book covers and interior design. Thanks, too, to my cousin, Pam Rossi of Pam Rossi Voice Overs, who has given "voice" to my novels on audiobooks.

Special thanks to Sharon Castlen of Integrated Book Marketing for getting what I do and helping me get it out into the world.

Most of all, I am grateful to the hundreds of survivors I have met over the last twenty years who have had the courage to become "thrivers" and overcome their past to find that living well is indeed the best revenge. You are my inspiration every day.

Let's keep on thriving!

Susan M. Omilian

Note from the Author

As I noted in *Awaken* and *Emerge*, the first two books in *The Best Revenge Series™*, the inspiration for this story told in a series of three fictional books was a true event. On October 17, 1999, my niece Maggie, a nineteen-year-old college student, was shot and killed on campus by her ex-boyfriend, who then killed himself.

As I wrote in those books, that story came to me by using one of the best tools that a fiction writer has—the "what if" method of finding the story. What if there was a young woman like Maggie who had been killed in a similar manner? What would happen to that person, her friends, and her family members? Would she ever rest in peace? How would they find a way to move forward without her?

With this book, *Thrive: The Journey of the Human Soul to Discover a Life of Purpose*, set twenty years after the death of Lacey, my fictional main character, I continue to explore those intriguing questions as well as others. Can Lacey's friends find a life of power and purpose after such a horrific event? Is that purpose to make the world safer and prevent what happened to Lacey – or is there a broader purpose? Can it be accomplished in twenty years, or will it have to wait for a future generation?

While these are great "what if" questions to speculate about in a fictional story, it is true that because this book is being published in 2022, you, the reader, already know what actually happened in the real world during that twenty-year period from 1999 to 2019. We know, for example, that the #MeToo Movement started in 2017 and spread virally on social media in the United States and around the world. It immediately made the public more aware that incidents of sexual assault, domestic violence, and sexual harassment were still very widespread and prevalent in our society. It also created greater empathy for the victims— mostly female—and a better understanding of the impact of these crimes on them physically, financially, and emotionally.

The impact of violence on women and girls that the fictional *Emerge* story describes in 2009 was eight years before the #Me-Too Movement exploded and terms like "trauma-informed care" and "survivor-centered services" entered the public discourse. In *Thrive,* the fictional characters face challenges still unmet in 2019 such as misogyny, gun violence, and the onset of a world-wide COVID-19 virus pandemic.

It has been my dream since I was a little girl to write novels with amazing characters and powerful plotlines that people will love. I hope this series of books, first *Awaken,* then *Emerge,* and finally *Thrive,* measures up to that dream. True, I didn't wish for something so tragic and sad as the death of my niece Maggie to happen. But good things can come from tragedy. After all, living well is the best revenge!

I will miss Maggie every day of my life, but I celebrate her life each day by living well—living my best life. I hope this book and its story will inspire you to do the same.

Susan M. Omilian

Go confidently in the direction of your dreams.
Live the life you imagined.

—Henry David Thoreau

Life isn't about finding yourself.
Life is about creating yourself.

—George Bernard Shaw

CONTENTS

Living well is the best revenge.
—George Herbert

The meaning of life is to find your gift.
The purpose of life is to give it away.
—Pablo Picasso

There are two powers in the world;
one is the sword
and the other is the pen.

There is a third power stronger than both,
that of women.
—Malala Yousafzai

October 26, 1999

A Shamanic Journey: Dreams from My Mother

With the insistent beat of Radiance's shamanic drumming, Lisette felt herself being lifted above the chaotic rabble of her own life and pulled into a different time and space.

To reach the Upper World, Radiance had told her to go to a high place that was familiar to her, and to her amazement, Lisette found herself in the mountains of Peru. That she went to the ancient city of Machu Picchu didn't surprise her. When she was a little girl, she and her mother had poured over picture books about this place. Lisette knew it well.

But Lisette didn't linger long there. As Radiance had told her to expect, she soon felt herself go up higher above the cloud line now, into a space she'd never seen before until she found herself in a deep, dark forest, green and fresh all around her. The only noise in this peaceful, quiet place was the gentle sound of water gurgling in a bubbling brook that flowed down through the piles of rocks at her feet. At first, she didn't notice a woman sitting on a rock a few feet away. She was dressed in a long, flowing green gown, the hues of which blended into the woods around her. When Lisette finally noticed her, Lisette exclaimed, "Oh my! Who are you?"

"I'm here to greet you," the woman said in a soft, friendly voice.

"But how did you know I was coming?"

"It is as it should be," the woman said, but her words confused Lisette.

"Are you my teacher?" she asked. "I could use some help."

In response, the woman stood, and a flock of birds gathered around her, lifting her up into the air. Lisette watched in amazement. Before she knew it, another flock of birds swarmed around her and lifted her up too. Suddenly Lisette was in the sky, flying over a canyon with such speed that the wind whipped her hair up so it trailed after her like a tail. Then the birds steered her down to the floor of the canyon, where that same woman in green was already waiting for her. The birds gently put her down and flew off in a clatter.

Lisette looked anxiously at the woman. "Where are we now? What is this place?"

"You'll recognize it in a minute," the woman replied as she led Lisette toward something far off in the distance. As they walked toward it, Lisette couldn't believe what she saw.

"That's the trailer I lived in with my mom!" she exclaimed. "What the hell is it doing here?"

Lisette rushed toward it, terrified that it would be just as she had left it – on the day of her sixteenth birthday and Ralph would still be living there with her.

So she turned and asked, "Is this a dream? It feels like a nightmare!"

"It's a waking dream. A chance for you to review your life's lessons."

"Oh, no!" Lisette snapped back. "That's not going to happen! The only thing I learned in that trailer was that I didn't want to be there."

"Then that's an excellent lesson to learn." The woman leaned closer. "Take a look inside. There's something there for you to see."

Lisette was leery about that. Radiance had told her that she hadn't come to the Upper World to find her mother, but if the thing she had to see was in the trailer, she had to go see it.

She walked up to the trailer and stood on her tiptoes so she could peek inside. It was amazing! Everything was painted a bright pink, and huge red-and-white peppermint sticks, her favorite candy, were hanging from the ceiling. Then there were all the toys, dolls, and playthings she had ever wanted. In the middle of it all sat a girl in a bright red dress, much like a dress like Lisette had wanted but her mother couldn't afford to buy her. The girl looked so happy! She had everything Lisette could ever have wanted.

Then the girl looked up at her, smiled, and waved her inside. Lisette felt a shiver run through her.

"Who is this girl?" she asked the woman. "What does she want from me?"

"The girl is you," the woman told her.

"She is not!" Lisette shot back. "My childhood was nothing like that!"

"Even if it weren't, you could still enjoy it now. Why don't you go inside?"

Lisette scowled, but she was curious. She opened the door, and as she stepped inside, the sweet smell of sugar hit her. The girl in the red dress was sitting on a chair in the middle of it all, eating candy from a bag.

She grinned at Lisette and asked, "Do you want some?" She held out the bag. "The red gumdrops are the best!"

Lisette's eyes grew big. She loved red gumdrops—yes, they were her favorites. Eagerly, she put out her hand, and the girl poured some candy into it. Lisette popped a piece in her mouth, and as she chewed it, a wild, wonderful flavor filled her mouth.

"These are amazing!" she exclaimed, tossing the rest in her mouth. Then she put her hand out for more. "I love candy! My mother used to get mad at me when I was a kid! She'd say . . ."

"Be careful, baby," a voice called out from behind her. "You'll get a tummy ache if you eat too much!"

Lisette knew that voice. She whirled around to see her mother.

"It's you! You *are* here!" But her mother looked so different! She was young, happy, and so full of life. Lisette wanted to touch her again. Did she dare try?

As if knowing her fear, her mother took Lisette's hand, pulled her close, and hugged her. Closing her eyes, Lisette let herself feel what it was like to be so close to her mother again. It was wonderful!

"Oh, Mommy, Mommy!" she said, sighing. "I've missed you so much!"

"Yes, my baby!" Her mother said, rocking Lisette in her arms. "I've missed you too. It's been a very long time!" Then her mother released her and held her at arm's length as she beamed. "Look at you! You are all grown up!"

"You look great too, Mom," Lisette gushed.

"I look pretty damn good, don't I? This place agrees with me."

"But what is this place? Where am I, and who is that girl?"

"That's simple. The girl is you."

"But I wasn't that happy, and our trailer wasn't the Candy Land Express!"

Her mother sighed. "It wasn't that bad, my darling, was it? I loved you." She touched Lisette's check softly. "I've always loved you."

"I know." Lisette's voice cracked as emotions welled up inside her. She couldn't blame her mother for everything that went wrong later in her life, but losing her mother when she was only ten years old had been hard. The cancer had spread fast, and her mother didn't have time to put everything right before she died.

"I wanted to come back and have you feel my presence sooner," her mother went on, "but I had to heal first and get stronger."

Lisette didn't know what to say. She was happy that her mother had healed, but in the meantime, she had been stuck living with Ralph. Then, as if her mother had read her mind, she added, "After I died, you went through hell, didn't you?"

"Oh, no, it wasn't so bad," Lisette lied, holding back her tears.

"But you see, Ralph was the only one I could leave you with," her mother said, gently pushing a loose strand of hair from Lisette's face. "Ralph was the only one who would love you because he was the only one who loved me."

Ralph loved someone! Lisette was shocked at the thought.

"I know you don't believe that, but in the end, he was the one who kept you out of jail for trying to kill him, right?"

"But Ralph didn't do that because he loved me," Lisette insisted. "He did it because . . ." Lisette's voice suddenly dropped off, and she was lost in thought. Then suddenly it came to her.

"*You* made him do it," Lisette said excitedly. "It was you, wasn't it? How did you do that? Why did you . . ."

"Don't try to figure it out," her mother said softly. "All you need to know is that I never left you and never will. I've been trying to tell you this for a long time, but you haven't been listening. It's been better, hasn't it, since Lacey has been with you?"

"You know about Lacey?" Lisette interrupted.

"Of course!" Her mother smiled. "I told you—I'm always with you. It's not for you to figure out. It's for you to live your life in the present. To live in the most conscious, purposeful way you can."

Lisette was confused. What was her mother talking about?

"Look, it's simple," her mother went on. "There is a reason you came into this world. There is something you can do that no one else can. You need to figure out what that is. It's your purpose in this lifetime, and then you must go do it."

"I don't know what that is," Lisette said, shrugging her shoulders. "I guess I could learn to read better. That might help and be a start."

Her mother's face broke into a big smile. "I remember how you loved reading all those books about Machu Picchu with me."

Lisette's face brightened. "I miss that. I don't read very much anymore."

"Why not?"

Lisette didn't know what to say. She had come up with reasons before, like she stopped reading because she was mad at her mother for dying and leaving her alone, but now those felt so childish that she couldn't even tell her mother.

"Oh, don't worry," her mother went on. "You're just out of practice. You'll learn it again. You always loved to learn. Just the other day you were reading about Atilla the Hun. That was good. Good for your new business venture."

Lisette stared at her in amazement. "How do you know about that?" Suddenly Lisette was interrupted by the sound of the drums beating softly but insistently.

"It's time to go." The woman in green was standing now at the trailer door, warning her. "The drums are calling you back. Remember, you have to go back when the drums call."

"But I don't want to," Lisette wailed. "I want to stay here. I have so many things to ask my mom. I still need to find out . . ."

"It's okay," her mother said gently. "Listen for me in the wind. I'll be there."

"I don't get it. What wind? Where?" Lisette could feel herself unraveling. She couldn't think of a time since her mother died that she hadn't felt lonely and scared. She needed her mother. How could she leave now? There must be something she could do!

"No, baby," her mother said. "Go now. Trust that you will see me again. Remember, never give up and always believe in yourself.

Can you do that for me?"

"But can't I stay a little longer? I didn't think you'd be here. I didn't believe it was possible."

"Then that's the lesson you've learned. Everything is possible, and you must keep your promise to return."

"Will I see you again?" Lisette asked, but the final call of the drums sounded—four long, hard beats.

"I love you, Mommy," she cried out. "I have to go!"

CHAPTER ONE

October 23, 2009

Finding Home

"All right!" Sophie exclaimed to Lisette. "You're staying! Best news I've had all week."

With that, the two women raised their wine glasses in a celebratory toast and then grinned and giggled like schoolgirls. Before this, the best thing going that afternoon for Sophie was the long, leisurely lunch she was having with Lisette, sitting out on the deck of her favorite restaurant on a warm afternoon in late October. It was the first time she had relaxed since the Tenth Anniversary Celebration Gala last week marking a decade since Lacey's death. That event had had more than its share of unexpected surprises.

For one, Ambrose, a ne'er-do-well homeless man as far as Sophie was concerned, had fallen off a catwalk in the backstage area of a hotel auditorium in the middle of the event. That would have been bad enough, but as he descended on the crowd, he screamed an obscenity and the governor's name, which sent her security team into a frenzy. Once they rushed Governor Jenny Jablonski out of the area, it was the end of a potentially successful fundraising weekend for her organization, SISTER—*Survivor Strong, Thriver Resilient*. Of course, the saving grace of the weekend was that her friend Lisette had a tender meeting with Brad Bufford, a man Lisette never knew was her real dad. She also reconnected with Erick, her on-again, off-again boyfriend whom she hadn't seen in ten years.

Not that Sophie hadn't planned—or maybe she could call it encouraged—Erick and Lisette coming back together from the moment Lisette had agreed to come from Los Angeles, where she was living, to attend the gala. Now, since Lisette had just announced to her at lunch that she was staying in town, Sophie wasn't sure whether that was to be with Erick or to spend some time with her biological dad who'd been absent in her life for almost thirty years. She hoped it was both, and she also hoped that Lisette might even consider helping her with SISTER, the work she did with survivors of abuse in honor and memory of Lacey, Sophie's best friend and college roommate. Whatever it meant, Sophie was just happy.

"I'm so excited you're not going back," she squealed. "I had a feeling about this with the way you and Erick have been canoodling around.""

Lisette gave her a puzzled look. "What's canoodling?" Then she added quickly, "And how is it spelled?"

Before Sophie could respond, Lisette whipped out a notebook, slapped it on the table, and sat there with a pen, poised to write.

Confused, Sophie had to think fast. "I think it's *C-A-N-O-O-D-L-I-N-G*. It means you're hanging out with someone hugging and kissing them. Having lots of "hot sex!"

"Really?" Lisette shot back. "There's a word for that?"

"Yeah, but what's the deal with the notebook? Are you taking notes on me? Only students are allowed to do that in class!"

"It's just something my dad thought would be good for me to do. You know he's helping me to read better. So, he says that if I hear a word I don't know or see it somewhere, I should write it down in my notebook and look it up later. Then when we meet for my lesson, we go over the list, and I practice spelling the words and using them in a sentence."

Sophie was smiling now, inside and out. "So, this is what you and your dad are doing together, huh? Of course, I know him more formally as Brad Bufford, first 'gentleman' of the state and husband of our governor," she said.

"We are not 'canoodling' together, that's for sure," Lisette said with a laugh. "But yeah, it's been great hanging with him. He's so different from Ralph, the fake dad I used to have to deal with. And I love Jenny too—my new stepmom. She's amazing!"

"*Hmmm*. That's the first time I've heard you talk about Ralph since you've been back here. Are you even in touch with him anymore?" Sophie paused for a moment and then screwed up her face and blurted out, "Shouldn't he be dead by now?"

Sophie wasn't trying to be tacky, but she knew Ralph's health wasn't good after having been badly injured in a fire at his bar years ago, a topic Lisette didn't like to talk about or be reminded of for a variety of reasons.

"No," Lisette said calmly. "I haven't seen Ralph since Sandy, my social worker when I was at the Susan B. Anthony Home for Girls, made me go see him to forgive him for all the bad things he did to me as a kid. She said that carrying around all that anger wasn't doing me any good. Now I don't even think about him. I've moved on."

"That's good. But let's get back to Erick."

"Why are you so interested in what's happening between me and Erick?"

"A girl needs to know, right?" Sophie said, giggling. "So, have you two made any plans? You know, like living together, getting engaged, getting married, and having kids?"

"Hey! Slow down. We just reconnected after ten years. We haven't gotten that far yet, if we ever will."

"But you've been talking about it, right? Like some 'pillow talk'?"

Lisette screwed up her face and asked, "What's 'pillow talk?'

How do you . . .?"

". . . spell it?" Sophie finished Lisette's sentence. "Are you going to do this all through lunch? Wow, I'm really going to have to watch my vocabulary."

Without missing a beat, Lisette started to ask, "What's vocab–"

That's when Sophie stopped her. "Look, let's do the spelling bee later, okay? Here's what I need to know. Now that you've decided to stay, what are you going to do about your business back in LA? Can you run it from here?"

Lisette smiled. "Yeah, in between all of our canoodling, the one thing Erick and I have talked about is business. Erick actually likes that crazy idea Ambrose came up with when he was trying to get Brad and me to give him a lot of money and if we did, we'd get to read my mom's diary and find out how we were actually related to each other.

"Yeah, yeah, I know all about how Ambrose tried to hustle you both," Sophie said, jumping in before Lisette launched into the whole convoluted story of what went on before, during, and after the Tenth Anniversary Gala. "But what was his idea?"

"Oh, he thought I could start a business offering pole dancing lessons to women for exercise. Strippers have done pole dancing for years, and women, young and old, could use it as exercise to get themselves stronger and keep going longer. Pole dancing studios are popping up all over, and Erick thinks it would be a good move for me. It could get me away from strip clubs and into the fitness business that he's in."

"That's right! Erick has a gym that he owns. God, I could use some exercise, something to make me strong and increase my stamina."

As Sophie spoke that last word, she watched Lisette's face twitch as she struggled to write something down in her notebook.

"Yes, the word is *stamina*," Sophie continued. "It's spelled

S-T-A-M-I-N-A. It's like when you run a long marathon without tiring. You can do that in your mind too—build your resiliency so you can face a lot of hard things in your life and still bounce back." Then Sophie winced. "Sorry, I keep dumping all these new, big words on you!"

"No, no, it's okay. I liked what you said about bouncing back from stuff. I've done that a lot in my lifetime, right?"

"Yes. You are very resilient. But I want to know what you think of Ambrose's-now-Erick's idea. Is that something you want to do—help Erick build out his gym with a pole dancing studio? Is that enough for you to really sink your teeth into? I mean, is it your passion and purpose in life? That's what you need to figure out here!"

Wow! Sophie could tell that the last part of what she just said got Lisette's attention because she jumped right back into the conversation, talking really fast.

"My mom talked about finding my purpose in life when I did that shamanic journey with Radiance right after Lacey died. Mom said to live in the present, not the past, and then find something good to do with my life."

Lisette leaned forward now closer to Sophie, her voice filled with wonder as she continued. "Mom made it sound so great, too. She said, 'Honey, there is something you can do that no one else can. You need to figure out what that is and go do it.' Is that what you mean, Sophie?"

"Yeah, exactly. So, what is your purpose in life, do you think?"

"I don't know. At that moment with my mom, all I could think of was to learn to read better." Lisette scrunched up her face as if that idea wasn't so great after all.

"That's not a bad idea," Sophie assured her. "You might even write a book one day about finding your passion and the journey your mom was talking about. You could do that, right?"

"Write a book? *Me?* I can't even read that good, let alone write a book! That can't be my purpose! There has to be something else. I have done some good stuff in my life so far. When I went back to LA after Lacey's death, I started that business, giving my stage name 'Attila the Hunny' to a chain of high-class strip clubs for men. It has been good for me because they paid me to use my name, and I make sure the girls are treated better in those clubs than I ever was as a stripper. I also donate a lot of my profits in the business to support your work, Sophie. But I'm not sure that's good enough."

"Yeah, that was a good thing. SISTER was able to grow by leaps and bounds because of it, but just giving away money doesn't feel like your passion in life. Not the way your mom meant it. What did she say? 'Something you can do that no one else can'? In my workshops, I call it 'manifesting a life of power and purpose.'"

Lisette sighed. "Yeah, those workshops and SISTER are your purpose in life, aren't they? You figured it out! Why can't I? I'm amazed at all you have accomplished so far. You got SISTER set up, raised enough money so you could work part-time at SISTER and teach at the college too. And before that, you got a law degree. I didn't even get through high school! How did you come up with all of this?"

"Starting SISTER was simple," Sophie said with a wicked grin. "You remember how angry I was about what Ari did to Lacey. I had to turn that anger into something positive or it was going to kill me. Since Lacey didn't have a chance to survive and move forward with her life, I wanted to help other women who could. With my workshops, I've taken all that energy and turned it into a passion to help others take the journey from victim to survivor—and then to thriver."

Lisette giggled. "I've never heard of that word *thriver* before. Where did you get it?"

"I don't know. Like so much of this, it just came to me, like I was guided to it. But when the women come to the workshop and they hear the word *thriver*, they love it. They want to be that, and not quit until they get there!"

Lisette laughed. "That sounds like me and my dad when he's helping me with my reading and writing. He's totally into it. He says I'm not 'illiterate'—that's the word he used—but a 'functionally illiterate' person. That means I've been taught to read and write, but I'm not reading or writing at my best. I always thought I stopped trying to read when my mom died. Before that we'd always read stuff together, and she was teaching me what we called 'big words' every day. But I haven't been the same since she died. Brad thinks he can get me going at my reading and writing again, though." Lisette giggled again. "Men! They think they can do anything even if they can't!"

"But that's good for you," Sophie reassured her. "It's time you had a dad looking out for you, and he seems to love it. He needs something to focus on now that his shopping mall design business has gone south after the shooting last week at the Westingham Mall, his current project. And the shooter was none other than Ambrose's son, Mark. Can you believe that? Ambrose scared us all with his hair-brained stunt at the gala—and just days later, his son shot and killed ten people at that mall."

"I know. Ambrose really is a mess, isn't he? But I feel sorry for them both," Lisette said quietly. "Ambrose really does love his son and is worried about him. He even called me to see if I'd go with him to the jail to talk to his son."

"You're not going to do that, right?" Sophie jumped in. "Everyone knows Brad is your father and Jenny, your stepmother, is the governor. If word gets out that you visited . . ."

"Don't worry, Sophie," Lisette interrupted. "I won't do anything stupid. But it's good that Ambrose is thinking about his son and trying to help him out of this mess."

"It was one of their own making though," Sophie replied. "Just remember, having that father and son duo be your life's purpose is definitely not what your mother had in mind!"

"I know, I know. But between me and Ambrose wasn't all bad stuff. Sure, he did do some pretty mean things to me, like take my mother's diary and not tell me that Brad was my real dad. And yes, it all got played out in public, but it turned out okay, right? I found Brad, and Erick and I got back together, so it's all good."

"I'll say it has," Sophie said, her eyes glistening with envy. "Good for you and Erick too. He is such a great guy."

"Yeah, he is," Lisette said softly. Just then, someone came up behind Lisette, reached around, and planted a big kiss on her cheek.

"Are you talking about me, Sophie? Am I that great guy?" a man's voice said as he pulled out the chair next to Lisette, sat down, and gave her shoulders a squeeze.

"Erick!" Lisette exclaimed. "What are you doing here?"

Then another man's voice chimed in. "What are we both doing here, right, Erick?"

Lisette looked up and saw Brad quickly grab another chair from a nearby table and sit down next to her on the other side.

"Dad! I thought you had a business meeting. Are you two goofing off?"

"No," Brad replied. "Remember, the other day Jenny said she wanted to see Erick's gym? I took her over there this morning, and we tried out every piece of exercise equipment in the place, didn't we, Erick? It was great! Then she had to go back to work, governing and crazy stuff like that. So Erick and I thought we'd go find out where the prettiest girl in town was lunching today."

"Flattery will get you everywhere," Lisette said with a grin, but then she gave Sophie a look. "So you told them where we were going to lunch?"

Sophie smiled wickedly, trying to look unshaken even though she had been unmasked here. "I told Erick that maybe he'd swing by toward the end of lunch and make sure I had convinced you to come to my workshop. I know you'd love it. You've given so much to the SISTER organization. I want you to see the work we're doing."

"And have you been convinced, honey?" Erick said, jumping in. "I agree. You'd love it."

"Geeze," Lisette said wearily. "So that's what this whole gathering is all about?"

"Of course not!" Sophie insisted. "We did talk about deep things, like finding your purpose in life. So maybe something in the workshop might help you with that . . . that . . . what did you call it—'something I can do that, right now, no one else can.'"

Lisette sighed and looked at Erick. "And what were you planning to do to convince me, hon?" She used that last endearing word with a little less endearment.

"I'm part of the SISTER team now, heading up its Male Initiative, and I agree with Sophie. Go to the workshop and see what it's all about. Your money supports it. We support you. It can't be as bad as you told me last night."

"What's bad about it?" Sophie asked quickly. "If there is a reason why you can't attend, I know we can work it out."

"Well," Lisette said hesitantly, and then looked at Erick. "I've heard you have the women in the workshops do a lot of writing and then they read what they wrote in the group. I just don't feel good about doing that right now. I'm working with Dad on my reading and writing, but I don't think I'll be ready that soon."

Brad looked at Sophie and asked, "When is your next workshop? How much time do we have?"

"It's next month on the two Saturdays in November before Thanksgiving."

"A couple of weeks? No problem!" Brad sputtered. "This is great, Lisette. It'll give you something to work toward. Look how much you've picked up already."

"Right!" Sophie jumped in again, "and some of my students will be there to help make it feel comfortable for you. They'd love to meet you. You are their role model as a woman in business. They want to be like you when they get out of college."

"Oh no," Lisette protested. "I'm far from a role model. Dad and I were just talking about that the other day. I consider all of you my role models! You're all doing great things and have a purpose in life. I hardly know what I'm doing."

"You know a lot," Erick jumped in. "And you'll get where you want to go, honey. Maybe with Sophie's workshop you'll get there sooner. You can try!"

As Lisette looked at the smiling, happy faces around the table, she had to admit she was lucky to have all of them cheering her on.

"All right!" she said, giving in. "Sign me up for the workshop, Sophie. But I don't want to stand out. I want to be like all the other women there. No big deal, okay?"

"You've got it," Sophie said with a grin.

Brad and Erick nodded their approval, and as Lisette looked around the table, she felt happy. Maybe she could really belong here.

But before things got too mushy, Brad shouted, "Who's for dessert?"

He raised his hand to signal a waiter and then said in a low whisper to those around the table, "Quick! Let's get dessert before my security team gets antsy and wants me back at the governor's mansion. They've been on edge ever since Ambrose played that stunt at the gala and everyone decided it was a threat on Jenny's life. It didn't go unnoticed that Ambrose's son was the shooter at the shopping mall where I had my largest business contract."

Sophie sighed. "Maybe it was better, Erick, that I couldn't convince Howie, Lacey's dad, to come mark the tenth anniversary with us at the gala. All that commotion Ambrose caused that night would have freaked him out for sure."

Then she paused for a moment and spoke as if just to herself. "It would have completed the circle, though—all the most important people in Lacey's life being there." Then she added with a sigh, "Except for one."

"You mean Jack, right?" Lisette asked. "Jack is the guy Lacey was dancing with at the Keg the night that got Ari all riled up, wasn't he?"

"Yes," Sophie whispered and then went on, holding Lisette's eyes. "Not sure where he is. Maybe it's best we leave him alone, dealing with what he's dealing with. I'm sure he'll let us know if he needs something."

Then with a sigh, she added, "I guess Lacey will see to that."

By the time Lisette met on Monday for her lesson with Brad after her Friday lunch with Sophie, he had already come up with what he told her was a "speed reading" lesson to get her ready for the first day of Sophie's workshop next month.

"Geez, Dad!" Lisette exclaimed, when he showed her all the reading charts and writing exercises he had ready for her. "You are really good at this. You could be a full-time literacy volunteer!"

Erick was really supportive of Lisette, too. They had picked up their relationship just where it had left off ten years ago when she had walked out on him in a huff. For years, Lisette had regretted how she had so brutally broken up with Erick back then and maybe missed the chance to be happy with him for the last ten years. But as they had discussed one night in their "after-sex" time, maybe it was good that they both had time to sort out who and what they were before they really became a couple. They needed time to miss and appreciate each other more for when they did get back together.

For one thing, she found Erick's way of living very easy for her to fall into. He was calm and cool, and he got what Sophie was doing with her workshops. And he totally supported Lisette finding what she was destined to do.

"We should all find a purpose in our lives," he said to her. "And look at all you've accomplished so far. You got through a lot of hard stuff and are still standing!"

The more Lisette thought about this, the more she wondered if her journey to find purpose in her life had started long before she encountered Lacey's spirit or met Sophie, Eric, or Brad. Maybe it started with what had happened to her earlier. A victim of abuse and neglect by Ralph, Lisette knew how much she was robbed of in her childhood. Her mom was the best ever, but she died of cancer when Lisette was only ten years old. After that she was "raised" (if you want to call it that) by Ralph, the man she thought was her real father for a long, long time.

Lisette could see that while she survived all that happened to her as a kid and even what she did to Ralph on the day of her sixteen birthday, what really put her life into a tailspin was coming to this town to dance at the Bare Bottom strip club near the college campus where Lacey was shot and killed by Ari on October 17, 1999. Having Lacey's spirit—caught between the two worlds after such a sudden, violent death—come into her body that night while she was being mobbed on stage by the college kids in the audience was what led her to all that was unfolding right now, ten years later.

it was Erick, the club's bouncer who got her safely off stage that night, but when she was confronted near her dressing room by a guy with a knife, it was there she first felt Lacey's spirit inside her, guiding her to safety. Then she met Sophie, Lacey's best friend, who led her to Radiance, the shaman, who got Lacey's spirit to leave her body and cross over into paradise where Lacey's mother, Marg, was waiting for her. Lisette knew that all this would sound crazy to some people in her life, but she believed it all and cared about these people—Erick, Sophie, and Radiance— who seemed to care about her. Now, after meeting Brad, her real dad at last week's gala that honored Lacey and her legacy, Lisette had all the more reason to stay.

It was an opportunity to grow, expand, and meet new people, and today she was taking on one of the most important projects in her life: learning to read and write better with a great literacy coach, her dad. He was helping her to get ready to take Sophie's workshop, but Lisette knew it was about more than taking the workshop. After talking with Sophie the other day, she wanted to be like Sophie . . . so smart, so daring. She loved how Sophie had come up with the whole idea of her nonprofit SISTER organization to sponsor and support *My Avenging Angel Workshops*™ based on the idea that 'living well is the best revenge." Since Ari killed Lacey and then himself, there was no way for those who loved Lacey to avenge Lacey's murder by getting him arrested and sent to jail for what he did. Instead, Sophie thought living well would be the best revenge and believed that something good would come out of what was horrifying and senseless.

Lisette wanted to be a part of what Sophie was doing, and she also wanted to be with Erick and work with him. He was smart like Sophie, and over the last ten years, he had successfully built a solid business with his gym. Now Lisette and Erick were talking about adding pole dancing classes and bringing in the right equipment and enough space so everyone stayed safe. Some nights they'd lie in bed during their "after-sex" time and talk about the people they admired and how they inspired them to do the things they both wanted to accomplish.

It was all part of what Lisette and her dad had talked about one afternoon in her literacy coaching session. Brad spelled out the two words to add to her list.

"R-O-L-E M-O-D-E-L-S. You know what I mean, right?" he said. "A role model is someone whom you look up to and admire, someone you want to be like. They inspire you to be more than you are and by their example, you get to be better than you thought you could be. They are the heroes you look up to in your darkest moments."

"Okay, then if that's true," Lisette said with a sparkle in her eyes, "you are my role model, Dad. I admire how you took me in as your daughter without question and are here for me in every way possible. Jenny too—she is amazing. I never met a woman like her before, at least not so up close. Even though she has all that power, she is a nice, good person."

What Lisette didn't say that day to Brad was how few role models she had for how good men act. Erick definitely was one of the good guys, and so was Brad. She loved how Brad and Jenny supported each other and were a team. She wondered if she and Erick could be such a team, too, making a life for themselves and maybe have children. What was she thinking? She never even wanted kids, not even a dog. Was she getting ahead of herself?

But she could see the possibility of a life with Erick and being able to help Sophie with her work, so attending the workshop was the place for her to start. She had to be brave. Otherwise she'd never find out if what the women said about the workshops was really true. Their comments were posted on the *SISTER* website.

"Attending Sophie's workshop made a huge shift in my mindset. Sophie reminded me that I am unique, valuable, and worthy. She gave me confidence to move beyond surviving, instilling in me the hope of an abundant and successful future as a thriver! I know that my best life is yet to come." —Gracie

"Sophie's workshops provide a safe environment where you can share feelings and feel supported. Your heart opens to possibilities and hope for the future." —Serena

"Sophie has helped me to learn how to search within myself to determine what I want out of life and how to set goals that enable me to take the steps necessary to reach them without feeling overwhelmed and too frightened to do anything." —Adele

"This workshop has totally changed my life. Sophie has started me on a journey to find the person I most want to be, and with the exercises she has presented, she is visually showing me how to get there." —Sherilee

Maybe going to the workshop could help Lisette figure out her next steps here and find what her mother had guided her to do years ago: find her purpose in life.

Her dad was by far the wisest about all this, Lisette decided. He said to be brave, be bold, and "if you can be as fierce and fearless as Attila the Hunny on the stage, you can do anything."

And he had other words of wisdom for her. "Don't worry what other people think about your reading and writing. You are making progress here," he said to her the last time they met before the first workshop session. "Most of them don't realize what you are going through to learn this now. They probably got it all handed to them at a very young age and don't appreciate it. But you do. You know the value and you will get there. Take it slow, and you'll get there, okay?"

Beside his guidance as her literacy coach, what she appreciated most about Brad was that he gave her a feeling that she was already a thriver. She had a father who was there to love and take care of her, no matter what she needed. He gave her confidence and believed that she could do anything she tried. That's how her mother, Marie, was too—always positive, always moving forward.

Lisette wondered, *What if Brad and Marie had stayed together? What if they had raised Lisette together? How would that have changed her life? Would her mother still be alive today? Would Lisette have ever met Sophie or Erick or known about Lacey?* But she couldn't change any of that now.

Thriving—that's what she wanted to do! Lisette never knew there was a word for it, but now she knew that thriving was more than surviving and that's what she wanted to do. There was one more thing Sophie had told her about the workshop that intrigued her. She told Lisette that she was the hero of her own story! *Imagine that,* Lisette thought. *So everyone else is the hero of their own story too. What if there was some way to write down these stories and inspire others to take the journey too?*

That sounded like a book idea to Lisette, and she wondered if that was what her mom meant when she said there was something Lisette could do that no one else could.

True, she wanted to find her purpose in life. Lately she'd been thinking it was to help women find true happiness in their lives. Would writing a book help her do that? It could be a start.

Wouldn't that be great?

CHAPTER TWO

November, 2009

Hanging with the Angels

Lisette didn't know what to expect when she entered the room where one of Sophie's *My Avenging Angel Workshops*™ was being held. While Sophie was so excited about her coming today, Lisette was more worried about how she would do in a room full of women all who could read and write so much better than she could.

As confident as Lisette was about coming to a workshop at her last session with her dad, she was a wreck today, thinking about all the ways she could mess this up.

"You'll be okay," Sophie assured Lisette this morning on the phone when she called Sophie in a panic and tried to beg off attending the workshop. "Just come, and you'll have a good time. No pressure, no problem. I know you can do this. Look at all you have done before this. Is this the hardest thing you've ever done in your lifetime?"

Sophie's question surprised Lisette. When she put it that way, no, this workshop was nothing. Maybe she'd embarrass herself a little because her reading and writing wasn't up to speed, but yes, she was going to be fine.

Still, Lisette wasn't totally buying it. She wasn't the type for this kind of touchy-feely stuff. But she figured the worst thing that could happen was that she would leave early and embarrass herself in front of everyone, and the best thing was that she could leave whenever she wanted to. Sophie would understand.

Lisette arrived at the workshop a little after the appointed time and was surprised how cheerful things were when she walked into the room. She had hoped that everyone would be there before her so she could melt into the crowd, but it didn't happen that way. Instead, she was the first one in the room except for a young woman busily removing things from boxes and bags and putting them on the tables set up in the room. The woman looked up, smiled, and walked over to Lisette.

"Hi, I'm Brooke," she said, extending her hand. "Nice to meet you."

"Oh, nice to meet you, too," Lisette muttered as she shook her hand. "I'm Lisette. I'm here for the . . . the . . ."

"Yes, the workshop!" Brooke said enthusiastically. "I'm helping Sophie out. She'll be here soon. So glad you could make it today." She pointed at one of the tables with a stack of notebooks and folders.

"Sign in here and take a notebook and a folder," she went on, as she picked up one of the folders from the pile and opened it. "On the right side of the folder is a survey," she explained. "If you could fill it out first, that would be great."

She paused and then added, "And let me know if I can help you in any way, please!"

Lisette nodded and then looked at the pink sheet, terrified at all the words, but before she could panic, she took the folder from Brooke and picked up a plain-covered notebook off the table. She signed her name on the attendance sheet, and then Brooke said, "Take a seat anywhere around the table. We're expecting twelve women total. We'll see who else shows up."

But before Lisette could take a seat, Brooke grabbed her by the arm and pulled her closer. Almost as though she wasn't supposed to be having this conversation, she whispered, "It is such an honor to meet you, Lisette. Professor Stratford, you know her as Sophie, has told us all about you. You are an angel investor in our *Survivor Strong, Thriver Resilient* organization, right? I've heard about how when you got rich, you donated a lot of money to SISTER. That's so amazing! I want to do that when I get rich or get married or something like that someday too."

Lisette gave her a weak smile. "Well, thanks! I'm glad the money has gone to a good cause. You said 'Professor Stratford'— are you one of her students at the college?"

"Yeah, I'm taking a women's studies class with her. It's called 'Women and the Law,' and I love it. I'm learning so much about women's history that I never knew before. And I'm an intern at SISTER, too, so I can help with her workshops."

Just then all of Brooke's attention and unbounded enthusiasm moved in the direction of several women who had just entered the workshop room, and she took off in their direction. Lisette took it as her cue to take her seat and fill out the survey.

She couldn't help but wonder if the women who had arrived were also agonizing about coming to the workshop. Things in their lives had probably been pretty depressing, sad, and terrible, just like hers had been in the past. They were probably thinking, as she still was, *How can one workshop really help a woman who had been abused or assaulted?* It had taken Lisette years to get through all the trauma and drama in her life, so she didn't believe it yet either. But she was here, and she could at least fill out the survey and see what happened next. What did they all have to lose? The workshop wasn't costing them anything and they were all free to leave anytime they wanted. But for many of these women, Lisette thought it may be that nothing, really nothing, that was going on here or anywhere else could make them feel better. She remembered all too well when her life, too, was a mess and she was miserable.

Lisette took a seat at one of the tables set up in a U-shape in the middle of the room—a seat where she felt she could make a quick escape if she got too embarrassed or overwhelmed. As she settled in, she could hear Sophie's familiar voice at the back of the room greeting other women who were entering and instructing them to fill out the survey first. So Lisette opened her folder and began filling out the survey sheet. While it took time for her to read all the statements there, so many of them fit her thoughts exactly.

I'm too busy for quiet time to think about where I'm going.

There is no way I can create the life I want right now.

I'll never figure out who I am or what I want to be when I grow up.

Abuse has always been a part of my life. I can't do much about it.

I don't take any big risks. Life is too scary.

There are some voices inside my head that are very critical of me, and I'll never get them to quiet down.

Sometimes I feel there's a happy person inside of me who wants to get out.

She picked out the ones she had felt strongest about at different points in her life, but many were still part of her thinking today. The last one, about the Happy Person Inside, intrigued Lisette. Was that true? Was there a part of her that was always happy despite all the challenges and trials she had gone through? Lacey's murder, even though it happened years ago, still haunted her thoughts and actions most days, and yet this idea of the Happy Person Inside stirred her.

Happy? Always Happy? No, she thought. That's not possible. But what Sophie promised with this workshop was that "living well is the best revenge," and Lisette knew she wanted some of that. She had come to this workshop hoping that promise was real and this woman, her friend Sophie, could deliver it.

So, yes, Lisette was ready to wait for that!

"What's your favorite fairy tale or children's story?"

This question from Sophie to the group as the session began got Lisette's attention. An answer immediately jumped into her head.

"Cinderella!" she shouted out enthusiastically, with a lot of more energy and excitement than she had imagined she'd have. But then, no one had ever asked her that question before, and suddenly she was having even more fun than she thought she might. The fun started when, after completing the survey in the folder, everyone was invited to decorate the cover of a notebook they were given for the workshop.

"You can't do this wrong," Sophie began, and Lisette immediately heard the negative voice in her head go off: *Of course, you'll screw this up. You always do.*

But Sophie's positive energy was infectious, so Lisette decided to go for it. She decorated the cover of her notebook with the scraps of bright papers, pictures from old calendars and greeting cards, stickers, glitter glue, and other items Sophie and Brooke had placed on the tables. Lisette also colored in a black-and-white computer sketch of an angel given to her for the cover. It was not particularly a religious-looking angel, but it had a happy, smiling face that Lisette felt spoke to her. So she colored it brightly with crayons and markers and glued it on the front cover along with the other decorations.

Feeling very successful and creative, Lisette's mood lifted, and she was open to writing about her favorite story. She listened intently as Sophie explained about the exercise.

"Everyone has a story from their childhood, and they are all different," Sophie said. Then she read aloud from the list she had written on the white board in the front of the room. "Here are some I regularly get from women in my workshops: Cinderella, The Wizard of Oz, Sleeping Beauty, The Little Engine That Could, The Little Mermaid, Mulan and so many more."

These are the stories that grabbed you as a kid," Sophie continued. "Now I want you to write about why." She went to the board and wrote on it two half-sentences: "I love this story because . . ." and "Lessons I have learned from it are . . ."

Then she explained. "These are writing prompts. Fill in the sentence and go from there. Whatever you are supposed to write about, you will. You can't do this wrong!"

Lisette knew immediately what she wanted to say. She opened up her notebook and wrote:

> *I love the story of Cinderella because . . . it makes me feel that no matter what, I can survive. Cinderella lost her mother, like me, and her father marries the wicked, cruel stepmother. Then her father dies, and she becomes a servant. One day a fairy godmother shows up and changes Cinderella's rags into a beautiful gown. She goes to the ball and finds her Prince there. They live happily ever after.*
>
> *The lesson that I learned is never give up. Magic can happen.*

Lisette couldn't believe what she wrote. Sophie was right. Somehow, she had that story inside her since she was a little girl and hadn't realized it. Suddenly, Lisette wanted to share with everyone what she wrote and was the first to raise her hand when Sophie asked who in the group wanted to read aloud their piece.

When Lisette finished reading, Sophie smiled broadly at her and then exclaimed to the whole group, "See I told you! These stories from our childhood have real meaning for us today. We actually do end up living these childhood favorites as adults."

"All these stories have real meaning for us," Sophie said after Lisette read aloud what she had written to the group at Sophie's urging and shared how her writing surprised her. "And we do actually end up living these childhood favorites as adults," Sophie added.

Lisette snickered out loud. "I'm sorry," she said quickly, still laughing. "But I don't see myself living in a fairy tale. People don't have happy endings, and if they do, they don't last very long!"

"Maybe not," Sophie countered. "But you do believe in the happy ending, right? We all do!"

The other women the room looked at Sophie, as glassy-eyed as Lisette.

"We do!" Sophie said emphatically. "Let me put it to you this way. The story of Cinderella has three parts to it, right? First, Cinderella had some challenges, some struggles in her life, right?"

Sophie wrote the word *STRUGGLE* on the board and then added words under it as she spoke. "Her mother died," she said, as she wrote *DEATH* on the board. "Then her father remarries the cruel and wicked stepmother." Sophie then wrote *CRUEL* and *WICKED* on the board, adding, "Then her father dies, and she becomes a servant and is abused." Sophie added *ABUSE* to the board.

Sophie continued, "We all have struggles in our life, right? That is the first part of our journey, like Cinderella's."

Next, she wrote the word *TRANSFORMATION* on the board as a second list to the right of the first, and below it she wrote *MAGIC*.

"Like Cinderella," she continued, "we all have that moment of transformation when a magical thought comes into our head that we can leave a bad relationship or get a better job. We get there because we realize that we don't want to give up, or we awaken like Sleeping Beauty and realized that we don't have to keep struggling anymore. We become empowered and ready to move forward." As she talked, Sophie added *AWAKEN* and *EM-POWERMENT* to the list.

"Finally," she went on, "we believe in the happy ending." She wrote those two words, *HAPPY ENDING*, on the board to form a third column. "In our Happy Ending, we are happy and free; we feel joy, abundance, and complete, just like Cinderella did when she found her Prince Charming." Sophie wrote *HAPPY, FREE, JOY, ABUNDANCE*, and *COMPLETE* on the board.

"Most of all we experience love—unconditional love—and feel connected to our family, friends, children, and loved ones." Sophie added *LOVE* and *CONNECTION* to the list.

"But I don't think Cinderella got all those things in her happy ending just by marrying Prince Charming. I believe that she completed herself first and then attracted a complete person into her life—and that was her happy ending."

Lisette looked at the whiteboard in front of her as though she were in a trance. Isn't that how it happened with her relationship with Erick? Erick was the most "complete" person she had ever met. He was kind, generous, thoughtful, and smart. Did she really attract him to herself? Could it be that simple—from struggle to transformation to happy ending? But how?

As if Sophie heard those questions inside Lisette's head, the next thing she said to the group was "What we are talking about here is a 'journey.' It is the journey that all of us go through in our lives. It begins with feeling like and being a victim." Sophie wrote *VICTIM* in the column above *STRUGGLE* on the board. Then she asked the group, "How does it feel to be a victim?" As the women responded to that question, Sophie added their words like *ANGRY, SAD, DEPRESSED, HOPELESS*, and *POWER-LESS.* on the board under *VICTIM*.

"I felt that way, too," Sophie said with emotion in her voice, "when my best friend in college, Lacey, was killed during her sophomore year by her ex-boyfriend, another student, who then took his own life. Lacey was only nineteen years old and didn't know she was being abused. She missed all the warning signs of verbal and emotional abuse; her boyfriend never touched or threatened her physically, so she didn't think she was in danger. But when he killed her and then killed himself in his dorm room, I became a secondary victim of a crime and began my own journey."

Lisette was stunned and loved the way Sophie told her story about Lacey. It was about a journey beyond the struggle of losing Lacey that Sophie had described so well earlier through Lisette's Cinderella story and it made sense. Something so awful had brought Sophie to do these workshops but because of it she found her purpose in life to help others.

"I'm so sorry to hear about your friend, Lacey," one of the women in the workshop said to Sophie. "That must have been hard."

"Yes," Sophie said quietly. "It's been ten years since it happened, and it still feels like yesterday." Then she cleared her throat and said more forcefully, "So I had a choice after Lacey's death. Was I going to stay a victim my whole life? Was I going to be able to move beyond this terrible thing that happened when I was nineteen years old or get stuck there in my anger? I know that Lacey wouldn't have wanted that for me. At the moment of her death, she realized that she was a victim, but she didn't have the chance to survive. I wanted to be a survivor for Lacey and for myself." Sophie stopped and put the word SURVIVOR above the column marked TRANSFORMATION.

"But that's only part of the journey. There's more," Sophie said, as she added the word *THRIVER* at the top of the column marked *HAPPY ENDING*.

"I believe," she continued, "that there is a journey from victim to survivor to thriver, and we are all on this journey. It's our choice where we take our journey, but I think thriving is the best place to be. It's where the Happy Person Inside lives, and I want to be there with her. And the way I honor my friend Lacey is that I want to help women, including all of you, to thrive, not just survive as Lacey could not."

Lisette stared at the board, at the simple listing of the columns marked *VICTIM* to *SURVIVOR* to *THRIVER*, and suddenly it all made sense to her. Yes, abuse had always been a part of her life. Ralph's behavior toward her was just one part of it, but for years and years, even after all that was over, she was still stuck in victim mode. No wonder she felt so lost about where her life was going. She was going back and forth between victim and survivor, wasting her energy when she could have moved on to thriving. There, she'd have a much better chance of finding that thing that only she could do – the purpose of her life. She deserved a great life, and she could get it as a thriver.

Lisette listened intently as Sophie continued talking to all the women in the room. She had never heard Sophie explain it so clearly before.

"We can't get back at the people that have abused us, and I can't get back at the man who killed Lacey. But that's not my revenge. Remember that living well is our best revenge. It's the one thing that those who have abused us most want us NOT to have. They don't want to see us do well, particularly not without them. They don't want us to believe in ourselves, to believe in our goodness, because if we do, then they will pale in comparison to us, and they don't want to work that hard."

Then Sophie laughed. "Think of it. We are born with wings. Why crawl through life? We are thrivers, not just survivors! So for the rest of today and next week's session, too, we are going to soar and explore what thriving after abuse means to us."

Wow! Lisette thought. *Wow!*

On the second day of the workshop, one week later on a Satur-day, Sophie introduced the idea of "manifesting" a life of power and purpose, and Lisette was ready for it.

She and Sophie had talked about finding a life of power and purpose at their lunch a few weeks ago when Lisette told Sophie she was staying in town after the Tenth Anniversary Celebration Gala. But Sophie had never used the word *manifesting* then, and Lisette was fascinated. Another word to add to her notebook.

She had been working all last week on getting her positive en-ergy going, an assignment Sophie had given them for the week in between the two sessions. They were to do something that week that made them happy and write about how it made them feel before, during and after they did it.

From there, Sophie introduced them to the *Journey to the Real YOU!™* She talked about starting with positive energy and a focused desire, then pushing through their fears and limiting beliefs about themselves, to find the Real You, a part of them untouched by all that had ever happened to them.

By the end of the session, everyone had a goal—something they wanted to work on using the "road map" of the Journey to the Real You™ that Sophie had outlined for them in the work-shop session. Some of the women said it was the same goal they had been working on for a while, like getting a new, better job. They needed one now that they had left an abusive relation-ship and were single parents. But other women came up with different ideas of what they wanted to do in their lives, things they said the past abuse had kept them from dreaming about, let alone doing. Several women said they wanted to go back to school and start a business. One wanted to start painting again, and several wanted to write their stories.

That last idea frightened yet excited Lisette. Someone—So-phie or Erick or Brad—had suggest that she, too, should write her story. But that meant she'd have to put her thoughts down in words, and she didn't know how to spell a lot of words good enough yet. Sure, she had been filling up that notebook Brad gave her for her reading lessons with lots of great words, but she'd need so many more to write a book.

"Some of those things could be terrible, horrible things that happened to you," Sophie explained, "and a reader might be interested in knowing how you moved beyond all that and reclaimed your life. They might particularly want to know how you got from 'survivor' to 'thriver.' How did you go from the impossible to something possible? How did you find a way to live the life of your dreams despite all that happened to you?"

But what Sophie said next was like magic for Lisette.

"Maybe their story is just like yours, or maybe it's very different, even more horrible. But if you could do that—leave an abusive relationship or move beyond the crisis of a sexual assault or a childhood of abuse and neglect—then they can move on, too, from whatever they've faced in life. They can thrive just like you and be the hero of their own story. Then you become a role model they can look up to. Win-win, all around."

Wow! Lisette thought. *Could I inspire others and be a role model?* She thought about the list she had made the other day of the role models in her life right now—Sophie, Erick, Brad, Jenny. But she had forgotten about Lacey. She was no longer alive, but her spirit and the way she died had been inspiring Sophie for years. Even after her physical death, Lacey made it possible for so much good to happen with so much more to come.

Suddenly, Lisette realized what had drawn her to come back to the Tenth Anniversary Celebration Gala of Lacey's death last month. Yes, she wanted to come celebrate all that had been done in Lacey's memory by Sophie, Erick, and so many others. But she was also here to—what was the word Sophie had used?—

manifest her own life of power and purpose. Maybe Lacey didn't have a chance to survive and thrive, but Lisette did. She could manifest the life of her dreams and help Sophie give that chance to so many other women too.

It was then that it came to her. There was a book she could write. She'd need a lot of help to get it done, but she was sure that her dad and Erick would help her. Besides, she wanted them in the book too along with Sophie and maybe others who could explain how they overcame that "fork in the road" of Lacey's unexpected and violent death.

Like Sophie said sometimes the fork in the road may be something out of our control—like being drafted into the military and going off to war or our mother dying when we are very young or the death of our best friend in college in a violence way.

Sure, we all have "what if's" in our lives, Lisette realized. What if my mom hadn't died when I was ten? What if Ralph never pretended to be my real father and I didn't have to live with him after my mother died? What if instead Brad had married my mom and I grew up with them as my family? What if Lacey had gotten safely away from Ari that night and she was still alive today?

But Lisette could see that there was another piece to the story here—the "what's next." What do we do next after that defining moment changes our lives forever? For Sophie, that has meant leading workshops for survivors and teaching them how to take the next bold step in their lives. Be big and bold, Sophie says, and make things happen. Make things change, make the world better, and find your purpose in life.

That's what Lisette wanted. She had wanted it long before she even knew Lacey or met Sophie, Brad, and Jenny, any of them in this amazing circle of people. She had thought bad things would always happen to her, and she'd just have to live with them. That's what she expected when Lacey was killed and her own life was impacted by the horrible, violent act that killed her. But being here now with Sophie, Radiance, Erick, Brad, and Jenny, she could see that there was an opportunity for her to grow, change, and heal as a thriver, something she had never imagined for herself. Surely none of them wanted Lacey to die and certainly not in the way she did, but even if that act was out of their control, together they could make something good come from it and find a life's purpose in what was next for all of them going forward.

True, Lisette still hadn't figured out her life purpose, but she had an idea that it might be somewhere in the vision piece she had written in last week's workshop. The exercise Sophie gave them was to imagine what they might be doing in the future but write about it as if it was happening to them in the present. Sophie started them off with what she called a "guided meditation." She had them sit quietly with their eyes closed, if that felt comfortable, and then she guided them with her words and some background music to move slowly into the future. How did they see themselves there? Who were they with, what were they doing and, most importantly, how it felt to be there, in the future, thriving and being all they could be—all that they ever dreamed of.

Lisette loved this exercise. Here's what she wrote as if it was happening today:

> *"I'm here feeling happy and free of all my past troubles. I'm in a great relationship. My partner is loving and sweet to me, and we have a great life together. We have a good business and great kids. Not sure how many, but there are other people in our lives too. We help and take care of one another. We are one big, happy family. We have a dog, too, and maybe a cat."*

Without any fear, Lisette read this out loud to the workshop group last week and surprised herself. She had never thought about a future like that. It seemed too normal, too easy, and something someone else could have, but not her. She wasn't sure why—maybe because she had never allowed herself to even dream it.

If you dream it, you can do it. That's one of the quotes Lisette pulled out at the workshop from Sophie's pile of quotes from famous people. It made sense to her now, while before it hadn't. It was such a simple step to just believe in a future where she could have a great life. Still, she wasn't sure what to do about it all now—particularly with the goal she had imagined for herself of writing a book. Sophie thought it was a grand idea, but then Sophie was so much smarter than Lisette. The bravest thing Lisette could do was to just sit in that moment without judgment and believe that if she could dream it, she could do it.

Why not? No one said she couldn't.

She'd do it, she thought. And she'd do it until it was done.

Sophie was thrilled when Lisette finished the two workshop sessions and officially became a part of what had come to be known as the ongoing "Archangel" community of the *My Avenging Angel Workshops*™ program.

The Archangel community came about because Sophie was clear about two things when she first started doing the workshops. First, she didn't want to have women come to a two-day workshop and then say "Goodbye, have a good life!" She wanted an ongoing program to support the women on their journey and help them accomplish their thriver goals after the workshop.

The participants loved this idea of an ongoing group. They even came up with the name for it. As they saw themselves graduating from "avenging angels" after the workshops, they wanted to be "archangels" in the follow-up group, and the name stuck.

The Archangel community of the *My Avenging Angel Workshops*™ was open to anyone who had attended both sessions of the workshop and wanted to join the follow-up group.

The second thing Sophie was clear about was that her workshops and follow-up sessions would be free of charge to all survivors. She didn't want her program to be a "luxury item," something that survivors couldn't afford after leaving an abusive relationship or coming through the crisis of a sexual assault. She believed that a lack of money should not keep them from healing or reclaiming their lives after abuse.

To finance this whole effort, Sophie started a nonprofit organization, today known as SISTER, standing for *Survivor Strong, Thriver Resilient* to raise money so her workshops and monthly gatherings of the Archangel community would continue to be free of charge.

She called her monthly gatherings "follow-up" sessions, so as not confuse them with the support groups women might find in a domestic violence or sexual assault crisis intervention program. Those support groups helped women through the crisis of a sexual assault or the process of leaving an abusive relationship that might include legal proceedings in a criminal case, a divorce, or a custody battle. While those support groups were important in helping women move from victim to survivor, Sophie wanted her Archangel community to be role models for them on their journey from survivor to thriver!

Eventually, the Archangels also had annual weekend retreats that gave them the opportunity to rest, re-energize and relax as well as holiday parties for women and their kids to get into the holiday spirit at the end of the year. But more recently, Sophie came upon the idea of doing individual mentoring sessions after the workshop. She thought that if she could work with each woman personally, she could help them pull together what they learned in the workshop and make a plan for how to accomplish the thriver goals they had set on the second day of the workshop. Usually, the plan came together easily, but with Lisette, Sophie thought that maybe she could use an extra boost.

Maybe she knew too much about Lisette—her background, her story. That made her different from most of the women attending the workshop since Sophie didn't have the women tell their stories of abuse as part of the workshop. They had told them too many times, and she knew that if they all started telling stories, they would get triggered, and everyone would end up crying. But with Lisette, it was different.

Sophie remembered all too well meeting Lisette ten years ago, broken and scared when the spirit of Lacey had come into her body. Lisette didn't understand what was happening to her or how to get Lacey's spirit out of her body so they came together in a sisterly way to figure it out. Each had a kind of intimacy with Lacey, Sophie's best friend, but it also complicated their relationship in Sophie's mind. They cared too much about each other without really knowing each other that well.

Sophie thought a mentoring session would put their connection on steadier footing and help Lisette do what she was most focused on right now—finding her purpose in life. Sophie had an idea how to help, but she wasn't sure she could sell it to Lisette.

At Lisette's mentoring session, Sophie put it to her like this.

"Remember how you did those shamanic journeys with my grandmother Radiance back when I first met you after Lacey was killed?"

"Sure," Lisette replied. They were sitting across the table from each other in a small private room that Sophie used as her office at the SISTER organization. They didn't have a huge staff, but there were student interns and volunteers that regularly filled the space, cheerfully decorated with artwork Sophie regularly used in the program.

"Yeah," Lisette continued. "I really loved your grandma. She's still around, right? I miss her! She saved my life! I don't know what I would have done without her."

Sophie smiled. She was used to people talking about Radiance like that, saying, "She changed my life" or "She helped me heal" or "No one can do what she does."

"Radiance is still going strong," Sophie continued. "I know she'd love to see you. She might have something that she can do for you, something I can't do."

"Really?" Lisette sounded skeptical. "Your workshop was so great. It made me see things I hadn't seen before. You were right! I've been going back and forth my whole life between 'survivor' and 'thriver.' So much wasted time and energy! I want to embrace my thriver energy, right? Isn't that what you call it?"

"I do, but I'm thinking about something Radiance taught me. Sometimes we have lost 'parts' of our soul. They've been 'split off' from us because of the abuse, trauma, and loss we've had in our lives. She says those parts go away to protect themselves from the storm around us. So they leave and won't come back unless we call them back."

Lisette gave Sophie a look as though she didn't understand. "Why can't those parts just come back by themselves?"

"They have to be convinced that they'll be safe if they do. So what Radiance does is a shamanic journey called a 'soul retrieval' to bring them back."

Lisette's voice got shaky. "Do you know anyone who's done this 'soul' thing with Radiance? Does it really work?"

Sophie could see the panic in Lisette's eyes, so she took a deep breath and said, "I've done it. Radiance did it with me."

"When? Why? What parts of your soul did you have to bring back? You're perfect, Sophie! What could possibly have happened to you that . . ."

Before Lisette could continue, Sophie blurted out, "My mother was a drug addict. She's dead now, but I lived with her when I was very little, and she couldn't take care of me. Radiance came and found me. She took me and raised me. My mother had no part of it. But the trauma of living in such a desperate situation with my mom and being taken away from her had an effect on me. Radiance and I did a soul retrieval when I was in my teens. Best thing that I ever did for myself."

"Oh wow!" Lisette exclaimed. "I'm so sorry . . . I didn't realize. I know you're close to your grandmother and your mom isn't alive, but I didn't know the whole story."

"It's okay. I'm over it. I live my life today in the present and with all my soul parts here in my body." Sophie laughed. "But you probably can't tell that from the outside!"

"Yeah, you're right. I've just never heard of anything like that—that some of my soul parts aren't with me. How did you even know that about me?"

"Radiance says she listens for when people talk about some part of their life that changed everything for them, that they can't seem to move on from. She says that those people often say, 'I haven't been the same since' or whatever. You said something like that to me at lunch the other day. 'I haven't been the same since my Mom died.' Do you remember that?"

Lisette sighed. "I don't remember saying that during our lunch, but I say it all the time. I feel that way. My life totally changed the day she died. I was only ten years old. So many things would be totally different in my life today if she had lived."

"There you go!" Sophie said with a grin, then she continued more seriously. "Look, I'm not saying you should do a soul retrieval with Radiance, but at least let's go see her. Talk to her; she'd love to see you. I told her you're staying, and she's thrilled."

"She just likes it when you and I hang out together," Lisette teased. "I bet she thinks I keep you in line!" Then she added, "Okay, let's do it. That soul thing, whatever you called it. I want to do it. I trust you, and I trust Radiance."

Sophie gave her a smile. "It's called a soul 'retrieval.' Would you like me to spell that for you?" She knew of Lisette's practice of writing down words she didn't know.

"If you don't mind," Lisette said with a giggle. "I want to tell my dad about it. I love it when I tell him things he doesn't know anything about. Keeps him on his toes."

CHAPTER THREE

December, 2009

Family Holiday Celebrations

It was only December 10, and Lisette had hardly been thinking about Christmas when she and Erick got their first Christmas card in the mail.

It was early to get a holiday card but she was excited that it was the first piece of mail that she and Erick had gotten as a couple. Sure, they had been together ten years ago right after Lacey was killed, but that ended quickly and rather abruptly with her yelling and screaming at him and then hustling herself back to Los Angeles. This time, after they reconnected in October at the Tenth Anniversary Gala, Lisette had moved from her hotel room into Erick's place almost immediately, bringing the few things she had brought with her from LA, thinking it would be a short trip.

But now, sitting here in Erick's small but nicely decorated apartment, she held in her hand their first-as-a-couple Christmas card. So, what did that mean, she wondered? She knew this was where she wanted to be—with Erick and her dad, and, of course, Sophie, her new best friend. But there was also Brad's wife, Jenny, governor of the state who at first was not pleased to have Lisette show up so unexpectedly. It seems that Jenny never knew there was even a possibility Brad had children of his own, let alone a daughter named Lisette. And what about the rest of the family? Were they as excited as Brad was about her coming into their lives? True, Brad had quickly taken on the role of being a father to her, someone he had no part in raising. Still, every moment she spent with him now, she could feel he was damned proud of how she turned out. She could see him being a part of all her triumphs, encouraging her to keep going, and telling her she could do anything. He'd be there, too, through hard times—and with him as her literacy coach, already her reading skills were much better.

Yet sometimes she could feel his guilt creep in—about how he screwed up by not being a part of her life earlier and how his mistakes and blunders were out there for all to see and judge. But he didn't really seem to care about that. He told her time and again that he wanted her in his life forever, and Lisette loved him for that.

Still, it was a lot for Lisette to take in. She was quick to point out a few of the deeper, darker spots she and Brad would have to work through from the very beginning.

"What about your wife?" Lisette asked him directly the night they met. "She's a politician. I'm an ex-stripper. That's not going to go well with the voters! Can she accept me and my past, or will she be like your parents with my mom?"

She had read in her mom's diary about the day Brad called his parents and told them Marie was pregnant. They weren't pleased with him for even dating her, so the news of baby Lisette being on the way didn't go over well.

Marie's Diary
Tuesday, September 25, 1979

Trouble. Brad's dad wasn't happy when Brad went to see him and told him about me and the baby. He didn't like that Brad had gotten involved with someone like me in the first place. I guess that's because I don't come from the same highfalutin neighborhood as they do. If they only knew where I really came from and what I did for a living, they'd really be upset. But they don't, and they never will. Hadley even asked Brad if he was sure he was the father. Imagine that. Of course, he's the father. But Brad told me not to worry. They're just upset, and they'll come around—particularly his father. He's the more reasonable one, Brad said. Brad is going to try to get them to meet me as soon as possible. That will help, Brad told me. "When they meet you, they'll love you as much as I do," he said.

Of course, Lisette knew it didn't go that way. From the day they first heard that Brad was dating Marie to the day she agreed to walk out of Brad's life, pregnant and alone, his parents never changed how they felt. But Lisette remembered that her mom had written in a more encouraging way about someone else in Brad's family:

Then Brad called his sister, Bethany, and he said she was so excited about being an aunt. All she could talk about was the baby . . . I think I'm going to like Beth.

Boy, was her mom right!

◈ ◈ ◈

November 26, 2009
Thanksgiving Day at Governor's Residence

As she and Erick drove to the Governor's Residence for Thanksgiving dinner, Lisette was thrilled that Brad's sister, Beth, was going to be there too. Desperate to meet an aunt that Lisette had never known even existed, Lisette focused her excitement on finally getting to know Beth rather than on her jitters about encountering Brad's entire family, possibly all in one day.

They had been at the Residence a few times in the past months, jokingly calling it "going to the Big House," but it still felt overwhelming to Lisette. Added to that, they had never been in the large, formal dining room where her dad said the main event—a family Thanksgiving Dinner—would be held. Lisette worried that she would feel out of place and uncomfortable with all that.

When they got there, people were gathering, and everyone was ushered into what Lisette would've called the "living room," except that it was quite grand. It had a huge open fireplace and a large mantlepiece that stretched across one side of the room. On the other side was a grand piano. Lisette wasn't sure that either Jenny or Brad played, but it sure looked fancy sitting there. This room led into a smaller room where before-dinner appetizers were being served. The wine and drinks started to flow.

One by one, Lisette met everyone who was there for the governor's turkey day festivities. They smiled, said they were happy to meet her, and asked how she was doing. Some were family; others were friends and "political allies" of Jenny, as her dad had explained to her beforehand. His business associates and partners were there too. They shook Brad's hand and smiled broadly when introduced to Lisette. Most would stay only for cocktails and appetizers, pleased to have been invited to hang with the governor before rushing off to have Thanksgiving Dinner with their own families.

Through it all, Brad stood next to her, beaming as he laughed and joked with everyone. He was a dad showing off his daughter and letting folks know that he was damned proud of her.

Lisette loved the meet-and-greet part of the day. She was relieved when it went so well and told herself that the next part which that was more of a family-only gathering would go well too. But she hadn't expected fireworks to ignite inside the Residence. It was the first time she saw how fiercely her dad was bent on protecting her from the mistakes of the past. His mistakes, not hers—but she still had to love him for it.

It all started out pleasantly. Once the cocktail-hour crowd thinned out, dinner was served in the dining room for the family and a few close friends of Jenny and Brad's who didn't have any other place to go for turkey and all the trimmings. Lisette saw this as her time to spend with Beth and she couldn't wait to call her "Auntie Beth" and her husband "Uncle Ben."

Lisette and Erick were seated for dinner near Beth and Ben, but with all the other conversations going on around the large dining room table, Lisette didn't have a real chance to talk to them. They did say some nice things to each other about how good the food was and asked "Does anyone want more?"

She learned, however, that Beth and Ben had three grown kids, two sons and a daughter, as well as grandkids, none of whom were able to be there that day. Beforehand, Brad had explained to Lisette that even if he and her mom hadn't married, Marie and Ben were still her aunt and uncle and their kids were her first cousins. Lisette marveled at how these family relationships worked and how long overdue this family reunion was.

But there was more for Lisette to learn about this family when the group dwindled down after dessert was served. Some guests headed home, while a smaller family group went back to the living room and sat down in front of a roaring fire for after-dinner drinks and coffee. It was there that Lisette was finally able to have the conversation with Auntie Beth she was dying to have.

Auntie Beth started by saying, "I remember meeting your mom. She was just amazing, wasn't she?"

Lisette was surprised. "Dad never told me what you thought of her. But my mom did write about you in her diary. When you met, you asked her how she was feeling, and you wanted to feel the baby kick. Do you remember that?"

"Of course I do, sweetie. And while I'm sure my brother has

no intention of keeping things from you, I have to tell you—the day I met Marie . . . and you, technically—it was something."

Brad groaned and Lisette could see her dad looking over at his sister now with a look of "Are you really going to go there?" Auntie Beth just smiled wickedly at him and went on. Lisette was all ears.

"It was Christmas Day, and your mom and dad had just started dating. At least that's what my parents told me before Brad and your mom arrived at the house. Uncle Alvin and Auntie Edna were already there. Uncle Alvin is my dad's brother, and he was always a little creepy. But their kids are cousins to me and your dad, so we always loved to see them. Of course, they are all grown up now—Cynthia, Charles, and Robert, with kids of their own. You'll meet them someday soon."

Beth paused and gave Brad another mischievous look, as though that was what he was hiding from Lisette.

"No, Beth," Brad interrupted. "I've told Lisette all about our cousins and how your kids are her cousins. First cousins, right? We already have a date soon for Lisette to meet Uncle Alvin, Aunt Edna, and their kids and grandkids."

"Great!" Beth chirped. "So, going back to Christmas Day . . . it must have been like 1979. When your mom and Brad came in the door at our house, your mom was already, I'd say, four or five months pregnant." Then she laughed. "You know, I was only in high school and not that experienced with that kind of stuff. But I knew that Brad and Marie had been doing so much more than just dating!"

Auntie Beth laughed, and Brad groaned. "Where is this story going, Beth?"

"Oh, I haven't gotten to the good part yet, Brad. Hang on." Then she continued talking directly to Lisette. "So, we had Christmas dinner, and things were going okay. Everyone was very polite, and no one mentioned that, you know, you, Lisette, were present, too, inside your Mom's belly, so it was a good day in the Bufford household. But then I guess—and I heard this later—that there was an argument in the kitchen while the dishes were being washed. Mom called Marie a whore, and Marie called her a bitch."

"That's it," Brad declared, agitated now and sitting up in his seat like he was ready to pounce. "Enough. Lisette doesn't need to hear any more of this from you."

"But I haven't gotten to the good part of the story yet," Beth protested loudly.

Brad snapped back, glaring at Beth. "There is no good part to the story. Enough!" he boomed again.

Suddenly, Jenny, who was sitting next to Brad, grabbed his hand and implored, "Let's see if we can lower the temperature of this conversation, okay? Maybe this is not the time to tell Lisette more about her father's family."

"Maybe Beth should just tell us whatever she is trying to tell us," Brad bellowed back. "What do you know about what happened that day after Marie and I left abruptly?"

"You left abruptly all right!" Beth retorted hotly. "And stuck me in the middle of it, asking me to tell Mom and Dad you left and had to get Marie home. I told them that, and a lot more."

"It was me," she continued indignantly, "who made Daddy go out to the car and apologize to you. And I told Mommy to stop treating Marie like something inhuman. She didn't like that and wouldn't listen, but I said it anyway. I told her I thought Marie loved you very much and that Mommy and Daddy didn't have any right to interfere."

Then she sighed. "Of course, that didn't go very far. Oh, Daddy did go out and try to make nice to you that night, didn't he, Brad?"

Brad eyed her carefully and then said quietly, "Yeah, he tried."

"And my performance got me sent me off to a girl's boarding school for my last two years of high school while the 'Marie' problem was dealt with, and after that, I never saw Marie again." She turned to Lisette and squeezed her hand. "And I never got to meet you until today. I'm so sorry my family treated you and your mother so badly. It was so wrong. What happened next, I don't know."

Lisette didn't know what to say. The diary said what happened next, but now Lisette had a little better idea of why her mom had made the deal with Brad's parents. But what did Beth know about that?

Beth's voice broke the silence in the room. "Those of us who have read Marie's diary—which Brad has shared with me so I'd understand more, Lisette, as you become a full member of this family—know what did happen next. My parents offered your mom ten thousand dollars to tell Brad that the baby wasn't his. Your mom, who was in a very bad financial situation with her baby on the way, did the right thing and took the money. She got it that my parents, particularly my mom, was never going to accept her in the family. They even paid good money to keep her—and you—out. I don't know what else to say except that it embarrasses me to this day, and I can't and won't defend my parents' position. They're both dead now and can't speak for themselves, but I think what they did was particularly cruel because there was a child involved."

The room was silent for a moment as everyone, particularly Brad and Lisette, took all that in. Then Beth continued. "But there were other payments as well."

Brad jumped in. "What payments? To whom?"

"I don't know exactly. Someone by the name of Ralph. And they continued for quite a while. I only know from some of the paperwork and receipts I found after Mom and Dad both passed away. Do you know who Ralph Rozniak was?"

Beth looked at Brad and then Lisette, who both sat there with stunned looks on their faces, not responding to her.

Finally, Erick said softly, "Ralph was a man who Lisette thought was her father for many years. He employed Marie as a dancer for periods of time before and after Lisette was born. Lisette was convinced that Ralph, not Brad, was her real father. She never knew about Brad until she read Marie's diary."

Beth sighed and looked at Brad. "So you didn't know about the payments either, did you? I didn't think to ask you. I thought it was an old debt Dad owed to one of his legal clients. I should've figured it had something to do with Marie, given that the payment started in 1979."

"Jesus," Brad said, letting out an exasperated sigh. "Is there no end to the misery that man caused?"

"I don't understand," Beth asked. "Do you mean our dad or this Ralph guy?"

"Both," Brad sputtered, then heaved a sigh and said, "They are dead to us now, so let's move on. I'm sorry to upset your festivities, Jenny." He squeezed her hand. "You planned such a great celebration for us all."

"It's all right," Jenny responded with all the charm of a true politician. "Every family has its—what shall we call it—'interesting history'—wouldn't you say?"

Then Lisette spoke up. "Auntie Beth, I want to thank you for telling me that story. I really like how you stood up for me and my mom. It has been difficult for me to hear all that went on before I was born, but I do want to say that no matter what, I'm so glad to have found my dad and to be part of his family, with you and all the cousins and everyone."

Erick raised his wine glass and added, "I'll drink to that." Then he clinked glasses with Lisette. "And to the lovely Lisette, who has blossomed from an embryo in her mom's tummy to the most beautiful, amazing woman on the planet! This family should be honored to have you in it."

"Here! Here!" everyone cried in unison.

Lisette blushed and hugged Erick as Jenny spoke above the din, asking, "Okay! Now, who's for turkey sandwiches? And there's lots more dessert! Come into the kitchen. I can dish out the leftovers to anyone who wants to take some home."

As Lisette got up to move with the crowd, she grabbed her dad's hand and whispered, "You know you don't have to protect me from all the family secrets. I can handle them. I'm a big girl now."

He smiled at her and whispered back, "To me, you're still my 'little girl.' Don't you forget that!"

December 24, 2009
Christmas Eve at Governor's Residence

BRAD

Brad knew that soon a whole cascade of guests would descend on the Governor's Residence for Christmas Eve dinner, so he took a minute to check in with Jenny to see what else he needed to do. She was in the kitchen getting last-minute instructions from the caterers who were obviously anxious to get home to celebrate Christmas Eve night with their own families. Usually Jenny cooked for family on nights like this, but this year, with the crowd expanding with each family event since Lisette came into their lives, this crowd was larger than the one she usually cooked for. Brad ventured a guess that anyone in his and Jenny's family who was available and hadn't met his daughter, Lisette, yet was coming, and that pleased him.

He and Jenny had talked about that last night. They agreed that Christmas was a time for family and for being happy. That hadn't been the case in his family or Jenny's for years, but maybe now, Jenny insisted, with no more family secrets to be let out of the bag, they could make that happen.

Jenny is right, Brad thought. A *Christmas Eve dinner is the place to start.*

JENNY

Jenny was nervous about dinner, but it wasn't about the food. The caterers had it all in hand so that it was ready to lay out on the table whenever dinner was to be served. But there was a special menu tonight, a part of her own family's Christmas Eve tradition, and Jenny had never cooked it all by herself.

Jenny thought she could get her daughter, Maryssa, who would be coming tonight and maybe Brad's sister, Beth, to help out when it came time to eat. The food was all prepared, and the large table in the dining room was set and decorated with all the festivities of the season. It would just be a matter of bringing out the platters of food, either chilling in the refrigerator or being kept warm in the kitchen ovens. So she sent the caterers off with a generous holiday tip so they could go home to their own Christmas Eve celebrations tonight. Hopefully, someone was cooking for them too.

But if not the food, Jenny did have two things on her mind that night. One she could do nothing about right now, so she had to let it go for the evening. The second was the exciting part of the evening, and she and Brad would just have to trust that it would come off without a hitch.

What she was letting go of for the entire holiday season was the dip in her political polls these last few weeks. She wasn't up for re-election until next year, 2010, when she was looking to be reelected governor for another term. But the slip in the polls from her usual 40 to 50 percent "likability" rating was unnerving. She was a very popular governor but going down to 30 percent likability . . . that she didn't like. Her disapproval ratings were up too.

Jenny suspected her sudden dip in the polls might be because of the obsession by the press over the last month that she was somehow connected to Mark Durocher, the shooter at the shopping mall in October. But that was crazy! True, when she was still on the bench, she had ruled on a motion for change of custody for Mark from Ambrose to Mark's maternal grandmother, Abigail, after Mark's mother, Betsy, had been killed in a car accident along with his younger sister, Jeanine. But that was years ago, and she hadn't seen Mark since. Nor was there any connection between Brad and the shooter just because Brad and his business associates had a contract to revitalize the mall—and yes, make it less susceptible to a mass shooting. But in the end, it was the mall owners, not Brad's company, that had rejected the changes needed to protect the public safety.

Jenny knew that's the way it was in politics. Having been in that world in one way or another for the last twenty years, it never got any easier, but her ambitions had gotten bigger. She wasn't interested in just being governor term after term. She had hoped to be considered for a national office by now. Her approval ratings were always good, and she had kept active in party politics on the national level and with the National Governor's Association. Surely it was time to consider a woman on the presidential ticket! Maybe not as president yet, but the first woman vice president might be possible for her. Then it was only a step to becoming president.

She and Brad had talked about this. He wasn't against it, although that was before his daughter, Lisette, came into his life. And Jenny didn't know what her daughter, Maryssa, might think of all of that. They had been estranged for so long, but maybe Maryssa coming to Christmas Eve dinner for the first time in years would provide an opening for Jenny, a thawing in their relationship that could lead later to a conversation about her mother moving into national political life.

Right now, Jenny's biggest concern was that Everett, her campaign manager, had told her that Ambrose, a lawyer with an inactive law license, was making noise about having his son, Mark, responsible for the recent mall shooting, sue the state for not providing him adequate mental health services as he aged out of the child welfare system into adult services several years ago.

Claims like that were not uncommon. Jenny knew that it was a rough transition for most kids when they reach eighteen years of age, usually because the child-now-adult may not reach out for help and in many cases, service workers can't locate them. So, she needed to do a little quiet digging around the holidays when the press wasn't paying attention. She would be asking the commissioners of the state child and adult services agencies if the system had broken down for Mark at some point. For now, Mark was in detention pending trial, and the proceedings had slowed as his defense attorney, perhaps with Ambrose's prodding, asked the court for a full psychological workup of his client prior to trial. Until then, Mark was being held without bail as a flight risk, and even if bail were possible, she was sure Ambrose couldn't pay it.

Tonight Jenny would be putting aside the worries of her political life and move on to being anxious about her daughter, Maryssa, meeting Brad's daughter, Lisette. God knows, Jenny thought, *I've never had an easy relationship with Maryssa.* Her daughter had been the sweetest, most sensitive little girl in the world, so happy, cooperative, and completely attached to Jenny, but, as a teenager, Maryssa was a terror. She was defiant, argumentative, oppositional, and at times, downright subversive. Jenny had even sent her to see a therapist to try figure out what happened to her daughter that could have caused such a complete personality reversal.

While Maryssa was generous and willing to share with anyone what she had who might need it, as a teenager and now as an adult, she had gone to the extreme. She'd given away most of her worldly goods, even pieces of antique furniture handed down from her great-grandmother that Jenny had given her. Maryssa also chose to work in global organizations—Red Cross, UNICEF, Doctors Without Borders, and others—that would take her to unsafe places, exposing herself to grave danger just to feel she was helping as many people as she could.

One of the therapists Jenny consulted during Maryssa's adolescence thought this anger and acting out, particularly against her mother, started when Jenny and her first husband, George—Maryssa's father—divorced. There was a lot of bitterness between George and Jenny, and joint custody hadn't worked, so Jenny fought for and won sole physical custody. She wielded her power over George with a fairly big stick. Maryssa saw her father being treated unfairly and her mother just being a bitch!

Over the last twenty years, while Maryssa lived all over the world working in so many out-of-the way places, she rarely came home. She hardly ever called Jenny either, telling her that in these primitive locations, the phone lines weren't great. But Jenny saw it as Maryssa purposefully staying away from her and not giving Jenny the one thing she really wanted: grandchildren. Maryssa never married, showed no interest in having children, and appeared not to care if Jenny ever got her wish.

Jenny's desire in having her daughter here tonight was not only to meet Maryssa's half-sister, Lisette, Brad's newfound daughter, but also to have both of the "daughters" embrace the family wholeheartedly. They were the future of the family, and Jenny didn't want Maryssa to think that Lisette was getting more attention from the family—or the media, for that matter— than she was. Jenny knew that Maryssa had never sought out or wanted to be known as the "governor's daughter." But she didn't want it to be a competition between them, or even a confrontation. That's the last thing Jenny needed in the press right now. Besides, Maryssa was probably living thousands of miles away from here right now. Why would she be so conspicuous in her absence for years and then now want the spotlight?

Only time would tell. Jenny finally resigned herself to that thought.

Only time will tell!

LISETTE

On their way over to the Governor's Residence for Christmas Eve dinner, Erick was unusually quiet. Not that he was ever a chatterbox, but usually he let Lisette know what he was thinking. Most men didn't do that in her experience, and of course, most would never talk about their feelings. That was unless they were angry— usually at her. But Erick was different. He'd talk about anything and tell her how he was feeling no matter what.

What amazed her the most about Erick was how gentle he was. He never let any of his thoughts or feelings provoke him to act against her or anyone in a violent or aggressive way. That was true not only in the way he was with her when they were out in the world, but also when they were alone together. He didn't want to just have sex with her. He wanted to make love to her. Imagine that!

Being with Erick was so different from all the experiences she had ever had with men before. She could trust Erick. He had shown her over the last two months that he did have her back. But what had really made a difference in how she felt about him and her emotional pull of their relationship was the soul retrieval session she had had with Radiance just last week.

Sophie had encouraged Lisette to work with Radiance, the shaman, who had helped Lisette ten years ago when Lacey's spirit had entered her body. Lisette had loved going on those shamanic journeys with Radiance then, and while the soul retrieval was a little different than that, it put her in the place she was tonight. Having parts of her soul retrieved by Radiance changed Lisette totally—both how she saw herself and how she connected emotionally with others. For the first time since she was a kid, she was loving people and feeling loved with her "whole soul" having had all the pieces of it that had been splintered off and lost over the years returned to her.

It was such an amazing experience that Lisette swore that one day she'd write about it. As she slowly began to think about it as a defining moment for her, she also thought about how she could ask others, particularly those who knew and loved her or were somehow attached to her life or memory, to write about a defining moment in their lives. The more she thought about the way the book could be laid out and who she might ask to be in it, the clearer it became that there was a book in her future after all.

All this led Lisette to feel *optimistic* for the first time in a long time. Yes, that was a big, new word she wrote down in her notebook and then used it in a sentence. The sentence read: "For the first time in my life I feel optimistic because I have so many good people around me who love me and want me to have a full and happy life." Then she quickly added two more sentences that said it all: "I am the hero of my own story. I am a thriver!" Sophie would be so proud of her for remembering that!

Forgetting that she was in the car with Erick headed to the Christmas Eve dinner, she was pulled back into it when Erick suddenly asked her, "Lost in thought there, Lisette? Are you okay?"

By now they had pulled into the driveway of the Governor's Residence.

Erick looked at her directly. "So, we're here, right? Why don't you bring in those flowers we got for Jenny as a hostess gift, and

I'll meet you inside. I have some things to take out of the trunk that Jenny asked me to bring."

"Oh, okay," Lisette replied. She wasn't sure what a hostess gift was, but since it was Erick's idea to get Jenny a big bouquet of holiday-themed flowers, the least she could do was carry them in and give Erick all the credit for them. Lisette guessed it would take her a while yet to get to know how to be the "nice person" Erick was.

He was amazing, and she knew she didn't deserve him, but there was no way she was letting him go. She had done that once before in their time together. This time, it would be different—she wasn't sure how—but it was Christmas Eve, she was having dinner with the only family she had ever known, and Erick was a big part of that.

She figured that qualified as some kind of a happy ending, if only for the night.

SOPHIE

While Sophie and her grandmother Radiance were not officially a part of the Bufford/Jablonski family, it was true in the Polish tradition of Jenny's family growing up that families are big, open collections of people, blood-related or not, who are gathered up and included in the family, especially on the big events like Christmas or Easter.

With Lisette now officially in the family as Brad's daughter, it was only natural that Sophie, who was Lisette's best friend, would get drawn into the family. Besides, Sophie had no other close relatives except Radiance, who had raised her ever since her daughter (Sophie's mother) had died when Sophie was very little. Sophie's father had disappeared long before that and hadn't been heard from since.

Radiance had no other relatives to be with on Christmas Eve so, of course, when Brad heard this at one of Lisette's literacy coaching sessions, he insisted that Sophie and Radiance join the party. Neither Jenny nor Brad had ever met Radiance, although Lisette talked about her as the "miracle worker" who got the spirit of Lacey out of Lisette's body. All they knew was that Radiance was a shaman, not the kind of person who regularly visited the Governor's Residence.

Sophie, on the other hand, welcomed the invitation. While she was really happy about Lisette finding Erick again, Sophie couldn't help but feel the incredible gap in her own life. The current relationship she was in—actually her marriage—was not going well. They had wed quickly, and Sophie realized later that she really didn't know the man she had married at all. It was a huge mistake, but not one that was easy for her to admit or for them to unravel. When the marriage soured, and it did quickly, her husband took off for some foreign country to do some kind of work and told Sophie he wasn't sure when he'd be back in the United States, if ever. Sophie found that a relief at first, but then she saw it as a trap. She had no way to contact him, no way to end the marriage unless she was willing to go through extraordinary measures to either try to find him or notify him that she had filed divorce papers against him. Neither option felt worth the effort at the time. She had dated a few men after that, and even a few women, but none of those relationships really stuck. Lately Sophie thought that maybe as a free, independent woman, she wasn't meant to have a relationship in this lifetime. Maybe that dream wasn't for her. Still, she longed for someone to love her, be a witness to all that she had done and been in this lifetime, but maybe that wasn't going to be a person with whom she had an intimate partner relationship.

Recently she had added one more thing—something even more demanding—to what she was looking for and had to have in any meaningful relationship. She was not sure any relationship would work if the person she was with didn't really understand her connection to Lacey, still her best friend and a spiritual relationship that was at the core of everything she would ever do until the day she died. When she thought about how intense that connection felt to her, how could anyone who didn't know Lacey ever understand that? Would they think she was crazy and weird to believe in spirits that haunted her life? Lisette got that. She felt haunted by Lacey's spirit too. After all, Lacey's spirit had inhabited her body right after she was killed and stayed there for a while until Radiance helped her cross over.

That kind of connection to Lacey was not something Sophie was expecting to find in any relationship going forward, but it felt like such a necessity. She could feel how deep Lisette's relationship with Erick was becoming. It had shifted so much even in the last week since the soul retrieval Radiance did for Lisette. Sophie had been there to drum for the ritual, and she remembered how much lighter and easier, more radiant and beautiful Lisette looked afterward.

But Sophie had all of her soul parts returned to her in the soul retrieval Radiance had done years ago for her. She had brought back the parts of Sophie's soul that were lost and left behind when her mother abused her, then abandoned her when Sophie went to live with Radiance, and finally when her mother died from a drug overdose. Sophie's soul was full and complete now and ready for love. But was love ready for her?

She'd definitely feel the love tonight at Christmas Eve dinner with Lisette and all the members of her newfound family. They were so gracious to invite her and her grandmother to join them in this holiday celebration. But Sophie knew she longed for more. She wanted to feel love with someone in the most intimate of ways.

She wasn't sure if her strong spiritual connection with Lacey stood in her way of getting that or if it was Lacey who would make sure that it happened.

No matter what, though, she was the hero of her own story. She was a thriver!

ERICK

As he arrived with Lisette for Christmas Eve dinner with Jenny and Brad, Erick was a nervous wreck. What he planned for tonight, he had never done before, and he wanted it to be perfect from start to finish. Lisette would remember it for the rest of her life, so it had to be good. He thought being spontaneous would be good. But maybe he should have rehearsed. Just winging it was a bad idea, right? Brad told him to speak with his heart, and he'd be great. Not to worry, Brad had told him.

Brad was the only one who knew what Erick's Christmas present to Lisette would be. Erick only hoped she'd want it as much as he did.

One could never tell with Lisette. She had shut him down before, but she did come back. She'd always fight for what was right. He knew that about her.

Maybe that was why he loved her so much.

Before the Christmas Eve feast began, Jenny announced how the evening would go and what everyone should expect.

Few people who had been invited knew much about Jenny's ethnic background except for her last name, Jablonski, which she had kept throughout her life. That name probably indicated to most people that she came from a Polish or Polish American family or, as a woman, had married into one.

But Jenny was a strong believer in women maintaining their birth name throughout their lives. Why change? While it was customary in most countries in the world, Jenny knew that if women should be required to change their names upon marriage, why not men too? Shouldn't they be willing to prove that they, too, were giving up their identity for the good of their union? Maybe both of them should take a hyphenated name. For women, it was an old vestige of a time when they were considered by law the property of their fathers, and upon marriage, that "transfer" of ownership to the husband was signified by the taking of his name. But those laws had changed so that all women, married or unmarried, could sign contracts, get credit, own property, and vote, all in their own name. Yet the "custom" of women, not men, changing their names at marriage had not changed, although many women chose to keep their birth names even after marriage.

Jenny had held on to her name for a number of reasons. One special reason that was most important to her tonight was that she wanted to preserve in some small way her heritage in the Polish American culture that had shaped her into the person she was today. Through her Polish family, she learned to work hard, be honest, and always believe in herself.

Jenny believed, despite being both a lawyer and a politician—two professions not known for upholding those values from her childhood—she had done much of what she aspired to do. Of course, there were moments when it all didn't come through, but she kept it as her goal, her highest aspiration.

One of the ways she remembered as a kid that she and her family—her mom, dad, and older brother, who had all passed now—would renew that commitment of love for each other every year was at Christmas Eve dinner, or what the Poles called *Wigilia.*

It was a special meal—all meatless, with the first course being mushroom soup or the special beet soup known in Polish as *barszcz.* For the main course, Jenny loved *pierogi*—Polish dumplings stuffed with cheese, sauerkraut and potatoes—and some kind of fish, although she could never eat the pickled herring her father had loved.

For the complete menu, Jenny relied on the caterers she hired, Polish American women from the South End of the city who kept these amazing foods and traditions alive. They were so pleased to bring this to the Governor's Residence for Christmas Eve, probably a first for this house and for many in Brad's family. She was sure that Maryssa would remember how she had Christmas Eve dinner with Jenny and George, her ex-husband who was Maryssa's father. She hoped that bringing back those good holiday memories would help "unfreeze" her relationship with Maryssa. It was worth a try.

But what Jenny was most relying on for bringing the group together around the dinner table tonight was the pre-dinner ritual for a Polish Christmas Eve that she remembered from her childhood. It was the sharing of the *oplatki*, the Polish word for a thin, flat, unleavened wafer made of flour and water. Each person at the meal would get a piece of the larger wafer and share it with others. The way the sharing would go is for each guest to approach another, break off a piece of that person's wafer and wish them something good for the coming year. Then the other guest would do the same, and it would continue around the room until all shared and received pieces of the wafer.

With the number of guests attending that Christmas Eve dinner, the sharing of the wafer and good wishes took a good half hour, but by the end, everyone was smiling, laughing, and looking happy as they returned to their seats, ready to eat.

All except for Erick, who suddenly jumped up out of his seat and, in a loud voice, addressed the folks around the table.

"Sorry, sorry! So sorry to delay everyone eating dinner, but I was so touched by how we all went around and wished one another good luck for the coming year, I just needed to do this now. I thought I'd do it later after dinner, but . . ."

Then he stopped and frantically searched one pocket after the other in his pants and jacket, looking for something he couldn't find.

"Oh no!" he muttered to himself and then louder. "I can't believe that . . ."

But before Erick could go on, Brad stood up from the other end of the table, walked calmly over to Erick, and said, "Is this what you are looking for?"

Brad handed him a small black box that looked like something that could have jewelry in it, and expensive stuff at that.

A *WHOOP* sound came up from some around the table who saw the kind of box that Brad slipped into Erick's hand. It's looking surprisingly like a—

"YES! Yes," Erick said, breathless and gulping for air as he grabbed the box from Brad's hand. "How did you get it?" Then Erick stopped, as if he realized that wasn't important but not before Brad added in a kind of stage whisper. "I saw you drop it when you came in, and I didn't just want to hand it to you because, you know, someone might see it . . ."

"See what?" Lisette jumped in, and suddenly she was standing up next to Erick, her napkin falling from her lap as she teased him, "Erick, what are you doing?"

Then she laughed, her face crinkling into a big smile.

"Oh, Lisette, I wanted to do this after dinner with everyone around us. . . . I wanted to make it real special, but I got so caught up with everyone going around the room wishing me—and us— the best of luck next year. I had to do this before all those good wishes went away."

Suddenly, Erick dropped down on one knee and opened the black box. As a beam of light bounced off the diamond ring inside, he asked Lisette, "Will you marry me? I love you so much. Please be my wife."

An audible sigh of surprise, excitement, and pleasure came up from all those around the table, and all eyes were on Lisette, awaiting her answer.

She blushed for a moment, then with tears in her eyes, she said, "Of course I will, you goof. How could I say no to someone I adore as much as you? YES! YES! I will marry you! YES!"

The room exploded with applause as Erick got up off his knee and slipped the ring on Lisette's finger; it was a perfect fit. Then they kissed, embracing each other and holding on tight for a moment, and then giving each other another quick kiss. By then, everyone had leapt out of their chairs and come up to embrace and congratulate the happy couple. The women had tears in their eyes, but Brad was by far the most emotional. With tears streaming down his face, Brad gave Lisette a kiss on her cheek and then a big bear hug.

"Congratulations, my dear. You'll be the most beautiful bride in the world."

"You knew about this, didn't you?" she teased him. "And you didn't tell me!"

"Of course I didn't tell you! This was Erick's secret, but I gave him a little help plotting this out so you wouldn't find out or see what he brought in tonight from his car."

Just then, Jenny came into the room carrying a big bouquet of red and white roses and handed them to Erick. He turned to Lisette and kissed her again.

"These are for you, my dear. I love you!"

"Oh my! These are so beautiful! Thank you, Erick. Hon, this is all too much, more than I have ever dreamed of." She turned to those gathered around them and shouted, "Thank you, thank you all so much!"

"When's the wedding?" someone shouted suddenly, and then the clanking of plates started.

"Yes," Jenny cried out, clanking her plate too. "Kiss her again for us, Erick, or we'll keep banging our plates until you do. Kiss your bride!"

Erick was more than happy to oblige. He was sure Lisette wouldn't mind another kiss. She knew how to play to the crowd, and this crowd was wild for them. So he leaned in to kiss her, all too happy to give them what they asked for because he was so happy. It was Christmas, and Lisette had said "Yes."

But when the clanking of plates didn't stop, Erick made a bold gesture of it. He pulled Lisette toward him, twirled her over his extended arm and held there as he kissed her until they both were quite breathless. The crowd roared their approval.

Erick was ecstatic. This year, he had gotten everything he had ever wanted for Christmas. He got the love of his life and the girl of his dreams.

And Santa had nothing to do with it.

CHAPTER FOUR

October 10, 2019

Before the Twentieth Anniversary

LISETTE

Lisette was having a crazy day.

With her two kids strapped into their car seats in the back of their SUV, it was hard for her to concentrate on her driving, what was happening with the two of them, and what was going on in the meeting she was now participating in on her cell phone in the front seat.

Just as a screech came up from her four-year-old daughter, Sasha, accusing her two-year-old brother, Jeremy, of taking her stuff, Sophie was reporting on the status of the celebrity guests coming in from Hollywood for this Thursday's October 17th Twentieth Anniversary Gala Celebration to remember Lacey on the date of her death.

Among those attending would be two actresses, friends of friends of Lisette from when she lived and worked in L.A. who had just come out with #MeToo allegations about male actors who had sexually assaulted them while working on films with them. Lisette knew that well-known celebrity guests like this at the Gala could take it over the top in terms of fundraising for Sophie's nonprofit, SISTER—*Survivor Strong, Thriver Resilient.* Lisette was equally excited that both actresses had done "cover blurbs," or endorsements, for her new book to be launched at the gala.

That book, an idea she first had had ten years ago when she took one of Sophie's workshops, had finally come together this year.

But right after the Tenth Anniversary Celebration Gala in October 2009, Lisette had come on board as the development director at SISTER, working full-time with Sophie. Lisette's job was to raise money, get the word out about what SISTER did and have the full financial support of the community for all its programs. Before that, the organization and staff had largely been living on the money Lisette had donated over the last ten years from the license fees she got for lending her "Attila the Hunny" name to that national chain of high-end strip clubs. But Lisette decided she didn't want to be a part of that kind of venture anymore, so she terminated the licensing agreement and let the clubs fend for themselves rebranding their image. That wasn't Lisette's problem anymore. She was clear that if she was working at SISTER, she didn't want to continue to support businesses that objectified and exploited women's bodies, making violence against women more possible in our society.

Instead, Lisette rebranded Sophie's nonprofit, running a six-month-long media campaign using "SISTER" as the identity of the organization since it had already been using that shortened name for years. Sophie added the tagline "Sisters Helping Sisters Thrive after Abuse!" and it stuck. From then on, the SISTER board and staff built a successful, ongoing fundraising campaign that provided a stable financial underpinning to SISTER's current programs and supported its ongoing expansion of services for men, women, children, and families.

Over the last ten years, Lisette also worked with her husband, Erick, to refocus his fitness club business. Freely borrowing from one of Sophie's best taglines, "Living Well Is the Best Revenge," they opened several Living Well Centers locally and in a few selected locations around the state. The new model added pole dancing as exercise and martial arts for protection and flexibility for both men and women. Erick added these programs to his ongoing classes and personal training sessions, and then, through SISTER, he began to work in groups with men and boys. He helped them to develop interpersonal communication skills to foster healthy relationships and build their fatherhood skills, and together they also addressed coercive control and toxic masculinity in personal and professional relationships. Erick also partnered with local businesses to bring in men from the community to be healthy role models to these men and boys on how to be successful in personal and business relationships.

Today was a particularly challenging day, though, because Lisette, as development director at SISTER, had taken the lead for planning and coordinating the upcoming Twentieth Anniversary Celebration Gala, which was only a week away. She really needed to listen to Sophie's report, but the noise from her kids in the back seat was just too much.

"Enough!" Lisette yelled. "Jeremy, don't take your sister's stuff. You have your own!"

Then she turned to her daughter, getting her attention by using both her first and middle name. "Sasha Marie! No more screaming. Mommy is in a meeting on the phone. I need you to shush! Now!"

Suddenly, a voice came on the cell phone with a shocked but direct tone. "Excuse me? Who are you telling to shush?"

"Oh no! No! Not you!" Lisette responded to one of the SISTER staff. "I'm sorry, Brooke. I didn't mean you. I'm talking to my kids. I'm driving them to day care and preschool today. My husband is out of town on business. He usually does the morning drop off. Sorry! I'm so sorry!"

Lisette suddenly realized that she was doing that "mom thing" again, going on too long explaining and apologizing about her kids. They were just kids, she had to remember. People would understand. Then Lisette recognized Sophie's voice on the line.

"Hey, kids, this is Aunt Sophie. I'm going to see you soon, right?"

Lisette grabbed her cell phone out of its dashboard holder and held it up for the Sasha and Jeremy to hear in the back seat.

"Auntie Sophie!" Sasha yelled out. "Yeah! I want to do an art project with you, okay? I can bring my crayons."

"Yeah!" Jeremy added, not wanting to be left out. "Play golf. Me play golf."

Lisette had to smile. Sophie had gotten these kids under her magical spell with art projects and sports activities, even if it was just with crayons and plastic golf clubs. She was sure that if she and Erick brought the kids along anywhere Sophie was, creative kid stuff was sure to be a part of that day's fun.

Lisette had to laugh at how she and Erick had adjusted to having kids. Not too long ago, Lisette would have been dancing in a strip club until the wee hours of the morning and Erick would be there as a bouncer. Now they were parents who had just as easily and happily adjusted their lives to two small kids, including adjusting the work they did.

For Erick, since the local wellness centers were open days, nights, and weekends, that meant having dependable staff on nights and weekends so he'd have time for Lisette and the kids. Erick was also getting more into the business side of things, expanding into some higher-end exercise equipment, wellness products, and online classes to give homebodies a chance to stay fit without traveling or paying gym memberships. He and Lisette were currently filming a video series for women, combining fitness, pole dancing, and martial arts for building strength and stamina with yoga for relaxation. The first of the videos would be out early the next year, but they also planned live virtual classes, hoping to change the way people exercised at home instead of going to the gym every day or on the weekend. If their business could go more virtual, it would allow them as parents a lot more flexibility and open up more family time.

After all, Erick had promised Lisette he would be a hands-on dad with the kids, but it wasn't him she was worried about when they talked about having a family.

"I don't think I'll be good at being a mom," she confessed to Erick back then. "I'll screw up our kids really bad, and you'll have to leave me and take them with you. You have to know that, right? I've told you more about my past than anyone else on this planet. You know that me being a mom is a nightmare just waiting to happen!"

But Erick saw it differently. "No, I don't know that about you," he insisted. "Do you really believe that or did someone just tell you that? I never did, and I never will. Besides, this is for us to do together. We'll figure it out . . . together, I promise."

So now they were doing it, and it was all new for Lisette. She wasn't used to the men in her life keeping their promises, but she did trust Erick. She just had to trust herself to trust him. Of course, she knew he'd be a great dad, and she wanted to be a good mom, but they both had had such dismal childhoods. It terrified her to think how bad they could have been at this. No kid deserved that growing up!

But then, she hadn't even figured on ever getting married. Now everyone around her seemed to be getting married, having kids, settling down, and enjoying a good, happy life, maybe even living their best life ever. Why shouldn't the two of them get some of that like everyone else?

That is, everyone except Sophie. A few years after Lisette and Erick married, Sophie married a guy she had only known for a short period of time, and as far as Lisette could see, it wasn't going well. Sophie didn't talk about it to her or admit to anyone that it wasn't working. Lisette guessed that Sophie thought any guy who would marry her and agree to change his name and hers to same hyphenated last name was the guy for her. But from what Lisette did know, he and Sophie hadn't lived together for more than a year. The Twentieth Anniversary Celebration Gala would be one more event that Sophie's husband would not attend, and no explanation would be offered.

Maybe he'd show up and surprise everyone.

For now, Lisette kept Sophie's secret because, above all else, she desperately wanted her dear friend Sophie to be as happy as she was in her marriage.

Living well was the best revenge!

SOPHIE

Friday, October 11, 2019

Late on a Friday afternoon about a week before the gala, Sophie was dog-tired.

There was still so much more to do before the big event, but she had promised Laura and Jennifer, friends of hers and Lacey's from college, that she'd meet them for drinks tonight at the hotel where the gala would be held. She wasn't that close with either of them now, as they both lived out of town. But every year they'd come to town for Lacey's anniversary and spend the day with Sophie. This year was a gala year, so they would help set up and coordinate the event.

Sophie knew they had their assignments for the week from the Gala Planning Team, so getting together tonight was more social than gala-related. It was their yearly girl-gabfest—talking about Lacey as if she were still there with them and remembering all the great times they had together in college. But most likely, they'd talk about how they had bonded years ago when the three of them were with Lacey at The Keg, a local dance club frequented by the college crowd. They had all gone there that night to dance and have a girls' night out.

That night, however, Ari had interfered with their plans to all go together to The Keg in Sophie's car, insisting instead that he drive Lacey to the bar. So they all stayed with Lacey, standing outside in cold waiting for Ari to show up. It was painful now for Sophie to remember the difficult conversation she had had with Lacey that night, trying to get her see how Ari was manipulating her. Because she failed at doing so, that night was forever etched in her memory as a "defining moment" in her life. It was a time, Sophie lamented, when everything changed and afterward none of them were ever the same.

Sophia also saw that evening as such a defining moment for her because, looking back on it now, she could see that she had realized then, months before Ari killed Lacey, how obsessed he was with her best friend.

She had written about it as if Lacey was telling the story, and it was now in Lisette's book, which would be launched at the gala next week. Sophie sat with that memory for a moment, but not too long. She knew that every time she let herself remember the conversation she had with Lacey about Ari and how he treated her that night, it reminded her once again, to her horror, that she might have saved Lacey's life. Sophie had clearly seen the way Ari manipulated Lacey that evening and on so many other occasions in the months that followed. But that night was the first time she had seen it the clearest. Why hadn't she just grabbed Lacey that night and thrown her in her car and left Ari behind? Why hadn't she and Lacey figured out a way to free her from Ari forever? Who else could they have turned to on campus to help them? Or could they have gone off campus, talked to Lacey's dad, gotten some other people involved? Why hadn't she saved Lacey? Why? Why? Why?

It took her a moment to stop and take a deep breath, the way her therapist had taught her to stop the negative talk in her head. Take a breath and let it go. Most days it only took a few breaths for her to do that, but today, maybe because it was closer to the anniversary of Lacey's death, it took longer. Still she couldn't let herself be drawn into that place, with all those questions and no answers.

And if there was an answer, Sophie had decided, it was "just because." All things happen for a reason. She wouldn't have found this work with women without the catalyst of Lacey's death. Did she want Lacey to die? No, but because Lacey died, Sophie was drawn to work that she never dreamed she would be doing. Yes, she was an advocate for women, but the women who participated in her workshops described them as "life-changing" and "providing a component for women recovering from crisis that has, until now, been virtually overlooked." Wow! Every time she read those kinds of comments in her post-workshop evaluations, she was stunned by how she had turned the tragedy of losing Lacey into a triumph for women alive today and struggling to move forward after abuse. Those women weren't all domestic violence victims either, but many had come out of a relationship marked by violence, trauma, and abuse. Many had long histories of trauma, including sexual assault, child abuse, and neglect.

As hard as it had been to lose Lacey, there were things that happened afterward that allowed goodness to come from such a loss. She could see it all now, particularly as Lisette had assembled for the book pieces from so many people affected by Lacey's life and death. The title, Sophie thought, was so appropriate: *Losing Lacey: Creating a Legacy of Goodness, Hope and Promise.*

Sophie liked that title. Maybe it was because she had helped

Lisette dream it up, but also because she and Lisette had known each together for the last twenty years, and for many of those years, they had been working either together or separately to make sure that Lacey would not be forgotten. They both wanted something to remain to reflect Lacey's spirit, her capacity to love, and her unrealized potential.

Sophie remembered the quote Lacey had put in one of her school papers:

> *I am no longer content to live a private life and concern myself only with affairs that affect me. The things I do in my public life can make a difference. I foresee myself raising a family eventually, and I do not want to pass on a world I have made no attempt to better.*

Sophie hadn't gotten around to raising a family yet, but she admired how insightful Lacey was about this and so many other issues at such a young age.

From that quote alone, Sophie realized that Lacey had more potential in her little finger than most girls her age would ever have had. She could have been so much, done so much in the world. She would have been a great attorney, teacher, or social worker too, but that wasn't big enough. She would have been an amazing public policy maker, a politician— or maybe the first female president of the United States? That's how high someone like Lacey could have gone, Sophie mused. How many people's lives she could have influenced for the good! And Lacey wanted to be a wife and a mom too. Have a family, change the world, and make it all better. She had so many dreams and possibilities!

Sophie had her dreams too. Of course, her marriage hadn't worked out. Maybe it was because she was too independent. She wanted to do what she wanted to do, and although her husband at the time professed to be an "enlightened" kind of guy, he just wasn't. He wanted things she didn't want ultimately—children and a quiet family life away from the horrors of the world, like Lacey's death. If Sophie could just stop talking about Lacey all the time, he'd tell her, they would have a happy life!

Not true, and she wasn't all that torn up that he was gone from her life, but tonight was one of those occasions when he might have come in handy. She'd like to have a husband to show off to Laura and Jennifer, even though she learned long ago that she didn't need a man to complete her.

She heaved a sigh and let go of trying to figure out a way to make her marriage work when the phone in her office rang. That was unusual. It was coming up on 5:00 p.m. on a Friday afternoon, and while technically it was still office hours, anyone who knew Sophie and how she worked would know she never kept "regular office hours." Sometimes she'd come in late in the morning, having worked late the night before on her laptop at home, or she'd stay late into the evening at her office to get stuff done. But she usually always left early on Friday afternoon for the weekend. Curious, she answered the phone.

"Hello," a male voice said. "Is this Sophie? Sophie Stafford?"

The voice didn't sound familiar, but still she assumed it was someone she knew. Before she could answer, the voice continued. "It's Jack. Jack Howe. I'm looking for Sophie, who runs . . ."

"Jack? Is that you?" Sophie jumped in. "I haven't heard from you in ages."

For a moment, a smile filled Sophie's face, and then she stopped short and asked, "Are you okay? Is everything all right? I can't believe you're calling me."

"Sure, sure," he said. "Yeah, I'm good. Look, I'm in town for the next week, and I was wondering if it would be okay for me to come to that Twentieth Anniversary thing you're doing. That 'Gala Celebration,' right?"

She winced at how he said those last few words. She knew it was a little weird to "celebrate" the day someone died, particularly giv-en the way Lacey had, but Sophie wanted those "every-ten-year" events to celebrate who Lacey was, what she could have been, and what had been accomplished in her name since she died.

But Jack was going on.

"I mean, I'm not sure that Lacey's family or friends like you would want me there. After all, I caused a lot of ruckus that night at The Keg with Ari. He was angry at me and at her. I'm sure people blame me for provoking what he did, and it's hard to face—. "

"Is that what you think?" Sophie interrupted. "Is that why you haven't come around here for the other anniversaries?" So-phie sighed and took a breath. "Oh, Jack! No one blames you for what happened to Lacey. That's crazy! Her relationship with Ari was rocky long before the two of you danced that night. She was ready to move on, but Ari wouldn't let her. It was his fault, Jack. Not yours."

"But I could've backed off, not been like some macho guy staking my claim to Lacey on the dance floor," he insisted. "Yes, I wanted to see her after that night, but she was trying so hard to let Ari down easy. I should've tried harder to—"

Sophie interrupted Jack again. "I'm going to stop you there. Have you been doing this to yourself for the last twenty years? You've got to stop. Lacey wouldn't want you doing that."

"I try; I really do," he said almost apologetically. "Most days I can, but when it gets close to Lacey's anniversary, I get pulled back into it. Usually I can work it out myself and then let it go for the rest of the year, but it keeps coming back. When I get the invitations to your anniversary events because they still come to my parents' house, I can't bring myself to attend."

"So why this year, Jack? What's different?"

Jack's voice filled with emotion. "My mother died this month.

She has been sick with cancer for years, but it was in remission. Suddenly, it came back full force, and she didn't have a chance. I came home to be with her and my sister, and I stayed for the funeral and beyond. One day I forced myself to go back on campus and sit there in Lacey's beautiful memorial garden. I thought maybe it was time for me to confront my demons. But I only went because the night before, I had a dream that my mother was talking to Lacey in the great beyond, and Lacey told her to tell me to get over it. Those were her exact words. 'Get over it, Jack, and move on.'"

Sophie laughed. "That sounds so much like Lacey, doesn't it?"

"Yeah, it does," he said with a laugh. "That's the only reason I believed any of it. She would come through like that, right?"

"And," Sophie continued, "if she were here right now, she would tell you even more. That she was so excited to have that dance with you that evening. She wanted it to go further, but she got stuck in trying to end it, and Ari was having none of it. And nobody knew—can I repeat this to you?—no one knew Ari would do what he did. The blame is all on him, Jack. You have to see that."

"I can see that now. But coming to the event, I worry what Lacey's family might think of me. They probably are still devastated and don't want to be reminded of—"

Sophie interrupted him again. "Look, I've had good conversations with Lacey's father, Howie, over the last few years and trust me, he's not focused on pointing blame on you or on anyone except for the man who shot Lacey. Yes, he's still healing. I think it's helped that he's been doing some legislative work with us, helping to change laws about violence against women in our state. His son, Jimmie, his only surviving child, was a soldier killed a few years ago in the war in Afghanistan, so that's been hard for Howie too, but he's been plugging along. He'll be here on the 17th for the gala. I know he'll be pleased that all of Lacey's friends will be there, too. So yes, please come next Thursday. How long are you going to be in town?"

"I don't know exactly. Things are changing right now in my life." His voice dropped a little bit. "I've got my mom's estate to settle, and I just retired from the Army. I'm still trying to sort out what's next for me."

"You've retired?" Sophie said with surprise. "You're not that old."

"Yeah, but you can retire with full benefits from the military after twenty years of service. I joined right after college and got my master's degree in the service. It worked out well. I was in military intelligence and spent only a little time in the war zones. I was in information technology—you know, the computer guy to the generals—so I was kept pretty protected and safe. That is, if you don't consider living in Washington, DC, as being in a war zone," he quipped.

"Good for you, and thank you for your service! So you'll come next Thursday? Please!" Then she paused, adding when Jack didn't respond, "Jack? You'll come? Be there, please. Lacey would've wanted it. You don't have to say or do anything if you don't want."

"What would you have me do or say? What kind of event is it?"

Sophie picked up right away that Jack was concerned about being drawn into all of this.

"No, no, it's not like that. But let me say this. There are two parts to the event. One is that Lisette is going to launch her book about Lacey. But it's more about how we—her friends and family—made something good come out of how and why she died. I started the organization *SISTER* for survivors of abuse, and we now have a Men's Initiative. Howie's just joined it. We want to work with men and boys to involve them in addressing intimate partner violence and promoting safety and awareness.

In particular, we've got to get the schools, like the college where Lacey was killed, to be more responsive to the violence, abuse, and trauma their students are experiencing. We're creating a model for how schools could do that, and we hope to duplicate it around the country."

Sophie went on. "The second part of our twentieth year 'celebration' will be to hear from celebrities who are abuse survivors, as well as some of the women who have taken my workshops—my 'thriver success stories'! They'll talk about the free SISTER program that changed their lives. You've heard about my workshops, right?"

"Yeah. My mom kept me up-to-date on all that and how positive it all was. She knew how I felt after Lacey's death. Like you, she didn't think I should blame myself, but that has been easier said than done."

Sophie was quiet for a moment, thinking of another way to get through to Jack. Then she said, "Look, I know Lacey was in contact with you in the months after that night at The Keg and before Ari killed her. We had long talks; she was in such agony. She wanted to pursue a relationship with you, but if she did, particularly in public on the campus, she was afraid Ari would find out and she'd never get him to calm down. No, she thought that if she just went at this problem slowly and methodically, she could solve it all herself. She told me about some of it, but I didn't know about the vile text messages she was getting from Ari over the last weeks of her life. I saw them after she was killed. Somehow she thought that if she went to see him that night, she could tell him one more time to leave her alone and that would be that."

Quiet again, Sophie waited for Jack to respond, but when he did there was such agony in his voice that it startled her.

"If I could just tell myself a story that she didn't die—that she lived," he began. "That someone or something saved her. I think about it all the time, but I can't construct a plausible scene in my head that would have made that possible."

Sophie jumped in, speaking rapidly. "I have. I have a scenario, and it's all written out. It's the 'what if' moment Lisette wanted us all to write for the book. I couldn't think what to write, but then one night it came to me. It was like a dream, but so real. I wrote it all down for the book. It's not available until the launch at the gala, but I have an early copy. You can read my piece if you want, but I don't think we should do this over the phone. It's intense."

Jack responded eagerly. "Yes, could I read it? Can we do it tonight?"

"I was planning to meet the girls tonight at the hotel, but I'll text them and tell them I can't make it. Where should we meet? It shouldn't be in public."

"I agree. We need some place quiet where no one else is around."

"Come to my condo. It's near the campus. You know the old Everett-Glenn Apartments near the football stadium? They used to be apartments. Got converted to condos a few years ago. I'm in #101. I'll leave my office right now and meet you there in about twenty minutes. Okay?"

"Yes, I'll be there."

Sophie ended the call, texted the girls that she wouldn't show tonight, and then quickly gathered her things, wanting to leave so she got to her place before Jack. She'd need to regain her composure. Talking to Jack after all those years brought up memories of that night at the Keg, but she had learned to let the memories come at times and knew it would be okay. So now she let the story come as if Lacey was telling it to her again.

It would get her through the drive home in heavy Friday

night traffic and ready to meet Jack. Soon it would be just one more year without Lacey. But this year, Jack, one more important person in Lacey's life, would be joining all of them—the survivors of a homicide of someone who was so very, very dear.

◈ ◈ ◈

A MEMORY
April 1999 at The Keg

Lacey sat alone at a table at The Keg with the loud music and noise of the college bar on a Friday night swirling around her. Her head felt light from the beers she had been drinking, one after another, since she and the other girls had arrived a few hours ago. Everyone but Lacey was out on the floor now. No one noticed that she had come back to the table by herself after only a few dances. She told herself that the music sucked and she was tired, but all she wanted to do was drink and stop the wild thoughts that were making her head throb. With each beer she downed, she felt some relief. Pretty soon, she figured, her head would be totally numb, and she'd stop thinking about how right Sophie had been about Ari.

The more she thought about it, the angrier she got. Why did Ari have to be so pigheaded about driving her and picking her up tonight? Didn't he trust her? Did he think he could have her all to himself? Things between them were getting too serious, too fast. She wasn't ready to settle down with anyone—and certainly not with Ari.

Suddenly Sophie's voice, yelling over the music, pulled her out of her thoughts. "What are you doing? It's not like you to sit in the corner and drink all by yourself. Why aren't you dancing?"

"I don't feel like it," Lacey muttered. "Go have a good time. Don't worry about me."

Sophie looked at her with a glint in her eye. "There's this cute guy up at the bar asking about you. He's in our history class. He's got a great smile."

Lacey gave her a disinterested look, but Sophie pushed on. "Why don't you go ask him to dance? His name is Jack."

Lacey scowled at her, and Sophie leaned in closer. "This is what he wants, you know, for you to mope around and not have fun. Stop stewing about Ari. He's not worth it."

Lacey wanted to argue that she wasn't doing that, but Sophie gave her a look that said it was useless to try. So, Lacey looked over at the bar and saw a guy with closely cropped blonde hair and a nice, easy smile looking at her.

"You say his name is Jack?" Lacey asked as she slowly got up from the table, trying to hold herself steady.

"Yup," Sophie said with a smile. "Jack Howe, and he's a cutie."

"Thanks," Lacey said, putting one foot carefully in front of the other as she headed toward the bar. Halfway there, she realized that Jack was watching her, and she liked that, so she slowed her walk down to a slink and stuck out her chest. She had forgotten that there were other men out there besides Ari who found her attractive. Jack evidently was one of them by the way he was looking at her.

When she got to the bar, she flashed Jack a smile and motioned with her index finger for him to come closer. "Would you like to dance?" she whispered into his ear in a husky, sexy voice.

"Sure," he said, taking her hand and leading her to the dance floor.

She felt his fingers warm and tight around hers, and as they walked, she checked him out. He was dressed in khaki pants and a blue shirt like most of the guys at school, but he looked really good in them. He had broad shoulders and a narrow waist, and she could see how tight his ass was as he walked. She thought he carried himself like someone who could take charge, but in a quiet, easy way.

He was so unlike Ari, and she liked that too. When they got

on the floor, the music slowed down, and Jack took her into his arms.

She put her hand on his shoulder and felt the muscles under his shirt. When he pulled her into an embrace, she felt his body hard against hers, and she allowed herself to relax.

The music that was playing was an old tune, "In the Midnight Hour" by Wilson Pickett, that made Lacey feel sexy. She had heard it played on the radio when she was a kid, and now she appreciated its slow, sultry beat.

As they moved to the music, Jack pulled her body even closer to him. Lacey was used to dancing slow and suggestively like this at The Keg, but she didn't expect to respond to Jack the way she did. With his hand on the small of her back and his body moving into her, she felt a spark pass between them. It was as if he was igniting her magic spot without even touching it.

Wow! Lacey thought. She closed her eyes, threw her head back, and let her body roll forward each time Jack pressed his body into hers. She imagined him getting excited by her body, and she wanted to kiss him so bad. Nobody had ever made her feel so wonderful just by dancing with her.

With their bodies swaying and moving in unison now, it seemed that their two separate existences had melted into one, like molten steel, and they were floating away as light as air. She couldn't explain it, but dancing with Jack made her feel as though she could fly. With her eyes shut tightly, everything but the music faded away. Jack's hands were moving slowly up and down her body now, and she wanted more. That was until another hand gripped her shoulder and spun her around, away from Jack.

"We're leaving now!" a gruff voice yelled coarsely in her ear.

Startled, her eyes flew open, and she saw Ari.

"What are you doing here?"

"I'm here to take you home. That was the deal."

"No, that was not the deal!" she yelled back. "And I'm not ready to go home yet."

Jack stepped toward Ari. "What's the problem? If she's here by herself, she can leave all by herself."

"You don't understand, asshole. She happens to be my girl-friend."

Ari puffed himself up against Jack as though he were as tall and strong as Jack, but Lacey knew there was no way. "You're dancing with my girl, and I don't like it."

"If she's your girlfriend," Jack fired back, "then why is she here with me and not you?"

Lacey could see that the two men were squaring off, so she stepped between them and put her hand on Jack's chest to hold him back.

"Please, Jack," she begged. "I have to go. I enjoyed our dance."

She smiled at him, but her lips were quivering, and her legs felt shaky.

She didn't want to leave, but she could feel the heat of Ari's hand on her arm and his anger coming right through it. She wasn't sure that she could get Ari out of there without him wanting to fight it out with Jack, and that would be disastrous. She didn't want to see either one of them get hurt, and Ari was her problem, not Jack's.

"You don't have to go anywhere with him," Jack insisted.

She looked at him, pleading her case silently with her eyes. *I don't want to go,* she tried to tell him, *but it's easier if I go. I'll explain it later. There will be a later. I promise you.* Instead, she simply repeated, "I have to go."

Jack grabbed her arm and held it tight.

"Are you sure?"

"Yes," she said with as much resolve as she could muster.

"Will you be all right?" Jack seemed to think that if he kept talking to her, she wouldn't have to go anywhere.

"Of course she'll be all right," Ari shouted in Jack's face. "She's with me. Remember, that's who I am, the boyfriend. You're the asshole."

Jack glared at Ari, and Lacey saw his nostrils flare for a moment, but then he backed off and released his hold on Lacey's arm.

"Until next time," Jack said, bending down and whispering in her ear so Ari wouldn't hear.

Ari tugged at her arm. "Let's go. The van's out front."

By now, Lacey could see Sophie rushing toward her from across the room, but she lost track of her as Ari pulled her through the crowd. She was relieved to hear Sophie's voice right behind them as they got near the front door.

"What the hell happened?" Sophie asked, grabbing Lacey's arm and spinning her around away from Ari. Then she hissed at him, "And what the hell are you doing here?"

Before either of them could respond, Sophie pushed Lacey toward the ladies' room door, only a few feet away from them. "You're coming with me!"

"And you!" She pointed at Ari. "You stay right there. Do you hear me? One more stunt like the one you pulled on the dance floor, and I'll flatten you. Don't think that I won't."

With that, Sophie pulled Lacey into the ladies' room and closed the door.

By the time Sophie got to this part of the story, it was no longer a memory she was telling herself in her head on her drive home. She was with Jack now, sitting on the couch in her living room, telling Jack the part of the story he didn't witness that night at the Keg. Sophie told him how she had confronted Ari that night, insisting that he leave Lacey alone, and how she knew for the first time—even before Jack had danced with Lacey at The Keg—how obsessed Ari was with Lacey and that he'd never let her go.

It was all about her guilt, and when she let Jack into her apartment about twenty minutes earlier, she had seen that same look of guilt on his face. Sure, she hadn't seen him in twenty years, and they had both aged, but he wore the pain of the trauma of Lacey's violent death, as she did, all over his face. It was particularly acute, she agreed, this time of the year near the anniversary of Lacey's death. It was as if they stored the energy of that pain and the sadness of their loss somewhere under the layers of their skin, but like a skin rash, it would come back again on October 17th each year.

She had hugged Jack and held him tight for a moment before they headed into the living room, Jack on the couch and Sophie in an easy chair nearby. They eased themselves into a conversation they should have had years ago about the worst thing that ever happened to them.

"You look like a mess," she chided him with a grin. "Like I usually do in October. You see why I insist on a 'celebration' of Lacey's death each year to buoy us all up? And every ten years, we definitely need a gala to get through it."

Jack laughed. "I'm glad to know I have fellow travelers in this war we wage with our guilt, loss, and grief. I don't know if I'll ever be able to shake this. Just when I think I've gotten through the worst of it, the anniversary of her death comes around again."

Suddenly, Sophie had to ask. "What is the worst of it for you?"

He sighed. "It's the guilt. That night at The Keg, I immediately saw Ari as a bully and a violent man. I should've whisked Lacey away with me to safety, gotten her off campus, totally away from him. I wanted to. I begged her the night she went to his room one last time. We had a big fight about it."

"So did we," Sophie responded.

For a moment, they sat in silence, suddenly overwhelmed by the common experience they shared. They had to live with what they didn't do and why they couldn't let go of that feeling of the "what if" they had.

"It's pretty clear now that both of us knew how much trouble Lacey was in and that she shouldn't have gone to Ari's room the night he killed her," Sophie said quietly, tears flooding her eyes now. "As if it makes a difference today." She looked up at Jack and could see tears in his eyes too.

"Yes," he said quietly. "The thing we loved most about Lacey was how strong-willed she was, doing what she wanted to do, never mind what others thought. Except that's the thing that killed her."

"Yeah," Sophie agreed. "That and a lot of other people who weren't protecting her that night. Some who knew her a little, like the campus security officers she had dealt with in the past but always felt that they, particularly the male officers, really didn't give a damn. And then others who were shocked to learn after it was all over how little had been done on the campus about abuse in relationships, let alone sexual violence and sexual harassment."

"But you've been working on that, Sophie, haven't you?" Jack said with a smile. "Amazing work with your organization. What's it called—SISTER?"

"Yes, that's it," she said, smiling back. "But it's what Lacey would have done for me, for all of us, if she were the one to have survived this kind of violence and we weren't. It's her legacy. And now, with a new president running the college, we're sure to get even further with the list of demands we've made ever since Lacey's death twenty years ago."

"That's great. I wholeheartedly support all of that. Let me know what I can do to help." Then his voice shifted. "There's something you said I could read from the book."

Sophie got up from the chair and went over to the table and

handed Jack a book with a bookmark sticking out of the top. "It's not a long piece, but take your time. It's my 'what if' from the night Lacey died."

Excerpt from

***Losing Lacey: Creating a Legacy of
Goodness, Hope, and Promise***

by Lisette Patterson Bufford

A "What If" by Sophie
Night of October 17, 1999

Neal really didn't want to check on Ari that night. He was his suite mate in an adjoining dorm room with a shared bathroom in between. Neal knew that Ari was agitated ever since what had happened at The Keg a few months ago, and he was trying to get Lacey back.

The agitation seemed to have subsided a bit when, earlier that afternoon, Neal walked with Ari to get a late lunch off-campus. But by then it was more like sadness, like Ari was depressed about his breakup with Lacey.

Neal had learned that lecturing Ari about letting Lacey go over the last few months didn't work, so they talked about other stuff. They had computer science classes in common, so they talked about how, when they got out of school, they were going to make video games for kids like them.

"Yeah," Ari said. "I'm going to do one about blowing people's heads off. That would be cool."

Neal thought that was an odd thing for Ari to say, but he was used to hearing Ari pop off at whomever he was mad at in any given week and then threaten—all in a fantasy, of course, Neal thought, that he was going to shoot someone.

By the time they had finished off a pizza at a place just off campus, it had begun to get dark on that Sunday night in October as they walked back to the dorm. Neal had homework to do for one of his classes, and Ari was talking about working on a paper that night too.

"Yeah," Ari said quickly. "Lacey is coming over to read it for me. She said she would when I talked to her yesterday."

"She's coming to see you?" Neal was surprised. "I thought the two of you had broken it off. That's what we talked about last night. You need to let her go. She's seeing someone else. She can do that, you know. Break up with you and move on to another relationship."

"Yeah, but we can still be friends, right?" Ari said with some clarity in his voice. "That's what she wants, and that's what I want too. Besides, she knows how to fix up English papers really good. With her help, I'm getting better grades now, and that, of course, always pleases my father."

Ari said that sarcastically, Neal noted. He knew that Ari had nothing but disdain for his father. And his father was never pleased with Ari or anything he did. Not ever.

So, Neal didn't even go there with Ari. But he did wonder why Lacey was coming over that night. Was she trying to dick around with Ari? Hadn't she been clear that she was done with their relationship? Did she really believe that Ari could be just friends with her? Neal didn't get it, but then maybe Lacey was coming to tell him one more time to leave her alone.

Good luck with that, he thought. *Not going to happen.*

At about 11:20 p.m., something else prompted Neal to check on his neighbor. Not realizing that Lacey was still there, he went through the bathroom and knocked on the door. He didn't wait for a response and stuck his head in.

First he saw Lacey, sitting on Ari's roommate's bed right next to the bathroom door. Her face was red from crying, but there was something more. She looked at him. She definitely looked at him, and that look haunted Neal. Like she wanted something from him—like she needed something, but what?

Then Ari got up from his computer across the room, waving some papers in his hand.

"Hey man, you're interrupting us here," he said, gesturing to include Lacey. "We're kind of talking right now. I told you, she's helping me with my paper."

Then Ari continued, rambling now. "Lots more to do. No time to waste. You know what I mean."

Ari stared at Neal, his eyes cloudy and threatening. Threatening toward him, for interrupting him while working on a school paper, Neal thought at first. Or was it toward Lacey, whom Ari had told him repeatedly had broken his heart?

Neal eyed Lacey again. When he did, she held his eyes and stirred in her seat. He knew Ari was trying to get him out of the room, but then another thought came to him, and he went for it as if by instinct.

He reached out, grabbed Lacey's hand and with one quick movement he pulled her off the bed and on her feet. She felt light and airy as her body came up close to his. He pushed her around him and into the bathroom.

Speaking rapidly now, Neal said to Ari, "Hey, I need to borrow Lacey for a minute. Be right back."

Before Ari could react, Neal dove into the bathroom himself right behind Lacey and slammed the door between the two rooms. As he locked it from his side, he yelled to Lacey.

"Get into my room quick—and lock the door to the hallway."

With some kind of instinct as sure as Neal's was now, Lacey moved swiftly, doing what she was told. As Neal came through the bathroom, he closed and locked the door leading into his room. Then he went to the window, the only one in his dorm room. It overlooked the yard between the dorm buildings.

As he unlocked it and threw it open, he yelled to Lacey.

"Come on, we're going out the window. You first!"

In that moment, a noise came from the bathroom that sounded like a bomb going off. Lacey reacted, but Neal didn't flinch.

"It's a ways down there," he continued. "We're on the second floor. You need to jump now!"

Lacey didn't hesitate for a moment. She grabbed the windowsill and leapt out, falling into the bushes down below.

Neal did the same, jumping out of the window just as he heard a second blast go off. He knew that sound. He had been hunting with his dad since he was a kid. It was a little distorted and exaggerated, but then he had never heard a rifle blowing through wooden doors inside a brick building.

Suddenly, he knew what had unsettled him from the moment he entered his suite mate's room.

Ari had a gun, and he meant to kill someone that night. With any luck, it wouldn't be him or Lacey. They'd just have to run for their lives.

It didn't take Jack long to finish reading, but Sophie could tell when he did because he looked up at her from where he was sitting on the couch in her living room. That first look was a haunted one, and it scared Sophie. Maybe it hadn't been such a good idea to have him read her "what if" scene.

As they sat there for a while just looking at each other, Sophie felt as if they were both taking in the idea that maybe, just maybe, right here, right now, Lacey wasn't dead. She was in the other room, and soon they'd both have the experience they hadn't had in twenty years of Lacey exploding into this room, bringing all her energy and excitement with her. The sheer potential of that, and the weight of all the potential in her as a lover and a friend, came with that idea too.

Tears were streaming down both of their faces. As they wiped them away with the tissues from the box on the coffee table between them, slowly the intensity of that moment of living in an alternative universe where Lacey was still alive sunk in.

Jack spoke first in a creaky voice filled with emotion. "If only it was me that was there that night to save her, not Neal. I should've figured out that she was in trouble. I was going to call her, see how she was doing that night, but she asked me to give her some space. You and I both knew she'd never get Ari to leave her alone. We should've gone with her to Campus Security and made them do something about it. But Lacey thought they were just a bunch of stupid old men who didn't think women should even be in college, let alone need their protection. They'd never been very helpful to her or any other girls in the past with security issues. She declared them all idiots, and that was it."

Jack stopped for a moment, his whole body shuddering as he bellowed out, "You and I should've helped her. Done more. It was our fault. We failed her. We did it."

By now, Jack was sobbing openly, his whole body shaking. He was hunched over, and a shrill sound was coming from his throat.

"You can't do this, Jack," Sophie yelled back at him. "You can't do this to yourself and certainly not to me. I showed you the book and had you read the scene to ease your mind, not to excite it. You have to let this go. Please! Tell me you'll be all right!"

By now she was at his side, sitting there on the couch and putting her arm around one of his shoulders. "Jack, Jack!" she shouted. "You have to calm down."

Instead of doing that, he turned and threw his arms around her, pulled her close and, still sobbing, he pressed his face into her chest.

Sophie let him hold her like that for a moment until his sobs subsided and he unwrapped his arms from around her. Then they sat side by side, breathing together in a moment Sophie knew neither of them really understood. Was it grief or healing or just utter confusion about how either of them should feel, given what they had just experienced together?

Unable to move, Sophie sat riveted to her seat next to him, not sure how and when this evening was going to end. Suddenly Jack turned to look at her, gazing deeply into her eyes, and as he gently grazed her chin with his hand, he leaned down and kissed her. The kiss was soft and inviting, but she broke it off quickly.

"Jack, I don't think we should be doing this. I think it's time for you to leave."

He looked at her sheepishly. "You're right. I should've asked you before I did that. And you must think maybe I thought I was kissing Lacey instead of you, but I wasn't. I was here with you. But you're right, I don't know what I'm doing. I should leave."

He stumbled to get up, but his foot got caught between the coffee table and the edge of the couch, and he almost fell. Sophie grabbed him and pushed him back down on the couch.

"No," she insisted. "You sit down. Let me get you a glass of water from the kitchen. Stay here. I'll be right back."

When she got to the kitchen, she grabbed a glass from the cupboard, and as she filled it up with water at the sink, she felt a wave of emotion come over her. She let herself feel it for a moment and then took a deep breath. She didn't expect this to happen tonight. What was she thinking, inviting Jack over to her place when he was still in such agony over Lacey? What was she thinking?

Before she could get herself back in the living room, Jack suddenly appeared at the door to the kitchen. "I'm going to leave. I

---

called my sister, and she's picking me up. I don't think I should drive home myself. Can I leave my car on the street overnight? I'm sorry for all this—and embarrassed too. My emotions are all over the place. I have to go."

Sophie looked at him for a moment and then said, "I just thought it'd help you to imagine another scenario, but that was crazy. You've got your own demons. I'm sorry."

"No, no. It's not your fault." Then he took a breath and added, "And it wasn't mine either. I got caught up in lots of feelings that I haven't dealt with for a long a time. I need to sort it out. I'll see you when I see you. I'll try to come to the gala on Thursday. I'll see what I can do." His voice trailed off just as the buzzer to Sophie's downstair doorbell rang out in the room. Although the sound was familiar to her, Sophie jumped as if it was one more surprise for her that night she didn't expect.

She looked at Jack. "Is that your sister? That was quick."

"Yeah," Jack said quietly. "She was in the neighborhood when I called her. She knows where you live." Then he touched her arm lightly. "I'll see myself out. Thank you, Sophie. Thank you so much."

With that, Jack Howe was gone, and Sophie stood there at the sink, still holding the glass of water. But then, suddenly overwhelmed, the glass slipped out of her hand as she collapsed onto the floor, sobbing hysterically. She hadn't cried like that—so intensely and forlornly—since she learned that Lacey was dead. It seemed to her that nothing she had done since, no matter how good or how substantial, had made the pain that this crying had brought on any less. She missed her dear friend Lacey, and once again, she cried as if there were no end to the measure and meaning of her great loss.

Except that there was one more person in the world who understood that.

And that was Jack Howe. She'd known for a while, that no one could or would sustain an intimate partner relationship with her if they didn't understand the intensity of the underlying reason she did the work she did and felt the same passion for it as she did. But she hadn't figured on Jack showing up, bringing up feelings in her and a longing for intimacy with someone who had actually known Lacey.

What would that be like? Would it be strange? Like he couldn't have Lacey, but he could have Sophie? Was that selling herself short, creating a weird triangle of love and attraction that included one part of the threesome who was dead.

She shuttered as she thought about it for a moment, like it was too maudlin or too strange. But then she felt the strong pull of the bond between the two of them—Jack and Sophie, alive and well today—and she longed for it so much. It was something she thought she'd never get to have in her life post-Lacey. She thought she was meant to sacrifice that kind of feeling because she hadn't been there to save Lacey. She could only write a scenario now that spelled out what could have happened if only she and Jack had been more aware, more capable, and more successful at saving the life of the one human being who meant so much to them both. They'd never forget her, but could they build a relationship in the shadow of such a tragedy?

Did she need to find out? Did she want to try, or should she just let it go?

She contemplated that as she picked up her cell phone and texted: "Jack. I think we need to talk. When? Where? Your place or mine?"

LISETTE

Monday, October 14, 2019

It was three days before the Twentieth Anniversary Celebration Gala and Lisette was now officially in a panic.

What was she thinking? Where did she get such a crazy idea that she was going to write a book? Was it even possible that she had actually done it?

Last night she lay awake in bed long after Erick had fallen asleep next to her, paging through an advanced copy of the book. *Oh God!* she thought as she read it. She knew from Sophie's workshop that her Inner Critic was now going wild, and she was unable to stop it.

This book is so stupid! Especially the part about a shamanic journey to retrieve my soul parts left behind when my mother died. No one is going to believe that. It's so crazy.

Why didn't all those people who agreed to write pieces in her book talk her out of this? Who was she kidding? She was no writer. Of course, she hadn't written the whole book. She figured out how to get them to write most of it, and then she put it all together in a book. Her dad helped her a lot with it too. He was her editor. He believed in the book, why didn't she? When she told him she was afraid of putting herself out there, calling herself an author when she really wasn't one, he was quick with his advice.

He told her, "Be brave, be bold. You were Attila the Hunny on the stage. If you can do that, you can do anything."

But even remembering that conversation and how her dad helped her thank everyone in the book's acknowledgments, she still didn't sleep much last night.

She woke up this morning in a sweat. It was so bad that Erick thought she was sick.

"No, hon, I'm just nervous—very nervous about what's going to happen this Thursday at the gala."

Now Erick was getting dressed as she laid in bed waiting for the kids to wake up. He usually fed the kids breakfast and got them off to day care and preschool, so he was up and ready to roll. Lisette, exhausted from not sleeping well, just wanted to pull the covers over her head and die! She was going to die of embarrassment anyway on Thursday when she got up to read the introduction to the crowd at the book launch part of the gala. Why not just die now? Get it over with!

Erick stopped in the middle of tying his tie and looked at her intensely. It was as if he hadn't really heard the panic in her voice, and suddenly now he did. He came over to her side of the bed and sat down next to her all curled up on the bed.

"Honey, you look like you've crawled back into your mother's womb and may be stuck in the fetal position for days!" Then he laughed. "And don't ask me about how to spell *fetal* right now. But you know what that's like. It's how Jeremy and Sasha were like all cuddled up inside you before they were born." Then he grinned at her. "I get that you are nervous, but let me help you think about this another way."

She looked up at him, full of hope. Did he have a way for her to get through the book launch without even getting on the stage? Was that possible? Someone else could be up there. Sophie could do it, she thought. *She's the one who should do it!*

Erick began with a question. "About how many times do you think over all the years that you were a stripper . . ." Then he stopped for a moment and asked another question. "How long were you a stripper?"

Lisette screwed up her face and gave him a look. "I started when I was seventeen when I got emancipated, and I was nineteen when I came here to dance and met you . . . and then Lacey died. I went back to LA and danced for another five years on and off while also licensing the Atilla the Hunny name. And then I danced—"

Erick cut her off. "Okay, we don't need exact numbers here, but let's say you danced for five or six years on the stage. How many times in those years would you say you danced and took your clothes off down to the barest minimum? How many hundreds of times?"

She gave him a puzzled look. "What you're saying is that if I could do that—take all my clothes off in front of all those creepy customers for years—I should be able to get up and read from my book?"

"No, of course this is different. Or is it? What did you do to psych yourself up every night? You must have gotten confident about your abilities to whip up the crowd, right? When I met you, you were the headline stripper of one of the most popular strip clubs in the area."

Erick made it sound as if it was something she should be proud of.

She laughed. "I don't know if I'd call it confidence, but I did get so nothing bothered me up there. I found a way to enjoy the more creative parts of the act. It's what got me in trouble so many times with the club owners. But when I could really feel the energy of Atilla the Hunny up on that stage, that was a good night. It was amazing."

Erick laughed. "So then I'd get into some of that warrior energy Thursday night. You can do this, Lisette. I can't think of an audience that is going to be more open to you and the book. You've got people coming who are in the book! They are going to own their part and add their energy to yours! It's going to be great, and most of all, it will be for Lacey. That's the best part. You are raising money for the incredible work that you and Sophie are doing in her honor." Then he added confidently, "And if that night anyone says or does anything other than give you love and respect for all your hard work, remember, once a bouncer, always a bouncer. I've got your back."

By now, the two of them were snuggled together, holding and kissing each other.

Then Lisette had an idea. "I know. I'll wear my Mom's furry white coat for the book launch, the one I used in my Atilla the Hunny act. It's always a showstopper. Remember how I'd take it off and toss it into the crowd? It could be my backup act Thursday night."

They laughed until they heard the pitter-patter of little feet coming through their open bedroom door and up to the foot of their bed. Suddenly two small bodies hurled themselves onto the covers, giggling and talking really fast.

"Daddy, Daddy," Sasha was saying. "It's time to go to school, right? I need to get to school early. We have our play today. The practice. That's what we are doing. My teacher said it's a practice, not the real thing yet. But soon. So we have to get it good."

Erick pulled himself out of bed and scooped his daughter and son into his arms.

"Okay, I'm ready to go into the kitchen to rustle up breakfast. Let's leave Mommy to luxuriate in bed for a little while more." Then, as they walked away, he looked at his daughter intensely. "Do you know what *luxuriate* means? Can you spell it?"

Lisette watched them as they headed to the kitchen. She knew that last remark was just Erick teasing her about her spelling. But then if her daughter, all of four years old, could be so excited about being in a play at school, Lisette could get up at the gala and read.

Right? No problem. You got this, Lisette, she told herself. You do!

SOPHIE

Monday, October 14, 2019

Today, in the office for the meeting of the Twentieth Anniversary Celebration Gala Planning Committee, Sophie was ready to report on who had accepted the special invitations she had sent out to Lacey's college graduating class of 2002.

These were the VIPs for this event. Because they had known Lacey, they might make some major donations to the SISTER organization. Many were now very successful doctors, lawyers, and businesspeople and Sophie wanted them to be acknowledged in a very special way on the night of the gala.

But more than anything else, she wanted to acknowledge publicly how brave they all were on graduation day. Of course, everyone in the audience knew why Lacey was not there, but the college wouldn't let anyone on the stage that day talk about how Lacey died and who had murdered her or share anything about the changes the school had made, if any, to have women students be safer on campus. So, although it was a crazy thing to do at the time because none of them had their diplomas yet after four long years of school, Lacey's friends and close classmates had agreed on a joint act of defiance. It would be a silent protest; they would ask all the graduating seniors to wear a purple ribbon, the symbol of the movement to end violence against women, on their gowns to honor Lacey and all victims of violence against women. While the school officials agreed to call Lacey's name along with the other graduates who were to receive their diplomas on stage, they refused the request by Lacey's friends to have the ceremony include remarks by a prominent local advocate against domestic violence or any other mention of that term from the stage. Sophie never forgot that deliberate omission by the college and the courageous activism of her fellow graduates in Lacey's name back then. It wasn't going to happen again.

Of course, things were different now that there was a new president of the college, this time a woman. The first in the history of the college! It wasn't smooth sailing yet, but things were getting so much better.

But what concerned Sophie more in making this report to the staff and gala volunteers about who was attending and exactly how they would be recognized from the stage was that she really needed to tell Lisette that one particular graduate, Jack, was coming on Thursday night and was, in fact, already in town.

If she were to add further details, Sophie had spent most of the weekend with him. Maybe it was all of the weekend, actually. They had been—and Sophie thought she could use this word with Lisette now that it was in her vocabulary—"canoodling" together all three days. Yes, that wild and unexpected kiss they had shared at her condo on Friday night had progressed into a full weekend of absorbing each other in every way possible. Sophie imagined that it started with their shared guilt and grief over what happened to their dear friend, Lacey, but that wasn't what it turned into by late Sunday night.

In fact, they had an impassioned discussion just before midnight about how they could work together to push Sophie's work in Lacey's honor even further. Jack was particularly interested in working with Erick on the Men's Initiative to add a program specifically for veterans. But he also had a sense that Sophie could approach some people in the government about her program and possibly get federal funding to expand it around the country. He was willing to contact some of the congressional staff he knew from his Army days to see what that might yield. He confessed that after all those years of computer work, he'd love to do some policy work to help advance Sophie's cause.

So all this was coming together nicely. Of course, Sophie wouldn't have even been able to get good mailing addresses for the graduating class if Lisette didn't have an "in" with someone in the "front office." When she went right to the President's Office to request current addresses for the alumni and it was granted, she thought it helped that the president of the school just happened to be Lisette's stepmother, Jenny Jablonski.

Yes, in the years since the Tenth Anniversary Gala, things had changed for Jenny and her husband, Brad. While Jenny had barely squeaked by getting reelected in 2010, she lost as governor in 2014 but was almost immediately hired to be the president of the college a short time later. It was a good connection for Sophie, not only because she had been an adjunct professor at the college teaching women's legal rights classes but also as the founder and now CEO of SISTER. Sophie was pleased that President Jablonski knew about, supported, and brought a sense of legitimacy to the topic of violence against women being discussed and dealt with on that campus. Suddenly school policies and practices on the issue were more aggressively being put in line with Title IX, the federal law outlawing discrimination on the basis of sex in educational opportunities. Yes, a new day had come to the college, and it was long overdue in Sophie's mind. If only those changes had been in place years ago, Lacey might still be alive, but Sophie didn't like to dwell on that thought. It was too heartbreaking for her.

In addition, Sophie was pleased that Jenny had written a piece in Lisette's new book about how her unfulfilled aspirations as a politician were a defining moment in her life and how her "What Next" was to continue fighting for equality for women on college campuses, particularly to ensure equal educational and career opportunities.

Sophie was also pleased with others who had pieces in Lisette's book, including Lacey's father, whom they all called Howie. He had been helping SISTER have legislative successes for a number of years. Sophie also shared her own pieces, as gut-wrenching as they were for her to write and put into print, but the process had also brought her to an amazing new place. It was one more unexpected thing to flow from Lacey's violent, senseless death. But as she pointed out regularly to the survivors in her *My Avenging Angel Workshops*™, sometimes we can't control what happens to us and others around us; we can only control what we do next in spite of it.

Now it looked as if she'd have Jack in her life to help her take her organization to the next level. It's funny that Jack talked about her going to Washington, DC, and getting some support from the federal government for her work. Sophie already had an idea about that, but it was bigger than the one Jack had put out there. In fact, it was her "What's Next" piece in Lisette's book that she had written before Jack reappeared in her life. Now, with Jack's help, she might be able to manifest this even sooner.

Sophie saw all of this as a way for her to position herself and SISTER in the next ten years so that at the Thirtieth Anniversary Celebration Gala, there would be so much more they would have accomplished in Lacey's name. But it wasn't a contest or about feeding anyone's ego or boasting about how smart they all were. Instead, she and all the others who knew or didn't know Lacey would carry on her legacy, being called to serve a higher purpose in life and having a positive impact on the world around them. Sophie had rarely shied away from an opportunity to do the right thing, even before Lacey's death, and now she was on this journey from victim to survivor to thriver, and she was going to make it big and powerful.

No way Lacey deserved anything less!

LISETTE

Monday, October 14, 2019

When Lisette arrived at the office for the Twentieth Anniversary Celebration Gala Planning Committee, she was thinking again about the launch of her book on Thursday. She was no longer nervous or afraid about putting her work out there. Instead she was thinking about how she got the idea for the book in the first place.

She remembered that it was a goal she had set for herself when she took Sophie's workshop for the first time ten years ago. It was almost impossible for her to imagine then that she could reach that goal because she wasn't much of a reader and hardly a writer at the time. Furthermore, she didn't have a thought in her head about anything she could write about that anyone would want to read.

But then one day, she realized that the book didn't have to be about her. What if it could be about other people, like the ones around her who had become her "role models" over the years? They all had "Defining Moments" in their lives that they could write about. Maybe it was something that put them on a new course in their lives or "defined" (or "redefined") their purpose in life. They could also write about situations they hoped could have gone differently. Those would be "What If" stories. What if this had happened differently? Where would they be today? Better off or not?

Those were two things she definitely wanted to know from her role models. Finally, she'd like to know "What's Next" in their lives. Where did they want to go? Had they had found their purpose in life or were they still seeking it? All these pieces might actually flow from what they had experienced because of and since Lacey's death. That was interesting to Lisette, too.

Of course, even if she had a great idea for a book, could she find enough people to contribute those kinds of pieces in a book that she could sell and raise money for SISTER? The first people she thought of asking to contribute a chapter were Sophie, Brad, Jenny, and Erick. She'd write something too—with Brad's help. Finally, she'd have to figure out how to get the work done for the book along with all the other things she was doing right now. She was sure that Brad would help her compile the book, and she could ask Brooke, now on staff at SISTER, to help anyone who needed assistance pulling their story together.

Her final and best thought about putting this book together was how she might have to "twist the arms" of a few people to be a part of her project. One person she definitely needed to get onboard was Howie Lockhart, Lacey's dad. He was working with SISTER now and had a story to tell about his journey of healing beyond Lacey's death. But the one that would be the toughest, Lisette figured, would be Ambrose.

God knows, Ambrose could use some self-reflection, or "introspection," in his life. Lisette learned that word and what it meant in one of her literacy sessions with her dad. Yes, that was exactly what Ambrose needed. She knew he was struggling with what was happening with his son Mark these days, having been charged with killing ten people in the mall. Through all the court hearings, appeals, and sentencing hearings, the case had dragged on for years, not counting the civil suits Ambrose had brought against the state for failing to give Mark adequate mental health services as a ward of the state. Lisette had talked to Ambrose on the phone a few times since the shooting spree, listening to him and trying to help. But she wasn't a therapist or a mental health professional; she just felt sorry for him. He wanted her to visit Mark, as if she could get through to him, but she didn't want to cause her mother-in-law any problems while she was still governor.

Now since Jenny had stepped down from that office, Lisette felt a little freer to approach Ambrose about writing something for the book. What he did write, Brad agreed, was definitely "introspection" as only Ambrose could do it.

Finally, the remaining question Lisette had about her book was who would buy it. She could get the local press any day to follow up about Lacey and her story, but she'd need the national press to give it a real boost in sales. She has some ideas about that. For starters, Sophie had made a real effort in this twentieth year to invite and encourage her entire graduating class of 2002. Some had been coming and helping out with the gala for years, and even more might come and share their journeys this year. Surely, there were books to be sold there.

With her book to mark the twentieth-year celebration, all of Lisette's thoughts and dreams about it had finally manifested. The book was done. It was finished, edited, and proofread. The title had been chosen, the photos on the cover selected, the dedication and acknowledgments complete. The chapters were done that contained the Defining Moments, What Ifs, and What's Next for each person who agreed to write and share their pieces in the book.

It was, as she wrote in the Introduction to the book, a labor of love for Lisette, and now that it was printed and ready to be launched this Thursday night, she wondered if this was her purpose in life. Could one book be someone's purpose—or was there more to it? After all, this book was meant to show the world how the violent, senseless murder of one person impacted so many good people who loved her. They, like Sophie, were inspired by how Lacey lived and died to want to bring something good into the world. But, Lisette wondered, was there more to her purpose in life than writing this book?

For Lisette, she wished she could ask her mother, Marie, that question right now. She would know, and at moments like this, that's when Lisette felt her grief over the loss of her mother more than ever. The loss would sweep over her like a blanket of gloom, trying to smother her and snuff out her breath. At those times, she had to stop herself, take a deep breath, and remind herself of what her mother had told her years ago on that shamanic journey, "I'm always with you. You just live your life in the present in the most purposeful way. That will be your perfect life."

Was this her perfect life? Was this her purpose? What Lisette did know is that she had kept her mother close to her long after her death. She named her daughter Sasha Marie for her grandmother, Marie Patterson, and Jeremy Brad for his grandfather, Brad Bufford. Although her children's last names were Larson, Erick's family name, she had kept her name as Lisette Patterson Bufford in honor of her mother, Marie Patterson, and her father, Brad Bufford.

In addition, often she and her dad would swap memories of Marie, the girlfriend and lover he knew so many years ago, and Lisette would talk about her mom who left her such a treasure of memories that filled her heart with joy, and gave her such wisdom.

Today, Lisette's loved teaching her son and daughter to become the best, strongest, and most resilient children they could ever be just as her mother had taught her. They wouldn't have to learn the hard way as she did after her mother died. For that alone, Lisette was sure Marie would be proud of her, and Brad was overjoyed.

But most of all, Lisette hoped the book she had compiled out of love and admiration for her heroes would inspire others to find their heroes and live their best life ever!

Living well was the best revenge!

PART TWO

The Book

Losing Lacey: Creating a Legacy of Goodness, Hope and Promise
by
Lisette Patterson Bufford

Dedication

This book is dedicated to Lacey, my inspiration and guide.

To Sophie, the one who has transformed me.

To my mother, Marie Patterson, and my father, Brad Bufford,

who have given me eternal and unconditional love.

To my beautiful children, Sasha Marie and Jeremy Brad,

and my husband, Erick, the love of my life.

I could never have done this without all of you.

Thank you!

Acknowledgments

This book has been a labor of love from the moment I thought of writing it to the day I held a copy of the finished book in my hand.

I want to acknowledge and thank the many people who agreed to contribute their writing to this book. I gave them an idea and the opportunity to write about some events that shaped their lives, recognize mistakes they wished they could have avoided, and contemplate where they might be going in the future.

Some of the pieces are surprisingly short and to the point. Others are longer and exquisite in detail. But there were no demands put on any of the contributors to this book as to the form and style of their writing. If they didn't feel they could write their story themselves, others stepped up to help. Chief among them was Brooke Halder, on staff at SISTER: *Survivor Strong, Thriver Resilient,* who helped create brilliant essays and novel-like scenes that bring the stories of this book to life.

As much pain as Lacey's death caused all of us, there have been many good and wonderful things that came to pass as a result. One of them is this book. I had an idea of writing a book about Lacey and what she has left behind, but as many of you know, I was functionally illiterate until a few years ago. Sophie's workshops inspired me to set a thriver goal of completing this book—and I did it!

Thanks to Brad Bufford, all-round good dad who was the editor of this book and my literacy coach. He has loved me unconditionally since the day we found each other ten years ago, and I owe him my life and everything good that has happened to me ever since. To Sophie, founder of SISTER, I love you like a sister. You inspired me to write a book and helped me manifest this one. Maybe there are more.

I am thriving every day now because of you. Thank you!

Introduction

Lisette Patterson Bufford

This is my book, and I hope you like it. I never thought I'd do anything like this. I never thought that I'd even have an idea about what to write in a book. But it came to me in a flash a few years ago when I was in one of the *My Avenging Angel Workshops™*, originated and facilitated for many years by my friend Sophie Stafford. In her workshops, Sophie taught me that "living well is the best revenge" and guided me about how to live well and have a fabulous life.

I met Sophie twenty years ago when I first came to town to dance at a local strip club. Some of you may know this about me already. I danced under the name of "Atilla the Hunny," and I'm glad that I did. Later, I made money lending my stage name to strip clubs across the country, but today I'm most proud of what I do with SISTER—*Survivor Strong, Thriver Resilient*, a nonprofit organization started by Sophie.

Through this book, you'll learn more about Lacey Lockhart, a nineteen-year-old student who was killed on a college campus by her ex-boyfriend twenty years ago. When I was dancing at a club near the college where she was killed that night, her spirit came into my body, and I didn't know how to get it out of me. That sounds a little crazy, I know, but it was a way for me to get to know Lacey, the people who loved her, and the magnificence of her spirit even after her death. In this book, you'll find out more about my journey and the journeys of many other people who were influenced by Lacey. She inspires each of us by how she lived and how she died, for—as Sophie says—we are all on a journey from victim to survivor to thriver.

Yes, we survived Lacey's violent, senseless death, but in her honor and memory, today we are thrivers! We have moved on to find our true value and purpose in life, and we are inspiring others to do the same. These are the stories of the defining moments of our lives, the "what if" we can only imagine, and the "what's next" we want to manifest in the future. May the experiences of our lives help you find a life of power and purpose in yours.

Be the hero of your own story!

Be a thriver!

Lisette

CHAPTER FIVE

Lisette's Journey

Late November 2009

Defining Moment

A Soul Retrieval

When she came walking into Radiance's workroom that afternoon with Sophie, Lisette felt as if she stepped back ten years in time.

Maybe it was because Radiance's workroom looked exactly as she remembered it, and it felt as magical to Lisette as the first time she had visited it. The walls were still lined with tall shelves of books, and mobiles made of paper and string hung from the ceiling. On the opposite wall, drums with brightly colored pictures painted on them were hanging above a stack of blankets and soft cushions on the floor.

Even Radiance looked the same: short, stocky, and as big around as Lisette remembered her. She still greeted them with the same big hug as they came into her apartment, pulling them both to her soft, fleshy body. Then she walked them back to her workroom, tempting them along the way with the same, tantalizing promise of a treat—chocolate chip cookies—awaiting them on a small table there. Lisette knew those homemade cookies usually made an appearance when her granddaughter, Sophie, came for a visit, but now it seemed that Lisette was also celebrated with this treat.

The only difference over the past ten years since Lisette was last in town was that Radiance's wild red hair was now silver, and her face was more lined and crinkled. But she was as positive and radiant—as her name suggested—as ever.

"Oh my, Lisette. It is so wonderful to see you again," Radiance gushed as the three of them sat for a chat on the soft cushions on the floor around that low table in the center of her workroom. "You look younger and happier than when I last saw you. Of course, then you were troubled by the spirit of Lacey stuck in your body, but we took care of that, didn't we?"

Radiance chuckled as she said that, but Lisette knew how serious it all was. She remembered how desperate she felt and how Radiance was the only person who could help her. She guided her through two shamanic journeys from this space, lying on a blanket on the floor next to her. Lisette remembered those journeys now like sleeping dreams but very vivid ones, as if they had just happened yesterday. In the first one, she visited with the spirit of her mother, Marie, who reassured her that she would find her purpose in life. That time with her mother eased Lisette's mind so she could let go of all that had happened to her after her mother's death when Lisette was only ten years old. In the second journey, Lisette was there to watch as Lacey's spirit crossed over and was welcomed into paradise by the spirit of Lacey's mother.

Today, Lisette was back in Radiance's workroom because Sophie had picked up on something during a mentoring session with Lisette after she had participated in one of Sophie's *My Avenging Angel Workshops*™. Sophie thought that maybe, with all the trauma in her life, parts of Lisette's soul had been lost and needed to be retrieved.

Sophie had explained it to Lisette this way: "Sometimes we have lost 'parts' of our soul that have been 'split off' from us because of the abuse, loss, and trauma we have experienced, and they need to be brought back to us so we can feel whole again."

Lisette didn't quite understand it, but she was impressed that Sophie had also done a soul retrieval with Radiance and gotten parts of her soul back. She said she felt so much better and happier in her life. Those parts of Sophie's soul were left behind after she was taken from her mother, a drug addict, and brought to live with her grandmother, Radiance. Sophie's mother later died of an overdose, so Sophie never saw her again.

While Lisette wasn't totally sold yet on what this soul retrieval could do for her, she remembered how Radiance had guided her through the other shamanic journeys ten years ago, and she trusted her. In fact, that experience of watching Lacey cross over was so emotionally powerful for Lisette that she was ready to try anything Radiance thought would help her, particularly now that Erick was back in her life. Lisette wanted to feel and cherish every emotion of the endless possibilities that might lie ahead for her in a life with Erick. But she couldn't always find a way to imagine good things coming her way without thinking about all the bad things that had happened and might happen again someday. Sophie was right. Lisette was holding herself back for some reason.

Lisette knew Radiance could help her find her way to true happiness.

When Sophie made the appointment with Radiance for Lisette's soul retrieval, Radiance suggested that Lisette bring with her an article of clothing or jewelry, preferably something she'd had for a while. Lisette wasn't sure what to bring.

She hadn't been able to hold on to many things in her life. She moved around a lot as a kid after her mother died and she went to live with Ralph. After being in several foster homes, she was finally sent to a home for girls. When she was emancipated at seventeen, she lived and worked here and there for a while until she started dancing at strip clubs. For those gigs, she traveled around the country, going from town to town, city to city—wherever she could get work. While her base eventually became Los Angeles, she was never there long enough for it to be home.

But despite all that moving around in her life, Lisette knew exactly what she could bring to the soul retrieval. She realized there was one thing she always had with her, no matter where she was. It was a short, furry white coat her mom had worn for years that Lisette inherited when her mother died. She still had that coat and took it everywhere. It was even part of her "Atilla the Hunny" act, the first thing she'd take off when she got on stage to dance. At times, when the crowd got really riled up, she'd get excited too; and she'd lose track of it on stage or toss it out into the audience. She'd be mad at herself for doing that, but each time, the coat would come back to her safe and sound. In fact, the first time she met Ambrose, he brought the coat back to her dressing room at the Pussycat's Meow Club, the new place she was working at about a week after Lacey was killed. Of course, Lisette learned later that wasn't the only reason he showed up that night, but for her, it was all part of the history of the coat.

Radiance listened to Lisette as she showed her the coat and told her its story. Radiance confirmed that it would be a good thing for her to watch for as she searched for Lisette's lost soul parts on her shamanic journey.

Then Radiance asked Lisette her mother's name.

"Marie," Lisette said. "Marie Patterson. Why? Do think that is important?"

"Maybe," Radiance replied. "I never know what'll come up in a soul retrieval."

"Then maybe this is important, too," Lisette added. "My name wasn't always Lisette. When I was born, my mother named me Lisa. I changed it to Lisette when I was emancipated."

"Good to know," Radiance responded. "That might be important. And I remember you telling me before that Ralph was the man you thought was your father for most of your childhood. Also good to know."

So while the girls consumed the plate of chocolate chip cookies in front of them, Radiance gave Lisette a little more detail about how the soul retrieval would work and Lisette's role in it. She would lie down on a blanket on the floor next to Radiance like the other journeys Lisette had done, but this time when Sophie started drumming, Lisette wouldn't be going into non-ordinary reality herself. Instead she'd stay there in the workroom on the blanket next to Radiance, with their shoulders, hips, and ankles touching. It was Radiance who would travel to non-ordinary reality and come back to ordinary reality in the workroom after she found one or more of Lisette's soul parts. The ritual would end when Radiance had blown all those soul parts back into Lisette through her chest and the top of her head.

Excited but unsure how all this was going to turn out, Lisette got into place. Sophie began the low, steady beat of the drum that reminded Lisette of how the human heartbeat. Lisette knew the drumming would allow Radiance to shift her consciousness and enter into non-ordinary reality, the realms where human and animal spirits dwell. As the session began, Lisette also heard Radiance rattling several times around her, and then, as Radiance had explained earlier, she sank into an altered state of consciousness while Lisette was lying quietly beside her.

While Sophie drummed, Radiance hardly moved a muscle for a good twenty minutes, but then as if her energy suddenly rushed back into the room, Radiance sat up and brought Lisette to sit next to her.

Lisette felt the warmth of a thousand candles suddenly flood her body.

"Oh my!" Lisette said with breathless excitement. "What did you do? It feels so wonderful. I've never felt like . . ." Her voice trailed off. She had no words until she asked, "Did you find my soul parts? Tell me, tell me. Quick! I have to know." Lisette exhaled deeply. "Oh my! This is so huge. I can't believe it."

Radiance then told Lisette and Sophie the tale of her hunt for Lisette's soul.

As I vibrate with the sounds of the drumbeat and connect with my power animal, I state my intention to locate the missing soul parts of Lisette and bring them home to her. With those words said, I find myself flying over a large city, looking down on all the buildings, streets, and people. I'm not drawn to anything in particular until I see a huge medical center with lots of buildings. As I swoop down to get closer, the building I am drawn to seems to be in a special wing of the hospital that deals with cancer patients. A sign to that effect is on the outside of this six- or seven-story building. Looking through the windows from the outside of the building, I can see into the rooms where patients appear to be very sick or dying. They lay motionless, hooked up to a lot of medical equipment, and in some rooms, I see doctors and nurses caring for them. In other rooms I see hospital attendants pulling white sheets over still bodies in beds and then wheeling the beds out of the room. I also see a larger waiting room where family members or friends are gathered, talking in small circles or sitting alone and crying. Others are being told by doctors that their loved one has just passed away.

I can see now that I'm probably in the hospice area of the cancer center where patients who are near death are cared for, and these family and friends are there to say goodbye. My eyes fill with tears as

I see so many sad, heartbreaking moments passing by the windows of these rooms, one after another. I'm amazed at the courage and unconditional love of these people for their loved ones, clearly being there so they will not have to die alone.

But while I'm watching a particular family holding hands in a circle around the bed of a patient who appears to be unconscious, I catch a glimpse of something white and furry in the next room. I move closer to that window and look inside. I see a young girl, about nine or ten years old, sitting at the bedside of a female patient. The girl is holding the patient's hand and quietly sobbing. My eyes are suddenly riveted on her, trying to determine the exact location of the room on what appears to be the second floor of the building. I need to get in there and talk to her before something or someone leads her out of that room.

I ask my power animal for help, and I'm lowered down to the ground to enter the building. I head for the elevators to go up to the second floor. I'm hoping I can find that room and that young girl. She may be the Lisa I'm looking for.

As I pass the front desk where visitors sign in and out, I hear a man wearing a "Visitor" tag asking the women at the desk when visiting hours are over. When he's told in half an hour, he tells the woman that he's been up on the second floor in room 201 visiting the patient Marie Patterson. Then he adds, "Look, I'm Ralph. I'm going out for a quick smoke and a cup of coffee. I'll be back. My daughter, Lisa, is up there visiting with her mom, but I'll be back soon. I don't know if it's going to take me all of that half hour, but I will come back and get Lisa. She thinks her mom is going to wake up and talk to her, so she doesn't want to leave. But the docs say Marie's on her last legs and so drugged up, she'll never be conscious again before she croaks. Lisa won't listen to me, though, and just come home with me. Geeze! The things I have to deal with!"

I'm astonished at this guy. First of all, it's like too much information to blurt out in the public area of a medical center, but it's also such a callous way to talk about Lisa. Second, who is he? Is he related to Marie? I'm shocked that he'd leave the girl up there alone with her dying mother, but the woman at the front desk doesn't seem concerned and just waves him off.

As Ralph goes off in another direction, I rush to the elevator going up and sneak in with the others getting on. I set an intention for someone to push the second-floor button, but no one does. Still the elevator does stop, and when the doors open, we are on the second floor. I'm thrilled, but the people in the elevator aren't. They look at one another and re-mark about why the elevator just stopped at the second floor when no one pushed the button for it. But in that moment, I take the opportunity to get off the elevator and head for room 201. When I find it, the door is open, so I step inside. There I see the girl, who I think is Lisa, sitting in the chair. I approach her cautiously and ask her name. Instead of responding, she asks, "Who are you?" I tell her I'm a friend of her mother's, and that her mother invited me to come see her today. Then, when I call her by her name, she looks up at me with a scowl on her face, and responds, "How do you know my mom? I've never seen you before."

Before I can say anything, her mother makes a kind of moaning sound. Her head shifts slightly in what I'd hardly call a movement, but Lisa, on the other hand, sees it differently. She is far more willing to see it as a positive sign of something that she wants very badly.

"See," Lisa yells. "She's waking up. I told you she would. I knew she would."

I look at her tormented face and want to be as positive as I can, but I know what is going to happen next, so I tread carefully with her.

"Honey, I don't think your mom is asleep. I think she is very, very sick and . . ."

"No, No, NO!" Lisa screams. "No, she is not going to leave me. Ralph says that just to be mean to me. She'll be coming home soon. I know. I know."

By now, Lisa is on the bed with her mother, coming close up to her *face and pressing her fingers on her mouth, trying to make her mother's lips move in response to her pleas.*

"You are coming home, Mommy, right? Soon. I miss you, Mommy."

Then her pleas get even louder. "Please, Mommy. Please, Mommy. Please."

Her voice is almost shrill.

At that moment, the noise Lisa was making must have been heard in the hall because a nurse appears at the door and asks, "Is everything all right in here?" Then she looks around the room and asks, "Where is your father, Lisa? I thought he was here with you. I told him kids aren't allowed in these rooms without an adult."

Lisa is confused. She turns and points at me, screaming, "She's here. She's with me." The nurse looks to where Lisette is pointing, but of course, she can't see me; only Lisa can. "I can stay," Lisa insists. "I promise I'll be quiet. Ralph is coming back soon. He said he needs a smoke."

The nurse eyes her. "Okay, but you need to get off the bed. Climb down now."

Lisa immediately obeys her.

Then the nurse adds, "Sit down here in your chair and quiet yourself. I'll go find out where your father is. He knows he's not supposed to leave you alone. "

Suddenly the room is quiet, with calm restored, but that's when Marie suddenly wakes up. Lisette is immediately off her chair and back up by Marie's bedside.

"Lisa?" Her mother's voice is creaky but steady. "Lisa, is that you?"

"Yes, Mommy. I'm so happy you are better. I love you, Mommy."

Marie says quietly, "I love you too, honey. To the moon and back, right? Like I always say." Then she gives Lisa a weak smile.

After a few short breaths that sound more like gasps, Marie continues in a voice a little stronger and steadier but still weak.

"Look, honey. I need you to go with this nice lady over there. Her name is Radiance. She is a good person, and she'll take good care of

you. She'll get you to where you belong with Lisette. Will you do that for me, sweetie? It's not good for you to stay. You need to go and do something that no one else can do in this whole wide world. I know you will—just for me, okay?"

Lisa looks a little bewildered, not sure what her mother is asking her to do, but she gets the part about having to leave and why.

"So I won't see you again, Mommy? That makes me so sad."

"I know, but I'll always be with you. You have my furry, white coat, right? Wear it always and think of me. I'll be okay. I'm leaving soon for a wonderful place, and you can't come with me. Lisette will explain it all. Go quickly before Ralph comes back, or that miserable man will try to convince you to stay. Ask Lisette about your real dad. She'll tell you all about him. He'll have Christmas presents for you, and he'll tell you all about the wonderful life you are going to have. Go now, my love. Remember, I'll love you forever."

I walk over to Lisa and ask, "Are you ready? If you are, we can walk together."

Lisa looks confused. "Who's that Lisette my mom was talking about? Is she the one who's going to take care of me now?"

I'm thinking I could try to explain to Lisa that she is no longer ten years old, that time has moved on. That she and Lisette are the same person, but instead I simply reply. "Yes, her name is Lisette. Isn't that a beautiful name? She is so much like you. I know you'll like her a lot." Then I take Lisa's hand to lead her out of the room.

"But I don't want to leave," Lisa tells me one more desperate time, pulling me back into the room. "You sound just like Ralph. He wants me to leave too. He says we have to leave right after he comes back from getting some coffee and having a smoke."

"Then maybe we should leave before he comes back," I counter. "Isn't that a good idea?"

Lisa looks up at me and begins to talk really fast.

"You know it's Christmas Eve tonight, right? Mommy promised

me something special for Christmas tomorrow. She needs to come home tonight so she can wrap it up, and we can give each other our Christmas presents tomorrow. My best Christmas present is for Mommy just to come home."

I look at this poor girl, and she is breaking my heart. I try again.

"If you come with me, Lisette will have presents for you. She is you now, only older and very pretty. She loves you just like your Mommy does."

Lisa turns back to look at her mother, who has mustered up her strength to wave at her daughter one last time.

"Lisette is a very pretty name," Lisa finally says. "Does she have a nice house to live in? Would I have my own room?"

"I think so. And she has a lot of friends, and you know what one of her friends makes for her whenever she comes by? Homemade chocolate chip cookies! Isn't that heavenly? Wouldn't you love to have some of those cookies with Lisette?"

I continue to coax Lisa. "You heard your mommy. She wants us to skedaddle. Do you know that word? Skedaddle? That's a great word, isn't it? It means we need to get out of here fast. We don't want to see that 'miserable man' Ralph, right?"

Lisa giggles and takes my hand.

As we walk out of the room together, Lisa wants to know if I know how to spell the word I have just used. "It's a big one, right? I know because I can spell and read real good. My mommy and I read together, and I'm learning more big words every day. Do you think Lisette would like to read with me too?"

"Oh yes," I say. "Lisette would love to do so many things with you. She's waiting for you, so let's hurry."

"I know how to skip," Lisa says, giggling. "We can go faster if we skip."

"Oh my gosh!" Lisette exclaimed after Radiance finished telling her and Sophie the story of the soul retrieval. "That is so amazing! I feel so good, so happy right here and now in this moment. It feels different, like something has been given back to me and my life can go forward. Like Erick and me are going to work."

"Oh yes," Radiance said. "I like Erick. He is a big hunk of a guy, isn't he? You two . . . I see a long life ahead for you."

"Thank you, thank you, Radiance. How can I ever thank you?"

"You will live a good life and have a lot of children!"

"Wow! That's quite a thing to say. Erick hasn't even asked me to marry him. I don't even know if kids are his thing. I'm not even sure I want kids!"

Radiance responded confidently, "So much doubt! He will ask you soon. Watch for it on Christmas Eve. There is magic in that day for you. And of course, he wants kids, and so do you." Then she added with a smile, "There are many blessings to come to you both."

WHAT IF . . .

Lisette (born Lisa) Lived with
Her Mommy and Daddy from Day One?

I woke up early on Christmas morning to open the toys I got from Santa plus all the other stuff I got from Marie, my mommy, and Brad, my daddy. I love the candy I got for Christmas, too, although I was a little sick from all the red-and-white peppermint sticks—my favorite candy—that I ate that day.

Mommy only gave me one candy stick, taped on the wrapping paper of a gift from her and Daddy, but Daddy snuck me a few more peppermint sticks throughout the day. He knows how much I love them. He does too.

That afternoon I wanted to wear the new bright red dress Mommy and Daddy had bought me to wear on Christmas. I love it so much. I know it cost a lot of money because I saw it in the store with the price. In the store, Mommy acted like it cost too much so she didn't buy it, but then she must have gone back later without me and bought it anyway. I know that my Daddy is what's called a lawyer and has a good job. He makes a lot of money, but Mommy always says that she didn't have a lot of money when she was growing up, and it doesn't grow on trees, so we have to spend it wisely.

I am so happy that I'm going to wear my new red dress when we go over to Auntie Beth's house for Christmas dinner later to-day. I love Auntie Beth. She is my favorite auntie. Mommy tells me I have other aunties, but they are the part of Mommy's family, and those people don't talk to us right now. I think we don't talk to Mommy's family because Mommy had to run away from home when she was sixteen, and that was "abandoning her family," so I guess that is something bad and they are still mad at her. "Hah! I think they abandoned her!" That's what Daddy told Auntie Beth a while ago when he didn't know I was listening. I won't ever be abandoned. I'm sure I won't because Daddy and Mommy always say they "love me to the moon and back," and I think that means forever and ever, which is a very long time. Or at least until I grow up and can make my own lunch.

I'm excited to see Grandpa Hadley and Grandma Marian at Auntie Beth's house and all my cousins who belong to Auntie Beth and Uncle Ben. I have such a large family, and it makes me very happy. I love them all, and they love me.

Signed, a very, very happy LISA

WHAT'S NEXT?

The Living Well Centers

Here's what I wrote in Sophie's workshop ten years ago for my vision for the future but in present tense, like it's happening today.

I'm here feeling happy and free of all my past troubles. I'm in a great relationship. My partner is loving and sweet to me, and he and I have a great life together. We have a good business, and we have great kids. Not sure how many, but there are other people in our lives too. We help and take care of one another. We are one big, happy family. We have a dog, too, and a maybe cat."

Here's my "What's Next" today—ten years later with a lot of changes and all the wonderful blessings in my life.

It's Christmas Eve 2019, and Erick and I are having the best day ever. It's ten years since we got engaged on Christmas Eve, and we've gathered all the best people in our lives to celebrate. This time we aren't at the Governor's Residence, but never mind—Brad and Jenny have settled into a sweet life outside of politics. Erick, the love of my life, is also the best business partner a successful businesswoman could want. We have opened up a chain of "Living Well Centers," which Erick and I dreamed up to showcase the best of both of our worlds. Of course, the base of the business is the fitness club concept that Erick developed before we were married, but we added the special element of pole dancing for exercise, strength, and stamina. That has worked well with many of the ladies, but I also wanted to incorporate some of the health and beauty products they'll need to stay young and look young. All of them come with positive messages and helpful tips about how to be safe in intimate partner relationships and resources if they are not.

Erick also teaches self-defense classes for men and women, boys and girls, in our Living Well Centers. An incredible selection of resources and groups for men and boys are also available. He works with men on healthy relationships, conscious communication skills, and how to be good fathers. I know he has a lot to share because he has been a great partner to me (a survivor of trauma and abuse) and also a great dad to our children. We are particularly pleased with how the men in the fatherhood groups have bonded with the other dads and their kids. We also invite women from the Living Well Centers to events with other moms and their kids. It's a family and kid-centered environment, and it is our pride and joy. We are ready to bring this new, exciting concept further out into the world and let it fly!

CHAPTER SIX

Brad's Journey

Defining Moment

Daddy's Little Girl

The day that Brad walked into the bridal shop with Lisette to find her a wedding dress was a day unlike any other in his life. It was a day he truly marked as the day he totally embraced being a dad, and from that day on, he never looked back.

Yes, he cherished the day when Lisette, the daughter he met for the first time only ten years ago when she was almost thirty years old, called him "Dad" for the first time. He thought maybe it was so special for him because she did it so easily. It was right after they had met, and they'd gone together to get their blood tested to show that their DNA really did match. The tests were needed mostly to address Jenny's concerns that as governor, her political enemies might use a story to her disadvantage about a mysterious young woman suddenly showing up, not only claiming to be her husband's biological daughter but also, more importantly, suddenly becoming Jenny's stepdaughter. It was bad enough for Jenny when the voting public learned that Lisette was an ex-stripper whose image still was emblazoned on strip clubs around the country. Jenny didn't need some enterprising reporter accusing Lisette of being a "fortune hunter" who was latching onto Brad's considerable wealth from a myriad of his business enterprises by pretending that he was her father. Besides,

Brad knew that under the watchful eye of the press, it would be hard for him to build a father-daughter relationship with Lisette if the press asked daily for proof that they were, in fact, closely related.

Brad knew there was no way the results of the tests were going to convince him that Lisette wasn't his daughter. From the first moment he saw her across the room at the Tenth Anniversary Gala, he knew who she was. True, she was the spitting image of Marie, her mother, but there was something about the way Lisette handled herself when he rushed up to her that night. Maybe it was the defiant look she gave him when he demanded to know if she was his daughter, Lisa. It was like she was saying to him, "Who the hell are you to even ask?" That, he knew, was all him.

She had that same sassy attitude in her voice, too, when she called him Dad for the first time. He realized that she said it like it was something she had called him ever since she was a little girl and had earned the right to call him Dad. Yet when she blurted out that word, Brad felt a bolt of energy pass between them, tying them together in a way neither of them had felt since Marie's death.

"It's okay if I call you 'Dad,' right?" she asked him. He could see tears forming in her eyes, and his heart swelled.

"Of course, honey. I love it," he said, his voice cracking. "I love being your dad." Crying now himself, he reached for her and pulled her into a big, bear hug. "I'll always be your dad."

Today, he had that same kind of heart-stopping moment walking into the bridal shop with Lisette on his arm. He barely thought he'd ever get anywhere close to having children of his own and yet today he was going to help his grown daughter pick out her wedding dress.

At first, he didn't think it was the right thing for him to do.

"Isn't there someone else you want to go with you, Lisette?

Sophie is your maid of honor, right? She should go with you."

"She's coming, but she agrees that you should be there too. Think about it, Dad. You are the closest living relative I have. Yeah, usually the mother of the bride helps out with this kind of thing, but Mom's not here, and you are. You are the most special person in my life right now besides Erick. Please, Daddy, won't you please come?"

And if that wasn't enough to convince Brad, Lisette added for good measure, "I need to find the perfect dress for a perfect day. Not only am I marrying my best friend forever, but I'm also having my daddy walk me down the aisle." Brad knew that when Lisette went from "Dad" to "Daddy," he couldn't say no to her. She was, after all, Daddy's little girl!

With that heartwarming thought, Brad was all in for this adventure. He insisted that his daughter was not going to buy her wedding dress from just any bridal shop. He wanted to take her to one of the really classy places in New York City, like in the reality shows on television. Of course, he didn't watch those shows, but he would rely on Sophie and Lisette to pick out the best one, and they'd all go into the city for a weekend adventure.

They arrived on what they were told would be a quiet Friday morning in the bridal salon. But as they walked in the door, Brad was hit with the reality of wedding dress shopping. First, he had never seen so many dresses in one place and so many women talking and fussing about. Still, he loved the bustle of it and how Lisette was so excited about picking out her wedding gown.

The number of choices for a wedding dress seemed unbelievable to him! How could there be so many different kinds of dresses and styles for a bride? First, Lisette tried on a "ball gown," a dress that had lots of layers of poofy stuff making the skirt stand out all around. But the dress was just too big, Brad thought, and her amazing figure was buried under all that poof!

"Honey," he said carefully when she asked his opinion of the dress, not sure he knew what he was talking about, "the dress is beautiful, but I don't want everyone saying that. I want them to say how beautiful the bride is in a dress. You should shine on your wedding day, not the dress."

Lisette took his advice, and the next few styles she tried on were "mermaid" and "fit and flare" dresses. They all liked one of them because it hugged Lisette's body so nicely, but the dress was just too simple. Brad and Sophie agreed that it needed more sparkle, or "bling" as she called it—and as Lisette's father, Brad thought it needed a little less shape. "No need to show every-thing you've got up there on your wedding day," he joked. It was a funny thing, he knew, to say to Lisette, an ex-stripper, but today he was her dad, and this was her wedding dress.

By then, the store stylist had exhausted her pick of dresses for Lisette and having heard early on in the appointment that her customer's dad was paying in full for the dress with no limit on the budget, she invited the group to look around the shop them-selves to see what they might like. Brad joined them, though he really didn't know what he was looking at. With Lisette by his side, they went through the racks of dresses until he stopped when he saw one he thought was perfect. It had some of the bling Sophie was talking about and something of a poofy bot-tom but not as big as the others. Most of all, he thought Lisette would look great in it.

"Oh, Daddy," Lisette sighed when she saw the gown that he held out from the rack. "I love that! It has everything I've been looking for." Then she giggled. "Wow! You really are good at this, aren't you? We should have had you pulling dresses from the start!"

With that dress selected, once again Lisette was swept away

by the store stylist to try on the dress as he and Sophie waited patiently but nervously on the couch on the showroom floor. Had Lisette found the dress of her dreams? The suspense was killing him until Lisette finally emerged with the dress on. But this time along with her came a whole entourage of salespeople, and Brad could tell the troops knew they were close to a sale. They were ready for it! One by one, they brought with them bridal veils, headpieces, jewelry, and fake wedding bouquets and then proceeded to do what they called "jacking up" the bride. Brad watched as Lisette was transformed into what she might look like in this dress on her wedding day.

When the process was complete and Lisette looked at herself in the mirror, Brad could see that she was beaming. Putting on that dress, more than any of the others before it, had made her glow. As she turned around to give him and Sophie a front view, Brad saw tears streaming down her face.

"Wow!" he said breathlessly. "You look beautiful, Lisette! Gorgeous! Just like a bride. You love this one as much as I do, don't you? I can tell."

"Yes, Daddy," Lisette said, her voice cracking through her tears. "It's perfect. I think this is my dress!"

By then Brad was crying, too, somewhat unexpectedly for him. As he jumped up off the couch and went to hug her, she whispered in his ear, "Oh Daddy, I knew from the start that you're a softy at heart. I love you!"

"Love you too," he said. He released her and took a step back, admiring her. "Oh my, my," he gushed. "You look like a million bucks." Then he laughed, tears still flowing. "Just wait until Erick sees us coming down the aisle. He'll be grinning and smiling, looking at you like he's never seen anyone so beautiful, inside and out. I'm so very, very happy for you both. I love you!"

WHAT IF . . .

Marie and Brad's Do-Over

April and May 1979

Brad fell hard for Marie. She seemed to be everything he had ever wanted in a woman and more. The first few months were like a blur to Brad after Marie walked into the SNAP (Stop Nuclear and Atomic Power) office where Brad worked on raising public awareness about the dangers of nuclear power. Marie was there to volunteer and help out. That time period, as Brad remembered it, had a dream like quality to it. Everything was so perfect.

By early April, Marie had started to come to the office to volunteer pretty regularly. She'd arrive about ten o'clock in the morning and leave around three o'clock. At first, she and Brad would find a few minutes to talk, getting to know each other here and there, but gradually they started taking breaks and even having lunch together. Sometimes they'd eat in the office if someone ordered sandwiches or pizza, but eventually they went out to lunch by themselves. By the end of May, two months after Marie became a full-time volunteer, working five days a week, she and Brad were what the others in the office called "an item." Brad knew he shouldn't favor one volunteer over the others, but he couldn't help it. More and more, he wanted to be alone with Marie, to get closer to her, and well, he had to admit it, to fuck her. In fact, he was so attracted to her from the very beginning that he would have fucked her a lot sooner except for the way it would look for the director to be in bed with one of the volunteers.

But at some point, he didn't care. He wanted to take her out on a real date and let whatever was going to happen just happen! But it was hard to get time with Marie at night. He realized that up until then, he had never seen her before ten o'clock in the morning or after three in the afternoon. She told Brad that her mother who was very sick needed her at night when her aunt couldn't be there. As it was, her aunt was there every day now in the morning until Marie came home from the office at mid-afternoon. But after pushing her every day for a week to go out to dinner with him, she finally agreed that she'd try to find someone to take care of her mom at least for one night. So, it was on a Thursday night in May that Brad and Marie went out on their first real date together.

They went to one of Brad's favorite restaurants, one that eventually became their favorite restaurant. Called Chez Jacques, it was French and very expensive. Brad's parents used to take him and his sister, Bethany, there for special occasions, and now he was taking Marie there. To impress her mostly, he guessed, but also to get her into bed. He had it all figured out. They'd do dinner and then go back to his apartment. He arranged it so Jimmy and Derek, his roommates, would be out that night, and they'd be alone.

When Brad and Marie walked into the restaurant, Brad watched Marie's eyes scan the place and then focus on him. Brad looked good that night. He was wearing a navy-blue blazer, a white shirt, and a pair of light beige linen pants. His tie was a little wild, kind of a paisley pattern, but he thought it looked nice with the outfit. He thought Marie looked smashing. While he wanted to surprise her about where they would be going for dinner, he did tell her that it was a nice place, one that she should dress up for. But he didn't expect her to look so good. She had on a tailored dress with buttons down the front that looked like something out of the fashion magazines. It was a light blue, a shade that caught the exact color of her eyes and made her face glow. It showed off her figure—not in an obvious way, but no one, certainly not him, could miss how perfectly she was shaped.

As they were seated and the maître d' gave them each a menu, Brad saw her open it while the waiter filled their water glasses and then breezed away to give them time to decide what they wanted to order.

"Oh my God, the menu's not in English!" Marie blurted out.

"No, it's in French," Brad said confidently. "And the waiters like it if you order in French too. You know French, don't you? Parlez-vous Francais?"

"Uh . . . uh," Marie stammered.

"I just asked if you speak French," Brad interjected.

"No, I've been taking Spanish," Marie said weakly.

"Spanish and French are a lot alike. They're both romance languages. You should be able to get some of the words."

"I don't know," Marie said hesitantly at first and then more strongly. "Why don't you order for the both of us? Whatever you think would be good is fine with me."

"You know what my favorite is here?"

"No, what?" Marie looked at the menu and then up at Brad. "I bet it's the beef."

"How did you know that?" Brad said with amazement in his voice. Sometimes Marie seemed to know exactly what he was thinking.

"Oh, I just do," she said coyly.

"I love the steak tartare, but I think that's kind of an acquired taste."

"What is it?"

"It's raw ground sirloin seasoned with salt and pepper and other things and then shaped into this mound . . ." Brad gestured with his hands out in front of him. ". . . with this hole in the top where they drop a raw egg yolk."

"A raw egg yolk!" Marie repeated, with disgust in her voice.

"Yeah. Like I said, it's an acquired taste. But I don't see in on the menu." Then he added disappointedly, "Maybe they don't serve it anymore."

Marie put down her menu and looked at him again. "Like I said, whatever you decide is fine with me."

Brad chose a simpler entree for each of them and then decided on a bottle of wine. He did all this in perfect French while Marie sipped her water and watched him in silence. When the waiter left after taking their order, Brad smiled at Marie.

"So, is this place everything you expected?"

"Oh yes," she gushed. "More than I expected. I've never been to such a fancy restaurant."

"Funny. You fit right in. You look incredible tonight."

Brad watched her eyes sparkle as she took in the compliment but then responded with a modest "Oh, thank you," drawing her eyes away from him again.

Brad reached his hand across the table to cover hers. "I mean it. You are beautiful. You know that, don't you?"

Marie cast her eyes shyly down on the tablecloth, and he tightened his grip on her hand.

"I'm really crazy about you!" he finally blurted out. "I've got this crush on you, you know," he went on with an impish grin on his face. "Can you tell?"

What he really wanted to say was that he was really in "lust" with her, but he knew that you should never tell a girl that you lust after her. Lust was a word that scared girls off, and he didn't want that.

"I like you too," she said demurely.

"That's all?" he said prodding her.

"Well, I'm not in love with you yet."

"You're not?" Brad was surprised. He thought girls always went for love first, then figured out how they really felt about a guy later.

"I like you a lot but I . . . I don't know what's going on in my life right now. With my mother and all—"

"Oh, I don't want to push you into anything here, Marie." He pulled his hand away suddenly, but she grabbed it back.

"It's not that," she said quickly. "I just want to be sure. I want to be sure about how I feel about someone before I do anything . . ." Her voice trailed off.

"Oh," he said, flatly at first, and then he repeated it with surprise in his voice. "Oh! I get it. You've never done it before, have you?" He lowered his voice and leaned toward her. "I mean, you've never had sex?"

She blushed and was silent.

"I'm sorry. I didn't mean to embarrass you," he fumbled, pulling his hand away from hers this time. "Look, you can tell me anything. I'm not going away. I promise. I just thought a girl like you, in college and all, well, that you weren't—I mean, you had, you know, I thought you had done it before." He took a few gulps of water while nervously twisting the napkin in his lap with his other hand.

Was he so wrong about her not being a virgin? Had he just blown everything here? But when he looked at Marie again, she was smiling warmly at him.

"I didn't say I didn't want to do it," she assured him. "You'd be my first. I'm saving myself for someone who really loves me. Someone I could love forever. Isn't that how you dreamed it would be?"

"Marie, that's—" Brad wanted to say that's not what he meant, but when he looked into her eyes, he knew that was not what she was expecting. Not what would make her likely to consider going to bed with him. So, she was a virgin and not the type to do it with the first guy who came along who wanted her as badly as he did. But she must have had other offers before. Someone who looked as good as she did should have had many men after her. Did she turn them all down with the same old line? Somehow, he had to get past all of that with her, or this was going to be a very frustrating relationship for him, not to mention a waste of a perfectly good dinner at a very expensive place.

"—that's exactly what I thought you were waiting for—true love," he said quickly, recovering himself in time. "I can understand why a girl like you would feel that way.

"So, you do feel that way about me?" she blurted out.

"I . . . I . . ." Brad stumbled over his words again until he gained control of himself and knew what it was he had to say. "I'm not sure this is the place we should be saying all of this." He looked around nervously for a second. "I was thinking that maybe after dinner, we could go back to my apartment."

"To your place?"

"Yeah, well, my roommates are out for the night, so we could just sit there for a while and talk." Brad grabbed his glass again and gulped down some water. God, his throat was dry. This was hard work here!

"We could do that," Marie said, smiling back sweetly. "I'd like that, but there is one thing. I'm not sure I know how to tell you this."

"What?" He stopped and put his hand over hers across the table. "You can tell me anything."

"I know, and you've been so nice to me. Bringing me to this big fancy restaurant. We could've just gone out for pizza. It would have been more like . . ." She stopped suddenly mid-sentence.

"More like what?" he asked. "Like being back in college? No, I wanted it to be special. I like you, Marie." He patted her hand again. "I like you a lot, and I don't usually like the girls that I sleep with. I know that sounds like I'm a real jerk. But then, so many of them lie to me about everything—including whether their breasts are real or not." Brad laughed.

Marie looked at him, and her face suddenly lost all its color. He saw the change and asked, "Are you okay? You look sick. Your face went all white, pale. Was it something I said?"

"No, no," Marie protested. "It's more of what I haven't said. What I haven't told you about myself. What I do for a living. Why I'm even here. I feel so ashamed."

Brad could see the anguish on her face. When she grabbed her water glass, her hand was shaking. Just then, the waiter swooped down on them with bread and wine, and Brad felt the pressure ease a little.

They both sat in silence for a moment until the waiter left, and then Brad continued.

"Is there something you want to tell me? Is that what this is all about? Look, I don't need to know your life history, but if there is something that might be like a deal breaker for us continuing along this path that we are on, it would be good to let me know. As the investigators in my dad's law firm always tell me, everyone's life has a secret in it somewhere. It's only a matter of time until it all comes out. Just wait for it!"

Brad managed a laugh on that last comment, and he had just picked up his wine glass when Marie blurted out, "I'm not who you think I am."

He put the wine glass back on the table with a thud and looked intently at her.

"Okay," he said slowly. "Then who are you?"

"To start with, I'm not a college girl. I've never been to college— probably never will. I never even finished high school." She was whispering now, talking quickly, and he could see her eyes filling with tears. "And that's only the beginning of what I'm not. I know if I tell you all this, you'll never want to see me again."

"Lots of people don't have a college degree, and you can get a GED these days."

"No. This has to stop, here and now," she said firmly. Then she began rambling. "I'm going to leave now before this gets way out of hand. It's okay. I can take a cab home. I do know how to get home. I've been in worse situations than this. Easily."

Brad was confused. "What situations? What are you talking about?"

As she gathered her things and stood up from the table, Brad stood up himself. He grabbed her hand and said in a voice filled with urgency, "Wait! Please don't leave. Just sit down, and we can talk."

She held his gaze but didn't relent. "Okay, let me put it this way. I'm a stripper. I strip for a living at the Baby Doll strip club down the block. I do lap dances, too, for the old guys who can't get it up most nights with their wives. I shouldn't have bet the girls in the club that I could meet and go out with a nice 'white bread' type of guy like you. What was I thinking? I let this go on for too long, and now it's time for me to go. Thanks for making me feel like a princess, but I have to go before I turn into a pumpkin."

He gaped at her for a moment and could see tears coming down her face.

"No, don't go! Please," he insisted. "I haven't been telling you the truth either."

She stopped and looked at him. "Why? What do you mean?"

"I made it sound like I bed a new girl every night, and they all have fake titties. I hardly ever date. I hardly find any women that I even like out there, but I like you. I don't know why, but I do like you. Are you really a stripper? Wow! I bet that's a first for a fancy restaurant like this!"

Then he sat down at the table and looked up at her.

"Hey, go if you want to. But I feel like the truth will set us free. Let's not stop here. I've got something else to say if you want to hear it. I think if we are going to be something, we should take the time to bare our soul and tell the truth. What do you have to lose? You've already told me the worst of it, the stripper part. After that, how much worse could it get?"

She looked at him and smiled as she slowly sat back down in her seat.

"I guess that's for you to judge," she replied. "But I guess it is time for truth-telling while the wine is flowing, and the food looks good."

"Okay, so let's start from the beginning. No more lies. Hi, I'm Brad. Nice to meet you, Marie. Tell me a bit about yourself . . ."

WHAT'S NEXT?

The Resurrection of Brad Bufford
October 2019

Sometimes the thing that brings you down can turn out to be the thing that moves you forward. I've learned that to be true several times in my life, and each time I've been able to resurrect myself. But it's not always been easy.

The first time was after I met Marie. I was very young, just out of college and naïve about relationships, but I loved Marie. My parents didn't like her, particularly after they found out that Marie was pregnant with a baby that she said was mine. I was really excited about the baby and couldn't wait to be a dad. But then Marie told me it wasn't my baby, and I had to move on. It was hard, and somehow deep down inside my being, I missed that baby every day of my life. That is, until almost thirty years later when my daughter, Lisette, showed up. We met across a crowded room at an event, but I knew she was Marie's child the moment I saw her. Lisette was the spitting image of her beautiful mother, and I was her dad. No question about it.

That was the second time I had to resurrect myself. After not being a part of my daughter's life for twenty-nine years, I had to make up for lost time, not only as a father but also as a grandfather. Today I have two wonderful grandchildren, Sasha, who is four years old, and Jeremy, age two. I adore them both, and I think they like me a lot. They call me "Popsy." I had wanted to be "Granddad" to them, but they decided on Popsy—I'm not sure why. But I like it; it has a certain class to it.

My third resurrection was how my wife, Jenny, and I have reconfigured our lives after some pretty earth-shattering events happened to both of us about ten years ago. While the good news at that time was that my daughter, Lisette, came into our lives, the bad news was that within days of meeting Lisette, a young man named Mark Durocher killed ten people with an assault rifle in a mass shooting at a local shopping mall. His connection to my family was distant at best, but nonetheless devastating. While Jenny was on the circuit court bench years before I met her, she handled a family court matter involving Mark and his father, Jeffrey Jerome Alexander, now known as Ambrose. She ordered the custody of Mark changed from his father to his maternal grandmother, whose daughter and Ambrose's wife, Betsy, were killed in the car crash along with Jeanine, their three-year-old daughter. Mark, who was six at the time, and his father survived the crash, but everything went downhill for the family from there.

At the time of the mall shooting, Jenny was still governor of the state, and, despite the tenuous connection between Ambrose's son and my wife, a torrent of media attention and publicity cast doubt on her credibility and ability to govern. It didn't help that at the same event that I discovered my daughter, Lisette, Ambrose was screaming threats at my wife which created an on-going security issue for her. While her poll ratings among voters dipped for a while, the following year she was reelected governor for her second term but after that, her high popularity ratings never returned. The criminal case involving Mark went on for years, as did the civil suit Ambrose brought against the state for failing to provide adequate mental health services for his son. Jenny was never out of the public eye and voters blamed her for all the chaos. She lost her chance to move into the national election spotlight as well as her reelection campaign for governor in 2014.

I was connected with the 2009 mall shooting by the fact that my business had been working to redesign the mall, particularly with an eye to making it less vulnerable to mass shootings. That part of the design, however, had been rejected by the mall owner over my company's protest, but when the shooting occurred, all the press cared about was making my business the "bad guy." The business deal fell apart, and my company's reputation plummeted.

Through it all, Jenny and I faced a tough couple of years, but I'll let her tell you later in this book how she has moved on. Today my business is booming, not so much in this country, but internationally. Right now, we are working with mall owners in the United Kingdom, Ukraine, and even in Wuhan, China. Most people don't know but Wuhan has some of the largest shopping malls in the world. While China doesn't have mass shootings like we have in the United States due to the proliferation here of military-style assault weapons, they are interested in security for their malls, and they love the designs we have come up with.

So today, my business is booming, my wife, Jenny, is happy in her new job, and I have the best daughter, son-in-law, and grandchildren ever. I am a lucky man. I have my life, my health, and a wonderful future ahead of me.

I am blessed.

CHAPTER SEVEN

Ambrose's Journey

When Ambrose learned that his son, Mark, was being sent to see a psychiatrist after the shooting at the shopping mall in October 2009, Ambrose felt a sense of déjà vu. Mark's visit to the good doctor was to see if he was competent to stand trial for the murder of ten people at the mall that day. Ambrose, on the other hand, had been sent as a kid to see one of those doctors, but he never meant to hurt anyone, particularly his cat.

Defining Moment
The Tale of Samson the Cat

When Ambrose was twelve years old, he went to see a psychiatrist about his obsession with Attila the Hun. Or, as his mother put it to his school counselor, why Attila made him kill the family cat, Samson. It was true that he killed the cat, but his mother just didn't understand about Attila the Hun. No one did. That's what Ambrose told the counselor, and when he did, she referred him to a child psychiatrist.

Ambrose had read enough about Sigmund Freud in a classic comic to know that he didn't want to be psychoanalyzed, and he sure wasn't going to tell his dreams to anyone. He liked to hear about other people's dreams, though, and make things up about what they meant. That's about what a psychiatrist did, he figured, so he agreed to see this psychiatrist out of curiosity. But he made a deal with his mom that she'd wait for him in the car in the parking lot while he went inside to see the doctor alone. He wasn't her baby anymore, and he didn't need his mother to hold his hand.

So, while she sat outside, he sat alone in the doctor's waiting room. He had his pack of baseball cards stuffed in the pocket of his blue jeans but instead he occupied himself by looking at the bright orange, red, and yellow paintings on the walls. He thought they looked like ink blots and wondered if the doctor would be testing him later on about which looked like elephants to him and which like gargoyles. So far, he only saw gargoyles, and he was interested to know what that meant.

After a while, the tall, skinny woman sitting behind the receptionist's desk came up to him and said, "The doctor will see you now."

She led Ambrose down a long, narrow hall into a big office that was dark and cool with wood-paneled walls and high ceilings. What impressed Ambrose most about the room was that it had two doors, one right after the other, when you walked in—as if double doors were the only way to keep the words spoken in the room from being heard outside. A nosy receptionist or curious patient might hear something they shouldn't, and that would be what lawyers called a breach of confidentiality. Ambrose knew that because he had read a lot about lawyers; that's what he wanted to be when he grew up. The rule was that doctors couldn't tell anyone the stuff their patients told them. He wasn't sure why, but he guessed that he didn't want the doctor blabbing about him to his friends and neighbors. That didn't make him feel any better about being in that room with the doctor, but at least he knew that the skinny woman wouldn't know any more than she should about him.

The receptionist went out of the room, closing both doors

behind her, with Ambrose left standing in the middle of the room, twisting his baseball cap in his hand. He watched the doctor, who was seated behind a large desk covered with stacks of books and papers. He was a large man with a big head that was bald except for a few stray white hairs. He had a long white beard that seemed to reach to the middle of his chest, bushy white eyebrows, and wire-rimmed glasses perched on his nose that looked too small for his large, full face. All the while, he scribbled into the pages of a book with a large black fountain pen.

My, my, Ambrose snickered to himself, trying to suppress a giggle. *Didn't the good doctor look just like Santa Claus making a list and checking it twice?* With a little more hair on top and a bright red suit on, Ambrose thought he could easily earn extra money playing Jolly Old Saint Nick in the department stores at Christmastime. He seemed to have been born to play the part. But when Dr. Kravinsky looked up at him, Ambrose could see that he didn't have Santa's rosy complexion or a twinkle in his eye. Instead he stopped writing, pulled off his reading glasses and eyed Ambrose up and down with a mean, Scrooge-like look.

"So, you're here to see me, young man," he barked at the boy.

Not sure whether it was a question or command, Ambrose remained silent, twisting his cap in his hand even harder and staring beyond the doctor to the large number of certificates hanging in dark frames on the wall behind his desk. Straining his eyes to read them, he could tell that some of them were written in a foreign language.

"Do you have a tongue?" the doctor demanded.

"Sir?" Ambrose said with a start, bringing his eyes back down to the doctor.

"I asked if you could talk. You do talk, don't you? Otherwise, you've come to the wrong person. I'm a psychiatrist, not a speech therapist."

"I can talk," Ambrose mumbled. "If I want to."

"Oh, so you think you have free will, do you?"

"Sir?" Ambrose asked sounding confused.

"Free will. I don't take much stock in that myself as a clinician anymore. Too much religious connotation attached to the concept these days for my liking. Wouldn't you agree?"

Ambrose wasn't sure what this guy was talking about, but he thought it was kind of neat that he was talking to him like he knew as much as he did.

"No, I agree. Free will is overrated," Ambrose said matter-of-factly, scanning the walls of the room again, this time for some more of those ink-blot paintings. When his eyes returned to the doctor, he added, "I think Descartes said it all when he wrote, 'I think, therefore I am.'"

"Oh, you do, do you?" Ambrose thought he saw the edges of the doctor's mouth curl up in a kind of half-smile. "They said you were precocious," the doctor snorted.

"Who are 'they'?" Ambrose asked inquisitively.

"Your school counselor, for one. She said—and I'm paraphrasing her, mind you—I have the report somewhere here, but I can't find it right this minute—that you're brilliant but misguided in insisting that Attila the Hun is your hero. Do you agree with that assessment?"

"That I'm brilliant or misguided?" Ambrose quipped cleverly, or so he thought.

"Either one," the doctor said flatly.

Ambrose looked down at his feet for a moment and then up again. "I have a very high IQ. No one will tell me exactly how high. I guess they're afraid I'll get conceited if I know how much smarter I am than the rest of my class. But they're all morons, so I guess in comparison that means I'm brilliant—wouldn't you agree?"

Suddenly Ambrose found himself enjoying this banter with

Dr. Kravinsky. There weren't many people in his life who were as worthy of his conversation.

"And what about misguided? Do you agree with that diagnosis?"

"I don't know if I'd call it a diagnosis, doctor, would you? But you'd know that better than I would, being a trained medical man and all. I'd say it was more like a label or even an epithet. I try to ignore what people call me because most times they don't know me well enough to judge accurately."

Ambrose sighed and shifted his weight from one foot to the other. "Am I going to have to stand up the whole time I'm talking to you?" he whined. He looked over at the couch in the corner of the room. "Don't I get to lay down on that and tell you my dreams?"

"Do you want to?"

"No, but I thought you'd want me to. After all, why else am I here?"

"Why do you think you're here?"

"Because I got sent here."

"And why do you think you were sent here?"

"Because people thought I needed help."

"Do you think you need help?"

"Do you?" Ambrose sputtered. "And why do you always answer a question with another question?"

"Do I?"

"Don't you?" Ambrose bellowed back. "You do—you know you do! That's because you don't have any answers, do you?" Ambrose was pleased with himself for figuring out the game the doctor was playing with him. "Isn't that what you get paid for? To have all the answers."

The doctor put down his pen and Ambrose saw that same hint of a smile around the corner of the man's mouth again. At least, he was entertaining the old guy a little. Maybe that was worth the money the school was spending on the session. Then the doctor got up from his chair and came from behind his desk to where Ambrose was standing.

"Why don't we come over here?" the doctor said gently, putting his hand on Ambrose's shoulder and coaxing him toward two large leather chairs on the other side of the room near a bay window. "Why don't you sit there?" the doctor went on, pointing to the chair on the right. "And I'll sit here."

No sooner had Ambrose sat down when doctor asked the question Ambrose had been waiting for.

"So I understand you killed your cat and Attila told you to do it. Is that true?"

"I didn't mean to kill Samson," Ambrose said quietly. "He just got in the way."

"In the way of what?"

"The battle. He walked through the battle lines and was crushing Huns with his paws, so I had to kill him. Kill the enemy before he kills you. That's what Attila says."

"With what? A toy sword?" the doctor asked incredulously.

"No, actually it was a kitchen knife," Ambrose muttered, feeling guilty about confessing to playing with something his mother wouldn't have wanted him to have in the first place. But he couldn't find his sword that day, so he used the knife instead.

"And you stabbed the cat because Attila told you to kill the enemy?" The doctor was repeating himself now.

"Yeah. That's pretty much it," Ambrose sighed and slumped back in his chair. "But it wasn't like I left him there on the battle ground to rot. I was burying him in the garden when my mother saw me. She didn't understand that I was giving him a full military funeral because that was the least I could do for the enemy that fought so gallantly."

Ambrose was becoming quite animated now, chattering on with a childish delight in his voice. "Not that Attila would've buried his enemies. Usually, he just let them bleed to death where they fell. Sometimes the battles were so bloody that bodies lying along the shores made the rivers run red for days. The carcasses would be there until the flesh rotted off and only bones were left to remind others of the consequences of challenging Attila the Hun. He was the most ferocious warrior in the Roman Empire, you know, and you had to do what he said or else."

Ambrose paused for a breath, and the doctor broke in. "I'd say you know a lot about Attila the Hun. Is he your hero?"

"I guess so. I mean, compared to Attila, Superman and Spiderman are just sissies. Attila was called the Scourge of God, and everyone was afraid of him."

"Is that what you want? For people to be afraid of you?"

"Ha! Who'd be afraid of me?" Ambrose snorted. "I'm just a runt of a kid. But it would be cool to think that someone wouldn't want to fight you just because you had a reputation for ripping the guts out of people. That would save a lot of time."

Ambrose noticed that the doctor's mouth did that funny little thing again like he enjoyed what he was hearing but couldn't show it. Why was it that adults never let loose? For himself, he found a good battle with his toy soldiers always made him feel better. Then the doctor went on. "If you could be one thing Attila was, what would that be?"

"Ah, now that's a good question, the best one you've asked so far. Let me see." Ambrose put his finger up to his mouth and thought for a moment. Then he said: "Loyal. Attila would beat the crap out of his enemies, but he was really good to his own people. I admire that. He had a soldier's fury but a savior's heart."

"Where did you hear that?" the doctor wanted to know. "That's very poetic."

"I made it up. I think that's what Attila would say about himself, don't you?"

"I don't know, but I'll take your word for it. You seem to be the one who'd know." Then the doctor shifted his body in his chair. "Let me ask you something I'm very curious about. How exactly did Samson—that's your cat's name, right? Samson?"

Ambrose nodded as he listened intently to the doctor's question now.

"How exactly did you kill Samson?"

"I stabbed him through the heart with my sword—I mean the kitchen knife. I was carrying it with me, like all Hun warriors have their weapons, in my saddle on my horse and when the battle started—" Ambrose demonstrated taking the imaginary sword in both of his hands—"I brought it out, raised it up over my head and plunged into it the heart of the enemy." Then his hands fell to his lap and rested there for a moment until he sighed and went on. "You know us Huns do everything on our horses—eat, sleep, even make love to our women."

"Oh, you do, do you?" The doctor sounded the most curious about the last remark. "Are you interested in girls?"

"No," Ambrose said quickly. "But you know what else we do? After we kill a boar or stag, we cut it up and carry the raw meat between our legs so it 'cooks' a little before we eat it. Did you know that, huh? Man, some of us Huns can't wait that long and just eat it raw." Ambrose threw his hands up in the air and slapped them down on his knees. "What can I say?" he chortled. "When you're hungry, you just gotta eat!" Then he let out a hoot and threw himself into the back of the chair laughing with delight at his own words.

The doctor's voice, stern and serious now, brought him back to their conversation. "Do you remember plunging the sword into your cat?"

"I–I don't know. It all happened so fast. I saw the enemy coming, and I had to strike quickly. A Hun has to be merciless. That's what Attila says." Ambrose puffed out his chest as if Attila had told him that personally.

"What else does Attila say to you? Do you hear his voice often?"

"Sometimes," the boy said in a small, tight voice. "He helps me figure things out."

"Like what?"

"Oh, you know, about stuff in life. Like how not to cry when my dad hits me."

"Does your dad hit you a lot?"

"Not anymore. He's not around much. My mom threw him out. He hasn't been to see me for a while. I don't think he knows where we're living."

"Did your mom do that on purpose? Move where he can't find you?"

"I guess so. He used to hit her too. And the cat. He hit everything when he got mad and was drunk."

"Do you miss your dad?"

"Sometimes. He used to take me for rides in his car and play with me."

"What did you play with your dad?"

"Baseball," he said twirling his cap on his finger now. "And guns. He liked to play guns with me. He liked cowboys and Indians."

"Besides your dad, who else do you play with?"

Ambrose didn't answer for a moment, and the doctor, taking it as a sign that he didn't understanding the question, added, "Do you have any friends, son?"

"Some at the school where we used to live, but then we moved. I had to start over again, and that's hard."

"Why is it hard?"

"Because a lot of the kids don't like the games I like to play."

"You like to play soldiers. Don't they?"

"Yeah, but they just blow up soldiers with their tanks, and that's it. That's no fun. I like to plan the battles and sometimes change the course of history. Like, what if Attila had conquered the Roman Empire? He got close, but then he made a deal with the Pope right outside the gates of Rome. I play that he took the city and became King of the World."

"That's very imaginative. Don't your friends want to play that with you?"

"Nah. The other kids think it's too complicated and could care less about Attila or the Romans. But I don't mind. I like my games better than theirs anyway."

"Do you play chess?"

"Yes, but the other kids would rather play checkers. I can play checkers okay, but I can usually easily beat them. They hate that. They say I cheat."

"Do you?"

"Of course not. I don't have to cheat to beat them. They're morons."

"Do you think everyone who's not as smart as you is a moron?"

Ambrose screwed his face up a little and thought for a minute. "Most people aren't as smart as me. I guess that doesn't make them morons, but I don't like the way they treat me just because I'm smart. It's not my fault either. That's all."

"Do you think Attila the Hun was smart?"

"He was the smartest man in the world," the boy said exuberantly.

"Do you think that people knew how smart he was?"

"They did then. He was a very wise ruler. But now people just think he's a bad guy who killed a lot of people."

"And you don't?"

"If he were alive today," Ambrose said with pride in his voice, "he would be President of the United States, and people would know how smart he was."

"Is that what you want to be when you grow up—president?"

Ambrose looked incredulously at the doctor. "No, that's a really boring job. I want to be a pirate."

"I don't think they are any pirates left in this world," the doctor said, chuckling.

"Of course there are. Lots of people steal other people's money every day and get away with it. With a fancy office like yours, I thought you'd know all about that."

Ambrose watched the doctor's face twitch again around the edges of his mouth, but this time it didn't seem like a smile. Instead, he cleared his throat a few times and then sighed deeply as he shifted his body in the chair.

"So, are you sorry that you killed Samson?"

"Oh, sure," Ambrose replied with great certainty and a wide grin on his face. "He was one of the best warriors I've ever known. I don't know how I'm ever going to replace him."

WHAT'S NEXT?

A Death Sentence

As Ambrose watched his son, Mark, his only child still living, standing there in front of the judge passing a sentence of life or death on him today, he felt the weight of all of the mistakes he'd made over the years.

Ambrose thought that the worst day of his life had been the day of the car accident that killed his wife Betsy and his daughter Jeanine. But today he realized it wasn't.

Today he wanted to stand up in court and explain to the judge why something like this couldn't possibly have happened to his son, his precious son, Mark. He would tell him what Mark was really like. He'd describe what he was like the day he was born, Ambrose's firstborn, and how the miracle of his birth had totally astonished and humbled him as a father. He'd tell the judge how cute Mark was as a toddler and all the toys and electronic gizmos he loved to play with as a kid. He'd explain how he helped Mark ride his first bike, took him for his first haircut, and taught him how to brush his teeth. Then he'd tell the judge it wasn't Mark's fault that he killed those ten people at the mall, and he didn't deserve the death penalty for what he did. Someone or something had taken over his mind and turned him into this monster.

Yes, he'd argue vigorously for Mark's life, as if he were one of his own clients back in the day when Ambrose still practiced law. What he learned as a lawyer then was that sometimes you'd have to look beyond the bad in a client and advocate for them, give them the benefit of the doubt.

But during the sentencing phase of Mark's trial, it was hard for Ambrose to hear what the families of the victims read to the court from their victim impact statements. It was sad and even more disturbing—shocking too—that Mark was so stoic as he sat there listening to the parade of people in their grief and sadness. He wanted his son to be more of a warrior and fight for his life, but Mark had little or no response to the proceedings around him.

He also had refused to let Ambrose visit him when he was detained prior to trial and sentencing without bail. Finally his lawyer, a public defender, convinced Mark to let his father visit to help in his defense. Hoping that his father could get through to him, his lawyer told Ambrose that Mark seemed to be confused at times about who was on trial here. Instead of him being on trial, he acted like Ambrose, his father, was being accused of killing his mother, Betsy, and his sister, Jeannine.

"Does that make any sense to you?" Mark's lawyer asked Ambrose. "You're the only other person besides Mark in that car that day who is still alive and can tell me this. Did something happen there? Something that Mark might have thought made the accident your fault. If so, in the sentencing phase in a death penalty case like this, I could use it as a mitigating factor, something in the defendant's background, record, or character that might mitigate or lessen the gravity of the offense and weigh against the imposition of the death sentence."

Ambrose wanted to help, but he couldn't figure out what had happened to Mark to put him over the edge. Was it that car accident so many years ago? He knew it had estranged him from his son, but was it true that Mark blamed him all these years for the car accident?

So, as Ambrose sat on a flat wooden bench waiting for his time to visit Mark today in the visitor's room of the men's prison, he thought about whether Mark blamed him; the media had certainly laid the blame on Ambrose ever since the mall shooting.

The *Capital News Enquirer* dragged out all the clips about Ambrose, from way back to the car accident on La Strada Street more than a decade ago to what happened at a local hotel only a few days before Mark's shooting spree at the local mall. But Mark was only three years old when the accident on La Strada happened, and Ambrose had never thought he was influenced by that.

Still the local press wouldn't let go of it. They decided that Mark went on this murderous rampage because Ambrose was a bad father. They went on about what lessons Mark must have learned from his father who was "a bad role model for a growing boy that anyone could get away with murder" just as he did for killing that little girl on La Strada Street years ago. Ambrose had been charged with a serious crime after that accident—negligent homicide with a motor vehicle with a sentence of up to six months in jail, a thousand-dollar fine, or both. The judge did let him off at sentencing with time served awaiting trial and a five hundred-dollar fine. The charge could have been higher if the police could have shown that Ambrose had been drinking excessively that night, but the cops screwed up on that. The trial judge ruled inadmissible the results of the breathalyzer taken that night at the police station because it was unreliable. The test equipment was faulty, the results were unreadable, and none of the attorneys at the bar association meeting earlier that night could remember Ambrose having had more than one drink. *Attorneys do stick together,* Ambrose thought.

But by then Ambrose had lost his job at the law firm, and he and his wife, Betsy, were struggling to make ends meet. To get back on their feet, Betsy went back to work full-time as a librarian.

With their roles reversed and Ambrose only able to pick up a few jobs consulting on tax cases with attorneys from out of town who didn't know much about the accident on La Strada Street, times were tough. To pay bills, they sold the sports car that Ambrose had been driving in that night and bought a used car with a stick shift. That's the car Betsy was learning to drive the day of the accident, the second auto accident, and the one that killed Betsy and Jeanine.

He and Betsy had tried their best, but none of it had kept Mark from this fate.

Now Ambrose was ushered into the room for visitors where he and Mark could only talk to each other by a telephone that hung on either side of the glass wall separating them. It wasn't an easy way to have a conversation, Ambrose knew, but he had to try.

"Mark," Ambrose began, speaking into the phone on his side of the glass. "It's good to see you, son."

Mark had no response, although he had picked up the phone on his side and was holding it up to his ear.

"How are you, son?" Ambrose continued. "How are you doing?"

Mark looked at him with a blank expression on his face. When his son finally spoke, there was a flatness in his voice devoid of any emotion.

"I told my lawyer that I'd see you, but it doesn't mean we're going to talk. Those days are gone for us. Don't you know that?"

"No, I don't know that, son. I know your grandmother must have told you all kind of bad things about me and . . ."

"Don't bring Grandma into this!" Mark responded sharply. "She's the only one who took care of me after you killed my mother and Jeanine. It's all your fault!"

Mark's voice was shrill, quickly getting to the crux of the matter that Ambrose was there to discuss with him.

"Look, Mark, I don't know where you got this idea that I killed your mom and Jeanine. I tried to save them. I grabbed the wheel and tried . . ."

"NO!" Mark exploded. "You took the wheel and sent us all into that ditch. I saw you. You thought I didn't, but I did. You did it on purpose, and I hate you for it."

Oh my God, Ambrose thought. *Was that possible? Did Mark see something from the back seat where he and Jeanine were sitting and misinterpret it? Did he think I would do that? Is that why Mark has been so angry with me all these years?* Maybe all this wasn't his grandmother's doing. Maybe someone should've realized that his son was carrying around all these crazy ideas in his head.

Now Ambrose remembered a day years ago when he did see his son and have a conversation with him, if you could call it that. It was on Mark's tenth birthday, and Ambrose had gone to his school playground to wish him a happy birthday. Although Ambrose was supposed to have visitation rights under the judge's order after the car accident gave Mark's grandmother custody, Abigail made it so difficult that Ambrose just stopped trying.

But that day, although he couldn't get into the school grounds, Ambrose stood outside the fence and yelled to get Mark's attention. Once he did, Mark recognized him but pretended he didn't.

"Hey, Mark," one of the boys near the fence finally yelled. "Do you know that guy? He keeps talking to you. He knows your name. He's calling you."

"That guy?" Mark's face was flushed, his mouth set in a scowl. "How would I know a bum like that?" Then he scooped by a handful of rocks from the ground and threw them over the fence at Ambrose.

"Get out of here, you bum," he screamed. "You're disgusting, and I hate you!" Then all Mark's friends started to holler at him. "Get out of here, you old coot, or we'll call our teacher. You some kind of pervert or what?"

"Don't you know that I love you?" Ambrose had shouted back to his son. "I didn't do anything wrong. It wasn't my fault."

It was Mark's parting shot that day in the playground at Ambrose that came back to him again now on the phone in the visitor's room.

"Nothing's ever your fault, is it?" Mark growled into the phone. "Well, it's not mine. I didn't kill my mother!"

"Of course you didn't, son!" Ambrose pleaded. "It was an accident. It wasn't anyone's fault."

But by then, Mark wasn't listening. He had slammed down the phone and yelled something to the guard. As the guard came behind him and Mark stood to leave the visiting area, Mark mouthed these words at Ambrose.

"Thanks a lot, Dad, for nothing."

Ambrose yelled back at him, too pissed to care who heard him in the visiting area. "So what do want from me, huh? I can't change what you did." Then he screamed at the glass. "It's your fault, not mine."

As a guard approached Ambrose from his side of glass, he said, "I'll have to ask you to leave, sir. Your visiting time is over."

"Fine, fine!" Ambrose managed to say, but his mind was reeling. *What did they all want from me? Mark and probably Betsy and Jeanine too. Some kind of a "what if"? Is that what this was all about?* his mind raged.

Fine! They want it. Then here it is—a "what if" for all of you! Then let's call it even.

WHAT IF . . .

An Alternative Ending and a New Start

About 1994

Everything in Ambrose's life that morning made him feel miserable.

His day started with the cries of his six-month-old daughter, Jeanine, in her crib right after dawn. It wasn't unusual that she would wake up so early and fuss a bit, but usually she'd either go back to sleep on her own or play quietly in her crib. But this morning, Jeanine was not going to be so easy. When Ambrose realized that his wife was not responding to their daughter's repeated crying, he assumed, although he could never keep track, that it was his turn to get up and deal with the baby.

As he jerked back the sheet that was over him and got out of bed, he turned to look at his wife, Betsy, sleeping next to him. She laid with her back to him, her body covered in a long, white cotton nightgown. Although it was early summer, Betsy was still wearing that damned gown to bed, he thought. She had taken to wearing it right after Jeanine was born and hadn't put on anything else at bedtime ever since. The weight that she'd gained in that her second pregnancy hadn't come off as easily as it did after the birth of their son, Mark, now three years old. The first time they had sex after Jeanine's birth, Betsy told Ambrose afterward that she'd start a diet soon.

"I'm not going to grow fat and ugly, honey," she had told him confidently. "I just can't seem to get the pounds off right now. The doctor says it's not unusual with the second child. But I'll get serious as soon as things calm down around here a little bit. I'll get back to a size six again, you'll see, like when we were first married."

At first, Ambrose had reassured her. "You were way too thin when we got married. I like you a little plumped up." He laughed and pinched her hips that filled out her frame in a voluptuous way. But this morning, six months later, Ambrose could see how the nightgown was tight across her back and her flabby arms pressed against the material of the sleeves. She was getting fat, he told himself, and consuming more and more food each day. He'd catch her stashing away food at night after the children were asleep, and he imagined her eating it alone during the day when he was at work and the children napped. For God's sake, couldn't she just stop?

This morning Betsy was lying in their bed, snoring and coughing, ignoring him and any problems he might have. Ambrose knew reality had set in where their marriage was concerned. Betsy was now so self-absorbed with her own problems, primarily her weight and overeating. That left little time for her to focus on his problems, which mostly centered on his job. Those problems were on his mind as he walked down the hall from their bedroom and entered the baby's room.

"Hey, pumpkin. What's the matter?" Ambrose cooed softly and gently to the small child sitting up in her crib. She looked up with big tears in her eyes. She was dressed in a yellow sleeper, and her face was flushed. She began to sneeze.

"Oh, God bless you! What big sneezes you have!" Ambrose said as he leaned into the crib, caressing the top of her head and rubbing her back in a soothing manner. He tried laying her down on her side and suggested, "Don't you want to sleep a little longer while Daddy gets ready for work?"

But Jeanine squirmed and wiggled out from under his hands and sat up again in the crib. A cranky, whiny cry came up from the back of her throat. Her hands fussed about her face and head, and she rubbed the snot running from her nose into her hair.

"No, I guess not. No more sleep today, I can see." So Ambrose picked her up and walked over with her to the changing table. "Let see if we can clean you up a little."

He laid her down and grabbed a tissue to wipe her nose. She reacted, turning her face away at the same moment so he fought with her and finally got most of her face clean. Then he threw the tissue in the wastebasket next to the dresser.

"How about getting you out of this sleeper? It's too warm for it this morning. I don't know what Mommy was thinking putting you in it last night."

Just then, Betsy's head popped in doorway, and she spoke to Ambrose in an agitated voice. "Did you leave your car outside all night?"

Ambrose looked up at her as he was removing Jeanine's sleeper and diaper. His daughter was lying on her back, playing with the rubber ducky he had given her.

"Yeah, I couldn't find the garage door opener last night. I don't know if Mark has taken it again."

His son, at three years of age, had already demonstrated a fascination with all things mechanical and electronic. "You know he hoards things in his room as if they were his toys, not the necessary tools of everyday adult life."

"Someone broke into your car last night," Betsy announced. "There's shattered glass all over the street." Betsy looked at him with irritation. "Why didn't you come into the house and get my garage door opener? It would have been so simple."

"It was late," he shot back. "The bar association meeting went on forever."

"What else is new?" Betsy said flatly. She started back down the hall, then turned back abruptly, adding as if issuing him a warning. "You can't take my car to work today. I have to take the kids to Mom's so she can watch them; I have to get to work early. I don't have time to drop you off at work either."

Shit, he thought. He needed his car today to go see a client at his house—a new wealthy client with kids who was interested in estate planning, an area of probate law Ambrose was becoming an expert in. He had a way to set up trust funds for children so the estates of their wealthy parents could avoid taxes. Tonight, he also had another bar association meeting right after work at a downtown hotel, his last one for the week. It was a lot, but those meetings were a great place to meet other attorneys whose clients were looking for the kind of specialized legal expertise Ambrose was developing and the only way for him to build a more lucrative law practice.

So, his only option was to take his precious 1959 Ford Thunderbird to work.

When Ambrose didn't have time to drop off his T-Bird after work and pick up Betsy's car to go to his bar association meeting downtown that night, he felt a pang of guilty pleasure imagining himself showing off his sports car to the world driving it with the top down on a warm early summer night.

After the meeting and a few drinks in the bar with colleagues, Ambrose brought several of them down to the hotel parking garage to look at the car. It was his pride and joy, a car he had found in a crumbled heap in a used car lot. It was still in running condition, and Ambrose bought it for cheap. Then he put all his spare time and money into restoring it the previous summer—not to its full glory but enough that he could sit behind the wheel and feel its power and majesty.

When he finally climbed into the car late that night, he gunned the engine, and the car bolted up the exit ramp of the underground garage. He turned on to Main Street and cruised the nearly deserted street with the top down, listening to Beach Boy tunes on the radio and singing along. He was headed toward the entrance ramp to the highway to take him back to his home in the suburbs.

But when he got to the highway entrance, he decided to keep going and drive home the long way, cruising down a few more streets until he turned right on to La Strada Street. With the wind blowing through his hair, he picked up speed. All the drama and trauma of the day eased out of his mind. Maybe he was cruising and speeding down La Strada Street that night to avoid going home to his wife and having to make up for the morning's thunder between them. But that didn't explain the sound he heard next.

It was a thump, a single, solitary sound that he could have ignored except that it was followed by a sharp, piercing scream from a woman standing on the sidewalk a few hundred yards behind him. He slammed on the brakes, and when his car careened to a stop, he sat frozen behind the steering wheel, thinking of what that thump on the side of a car might mean. Had he hit a dog? That's what it sounded like, a small one.

All at once, the noises and smells of La Strada Street at 10:00 p.m. on a summer evening came flooding into Ambrose's consciousness. It was the central business district of a close-knit Hispanic community as well as a residential area. The men and women, boys and girls, who lived, worked, and shopped there were out on the streets tonight, even at this late hour.

As Ambrose turned his body in slow motion and took in this scene around him, the piercing scream came again. "No, not my baby! My baby!"

It was then that Ambrose saw the crumbled body of a small

child lying on the pavement. The girl's dark tresses, curled and tied with hair ribbons, were covered with an oozing red liquid that Ambrose could only imagine to be blood. Now the woman with the piercing scream was cradling and coddling the limp body in the street, wailing and crying in terror. Ambrose could see tears streaming down her cheeks and falling on to the dead girl.

Ambrose felt his own terror. *What have I done? Did I do this? How could this happen? Is this really happening to me?*

Ambrose stood up in the car and held on to the top of his windshield. Like the other spectators around him, his eyes were glued to the accident scene. But he was not like those around him. They had come to find a little girl dead, killed by a gringo driver in a red sports car, and they were mad. He wanted to cry out, "I am not a man of privilege or wealth. I am like you!" But he was not like them. He had run down one of their own, and now she was lying dead in the street. And despite the wails and pleading of the girl's mother to God for mercy, there would be no miracles performed on La Strada Street tonight to bring this child back to life.

As the angry crowd moved closer and closer to him, he was relieved when he heard a booming baritone voice behind him.

"All right," the man bellowed. "This is the police. Let's get away from this car and move back from the scene." He repeated the instruction in Spanish. A second police officer appeared beside him, and she began to disperse the crowd by putting her arms in front of her and pushing the crowd back to the curb.

The male police officer approached Ambrose in his car.

"You the driver of this car, sir?"

"Yes." Ambrose looked blankly down at the officer. Of course he was. He was still standing on the front seat of the car.

"I'll need you to step out of the car, sir, and show me your license and registration."

Ambrose climbed out over the front driver-side door of the car without opening it and when he hit the ground, he was standing next to the officer. He reached back into his pocket to retrieve his wallet. He pulled out his driver's license and handed it to the officer. "My registration is in the glove compartment. I can get it for you."

The police officer nodded, and Ambrose walked around to the passenger side of the car and leaned in to open the glove compartment. When he had retrieved a document from it, he slammed it shut and turned to find the officer at his side. He handed the officer the registration information.

"Thank you," the officer replied.

Ambrose nodded at him.

"Okay. Are you Jeffrey Jerome Alexander?"

"Yes," Ambrose said.

"Then I'm placing you under arrest for vehicular homicide." He turned him around and grabbed his hands behind his back. As he placed the handcuffs on his wrists, the officer intoned, "You have the right to remain silent. Anything you say can and will be used against you." He droned on for a bit more as he read Ambrose his Miranda rights.

Ambrose was silent until he finished, then spoke in a flat, low voice, looking the officer squarely in the eye. "I want an attorney."

"You can arrange for one as soon as we get you down to the station and do a breathalyzer on you. Have you been drinking tonight, sir?"

Ambrose had a quick thought. If he said no, that would be a lie. If he said yes, he was sure, although he had never practiced criminal defense law, that if he were intoxicated, it might bump his vehicular homicide case to a higher charge that carried more prison time. So he took a lawyerly approach to that question.

"No comment, officer," he muttered. "I have nothing to say about that."

The officer gave him a look, then spun him around, led him toward his squad car, and put him in the back seat.

As they left the scene, Ambrose could hear the crowd they left behind jeering and screaming "MURDERER!" at the top of their lungs.

All he knew was that it wasn't his fault, and he wasn't going to admit anything. Let them prove something in court. He didn't do anything wrong. That little girl ran right in front of his car. Her mother should have been watching out for her. That wasn't his job. It was hers.

He was innocent of all charges! He'd prove it in court.

It was five years later before Jeffrey could breathe the calm, cool air of freedom again. He had gotten off, many people said, with a light prison sentence for what he did that night on La Strada Street that resulted in an innocent young girl losing her life.

But his time in prison was not easy, that he knew.

First, the judge threw the book at him. Things had gone bad when the prosecutor decided to make an example of a rich, white lawyer who—in his words to the press and in his opening statement to the jury—"mowed down an innocent Puerto Rican girl in the middle of a street in the very neighborhood where she lived happily with her mom, her dad, and her sisters who loved her so much."

The penalty in the state for vehicular homicide depended on the circumstances. He learned that at trial and then later as he poured over legal books in the prison library while he did his time and tried to find some way to get himself out of there.

What he learned was that negligent homicide with a motor vehicle only brought a sentence of up to six months in jail, a thousand-dollar fine, or both. That charge was brought when, because of the "negligent operation" of a motor vehicle, a person causes someone's death. It occurs, according to the statute, when "someone deviates from the standard of care or conduct a person should reasonably follow under the circumstances."

But if while driving under the influence of intoxicating liquor, a person causes the death of a person as a consequence of such liquor, that turns into another more serious charge of manslaughter in the second degree with a motor vehicle. It's a Class C Felony that is punishable by a prison term of up to ten years. That's what Ambrose was ultimately charged with and found guilty of.

The facts weren't hard to prove. Yes, he hit and killed the girl with his car, and yes, he had been drinking that night—maybe he'd had a few more drinks than he should have before he made his way home. The breathalyzer that night that the police properly administered on him at the station showed he was over the legal blood alcohol level. And finally, there were witnesses who came forward, mostly to support the girl's family, and testified that he was driving too fast at a time of night when he could see that there was a lot of activity on the streets. The jury concluded that he was negligent in not being more cautious operating his motor vehicle that night.

What got trickier, however, was how the girl got from the sidewalk into the street, and no one could say at trial, including her mother. The mother's testimony of what she saw and how her daughter was killed was especially hard for him to hear. He realized then that his actions had consequences—tremendous consequences—and there was no taking them back.

There was nothing he could do or say to that mother or the rest of the family or even the entire community there on La Strada Street that could bring her back. He shouldn't have been driving so fast. He should've gone straight home on the highway, and he shouldn't have had so much to drink before he got in his car. He didn't need all that alcohol in his system to make a good impression on the other lawyers in the first place.

He had screwed up, and what happened that night was his fault. For the last five years, he had paid for his crime, and so had his family. He missed his children desperately. He lost the chance to watch them grow up and teach them how to be good people. He missed his wife, although she visited him every week without fail at the prison and always brought him photos or drawings by the kids whenever she could. He didn't want the kids to see him there. They were too young anyway, but he did want Betsy to tell them where he was and that he was there because he had done something bad to hurt someone and so he had to be punished. He wanted her to tell them that he would be home soon, so they should listen to her and be good.

Of course, he lost his marriage in the process. With all the legal bills and costs and the wrongful death lawsuit brought civilly against him by the girl's family, the only way to shield Betsy's small income was to have her divorce him. He insisted; she resisted. Finally, his lawyers convinced her it was best. Still their relationship grew stronger and stronger, and he longed for the day he could see his kids again.

He would face the consequences of his actions, and he would live a better life when it was over. He couldn't get away with it like he did with killing the cat all those years ago. Sure, he fooled his psychiatrist as a kid, but he knew his son, Mark, needed to see how to be a real man, a good man, and do the right thing.

It was never the right thing to harm another person, even by your negligence. He had learned that lesson the hard way. He would make sure his kids would learn it by his own example.

He would show them the way.

CHAPTER EIGHT

Howie's Journey

Defining Moment

Just a Moment at a Funeral

October 1999

Weighed down with the sorrow that had invaded his body and exploded his mind since the phone call he received a few days ago from the police telling him that Lacey had been killed, Howie walked slowly down the steps of the church where he had just attended the funeral service for his daughter.

It was still unbelievable to him that she was dead, and now he had to bury her body, her face maimed and unrecognizable from the gun shots that maniac had pumped into her. Wild, crazy thoughts ran through his head. *What was wrong with this world? How could this have happened to my little girl? That bastard! He's lucky he killed himself. I'd have killed him myself with my bare hands. Oh, Lacey, Lacey! How could this have happened to you?*

At the bottom of the steps, a crowd of people surrounded him. Some were friends who had been supporting him and his son, Jimmie, through this nightmare, but he couldn't deal with all of them right now. Still, they thrust their hands at him and poured out their sympathies. All he could do was respond weakly with a thank-you. He could have said more, something like "Thank you for coming today. It means a lot to me and my son, Jimmie." But he didn't.

Others that he didn't know were pushing their way into the crowd. Through the din of voices shouting at him, he heard someone say, "Excuse me, sir? Mr. Lockhart? Could I talk to you?"

By then, he had reached the limousine that was to transport him and Jimmie to the cemetery. His son must already be in the car, but in that moment, he didn't have the strength to open the door and get in himself. Instead, he rested against the door and stared back at the crowd. *If Lacey were still alive,* he thought, *she'd be hanging out with all the young people, her friends who had come to show how much they loved her.* Oh God! he wailed inside. Lacey would never finish college or graduate with her degree like her friends. She'd never marry, have kids, or get a great job! Suddenly he felt a severe pain inside him. It was so intense. It was too much!

Then a voice came at him, interrupting his thoughts.

"Excuse me, Howie," the voice asked. "Could I talk to you for just a moment?"

That voice from a young woman, probably close to Lacey's age, was louder than those who had just spoken their words of condolence in hushed tones. But that wasn't what got his attention. What had she called him? How could she know?

The young woman went on nervously, "Look, I'm really sorry about your daughter. It's a terrible thing. But I need to . . ."

"You called me Howie," he broke in. "Only my wife called me that. Do I know you?"

"No, but . . ."

He gaped at her, trying to figure out who she was and what she knew.

She took a breath and continued more calmly. "I know this sounds a little weird, but Lacey has something she wants me to tell you."

He looked at her, stunned, and then closed his eyes for a moment. This was too much. He had had enough. He had to get out of there. He moved toward the back door of the limo, but the young woman grabbed his arm and went on talking.

"You don't understand. Lacey's here. She can't talk to you, so I have to . . ."

He pulled his arm away from her and sputtered, "If you knew Lacey, you'd know she'd never play a hairbrained trick like this on me. Not me, not on her father. She loved me, and now she's gone." His voice cracked as he continued. "Lacey's dead. She's not talking to you, and you're not talking to me anymore."

Then he moved away from her, but this time she grabbed the edge of his suit coat and yanked him back like some kind of crazy, desperate person.

"Listen, you sorry son of a bitch," she whispered hoarsely. "Why else would I know to call you Howie if Lacey hadn't told me?"

He looked at her. *Was Lacey still here? Where was she? Where?*

"Here's what she wants me to tell you," the young woman continued. "Lacey forgives you for lying to her about how her mother died. If you had told her the truth when she was back in high school, maybe all of this would've worked out differently. But you didn't, and she's sorry about that too."

Then she went on. "So, let's cut the crap. Lacey is sorry. She forgives you. There, I delivered the message. Do you think I like having dead people talk to me? Or that I want to talk to pighead-ed idiots like you?"

"You're crazy!" he screamed at her. He felt his face burning with rage.

"Me, crazy?" she yelled back. "It's your daughter who's mak-ing me crazy."

"You leave Lacey out of this. Do you hear me? You're a lunatic!"

In one quick motion, he yanked his coat out of her hand, opened the door of the limo, and jumped in. As the door slammed shut, she lunged for him.

"No, wait, Howie," she wailed, her face at the window. "Mr. Lockhart! Please wait! I just need a moment to talk to you!"

But he was in the car now and had pushed the automatic lock. Still, she pressed her face against the car's dark-tinted glass window.

"Please, I'm sorry I upset you," she went on. "But Lacey's stuck in my body, and she won't go away. If you don't forgive her, she'll never go!"

Now, as she was yelling and pounding her fists on the window, he could see a crowd of people quickly gathering around her. Then two men in dark suits came up behind her, grabbed her by the shoulders, and pulled her off the car.

One of them shouted at her. "What the hell do you think you're doing? Can't you leave the poor man alone? He just lost his daughter."

"I know that, you asshole," she snapped back. "That's why I'm here. Lacey sent me. I'm telling you. I've talked to Lacey."

Damn, she was persistent, and suddenly Howie was intrigued. What if Lacey was trying to reach him from the beyond? Was that possible? It couldn't be any crazier than all that had happened since that night Lacey was killed. Maybe this girl could explain to him what happened.

All he had to do was to let her into the car and take a moment to talk with her. But by now, she was being carted off by someone from the funeral home doing crowd control.

What if he had told Lacey the truth that day when she had asked him for a full explanation of how her mother died? Why did he think that she wasn't ready to hear that from him then just because she was still in high school? If he didn't tell her, no one would. Or was Lacey, now dead, already hearing it from her mother somewhere in the afterlife? How would she describe it he wondered?

What if he had tried to tell Lacey back then? Could it have

changed anything? Would she have trusted him more and come to him for help to get away from Ari?

He sighed as he realized that now he'd never know. Maybe he could have saved his little girl's life that day.

If only.

WHAT IF…

Come to Daddy

He came home from work that evening, expecting Lacey to be there. Now in high school, she was old enough to take care of herself after school, start her homework, and rustle up something for their dinner. Or she could let him know if that night was a takeout night and what kind of food she'd like to order. This was their routine on school nights when they were alone together in the house and Jimmie was away at military school. He boarded during the week and came home on weekends.

When Howie pulled into driveway that night, he pushed the button in his car to open the automatic garage door. It started to grind open as it usually did, and the sound—the thumping, bumping, and thumping of a garage door—always reminded him of that horrible day years ago in another garage at a house clear across town where his wife, Margie, had died.

In order to avoid his own memories of that day, he immediately moved with Lacey and Jimmie into a new house, where they lived now. He purposefully chose a house with an attached garage so what happened that day to his wife in an unattached garage couldn't happen again.

He told Lacey, who was five years old at the time, very little about how her mother died except that she was in heaven now with the angels and would always love Lacey very much. Jimmie was an infant when Margie died, so he had no memory of his mother, and as he grew up, he never really asked Howie much about her.

So it was Lacey who bore the brunt of what happened to her mother. She cried for her mother every night for months afterward. Eventually, when she was older, Howie added a little more to the story if she asked how her mother died, and it seemed to satisfy her at the time. But he dreaded the day when she would want to know more.

Tonight, as he got out of his car and headed into the house through the door from the garage into the kitchen, his voice boomed out, "Lacey, I'm home."

When there was no response, he called out again, "Lacey! Daddy's home." But his voice merely echoed through the empty house. He remembered how, when she was a little girl, Lacey would run and hug him the moment he came through the door. But tonight, she wasn't cooking in the kitchen or sitting at the breakfast nook doing her homework and waiting for him.

"Lacey, where are you?" His voice grew heavier and more insistent. When he appeared in the living room doorway, he sighed as he saw her sitting on the couch. "There you are. You're so quiet. I didn't realize you were in here."

He walked over to the dining room table, took off his suit coat and threw it over the back of a chair. Then he loosened his tie and picked up the mail left there for him on the table. This was his daily routine, and they both knew it well.

"How was school?" he asked her absentmindedly as he flipped through the bills and catalogs, discarding what he didn't want back on the table.

Still not responding, she sat still without moving. He gathered that her silence had some significance, and he was supposed to pay attention to it. Throwing the rest of the mail on the table and stepping back into the living room, he looked at her carefully for the first time since he came into the house.

"Lacey, are you all right? You haven't said a word to me."

She looked up and stared at him, holding his eyes with hers without flinching.

"What's with the silent treatment?" he quizzed her. "Is it going to last all night?"

"It depends," she said in a low, coarse voice.

"It depends on what?"

"If all subjects are open for discussion."

"Sure," he said with a smug grin, and then he went on as if he knew what this was all about. "We can talk about the car, but you're still not getting it until graduation. You have to wait three more months."

"No," she replied, then blurted out, "I want to talk about my mother."

"Oh!" was all he could manage to say, and that came out of his mouth like a sound, not a word. His face went pale, as he sank down in the armchair next to her on the couch. "What about your mother?" he finally said, barely able to look at her.

"I want to know how she died."

These words stunned him even more, piercing him right to his heart. He tried to look away from her, but she held his eyes and commanded his attention. He squirmed in his seat, took a deep breath, and then let it out slowly. His voice was low and tight when he said at last, "I told you a long time ago—the day she died. She died in the car from carbon monoxide poisoning."

She glared at him. "Not that old story about the gas cap falling off, Daddy! I might have bought it when I was a kid, but now I want the real story. Or did you think I was so stupid that I'd never figure it out?" Then in a flash, she went for the jugular, blurting out before he could blink again, "Why didn't you tell me that my mother killed herself?"

With those words, Howie's eyes darted back to hers and all the color drained out of his face. For a moment, the question hung between them. He felt his face twitch as though he was going to say something. Finally he sighed and drew a hand through his hair and then let it drop in his lap.

"She didn't kill herself," he said in a shaky, muffled voice. "It was an accident."

"You expect me to believe that?"

"You can believe what you want. I can't tell you any more than that."

His voice was steadier now, and he could see that infuriated her even more.

"You can't, or you won't?" she bellowed. "I want to know how she died. Don't lie to me, Daddy!"

"Your mother's death was a terrible accident. There's nothing else to say." He stopped talking but then added quickly, as an afterthought, "I'm sorry."

"Sorry?" she screamed, and her voice went shrill. "All these years I thought Mommy's death was my fault. *What did I do wrong that God took my mommy away from me and she's with the angels now?* Now I find out that something else might have happened, something that maybe I had no control over, and I have to know how my mother died. I have to know, and you have to tell me!"

He looked askance at her because he hadn't really thought that Lacey might blame herself. But then his eyes glazed over, and he responded in a stiff, tinny voice.

"Life has a very slippery edge, Lacey. What difference does it make how your mother died? She's dead. She wouldn't want you going over and over this. Life is hard enough, and it will only get harder as you get older. But there are wonderful things about life, too—things that you can only imagine but can't possess right now."

They both sat there for a moment in silence, each thinking their own thoughts. He imagined that she was at a loss as to how to reach him, and that he deserved what he had gotten from her. His thoughts were much more conflicted.

He leaned over in his chair to where she was on the couch and touched her shoulder lightly. Then he said in a whisper, "Your mother is gone. When you die, you'll see her again. She'll be waiting for you. Remember that. Everything else is just not important."

Suddenly her voice shifted. "Fine, Daddy. Don't tell me what I need to know. You can do that. But you know what that means from now on between us, you and me?"

He looked at her and asked, "No, what does that mean?"

"I don't trust you. I never should have trusted you about what you told me happened to my mother, and I'll never trust you again. Ever! You know what that means, don't you?"

She didn't wait for his response and went on. "It means that if I ever have a problem now or in the future, something that I really need to share or need to figure out what to do, I won't be coming to you. You're a liar, and I hate you for lying to me."

Oh God! he thought. That's not what he wanted. He was there to protect his little girl. No matter what the trouble. He couldn't bear it.

Suddenly he stood up and moved to sit down next to her on the couch. He put his arm around her and let her head rest on his shoulder. She cried silently there for a moment, and then he reached down, put his hand on her chin, and lifted her face up to his as he spoke.

"I'm so sorry, Lacey. I should have told you about your mother sooner. I didn't realize all that you were holding inside yourself about her. That must have been so hard for you. But I thought you were too young to know. I wanted to protect you for as long as I could. But I can see now that you are a very smart, very mature young woman, and you should know everything. That's what I need to do for you. Tell you all I know. Everything. Okay?"

Lacey nodded and said in a hushed voice. "Yes, Daddy, I need to know. I do."

"Fine, but here's what I need you to do for me."

"What's that, Daddy?" she said, sounding surprised.

He gripped her hard, holding her close.

"I need you to promise me, Lacey, that if you are ever in trouble, if anyone—man woman, or child—is ever hurting you or threatening to hurt you or you're just confused and not sure about what is going on, you will come to me. You will not think twice about it, and you'll tell me everything. Do you understand? I will help you. I will not judge you or yell at you or blame you or anything else like that. I trust you to tell me the truth, and you can trust me to be there for you. That's the rule between us. No exceptions, okay?"

"Yes, Daddy," she whimpered, her tears subsiding. "Yes, I can do that for you. I love you so much."

"Me too. I love you too."

Then he hugged here again and repeated. "Remember, whenever you needed me, I'll be there. All you have to do is ask."

WHAT'S NEXT?

Making Changes

The hearing room felt familiar to Howie now. It should; it was the fourth or fifth time he was there at the legislature, and while it wasn't feeling like home to him yet, at least each time he appeared at a public hearing, he was a little less nervous and a little more confident. Today, he was actually feeling kind of bold and outrageous because today they were going after the guns.

The first time he was there for a public hearing, he had accompanied Sophie, his daughter's best friend. She had asked him to come with her to ask the legislature to include dating violence in the statute that addressed domestic violence in the state.

"I'm sure if you tell your story about Lacey, they will listen."

He was skeptical and terrified, but it worked. The law was passed that session.

The next time, emboldened by the power of the story they could tell, they took on gun violence more generally, supporting a bill to do more research into gun violence, its causes, and its impact on men, women, children, families, communities, schools, and churches. That time he came with Sophie and Lisette, who had known his daughter in a most unusual way, and he testified about how Lacey was murdered on the campus with a hunting rifle that the perpetrator had easily obtained at a local gun store using a college dormitory address.

The successful passage of the bill, bolstered by Howie's testimony, ingratiated him with the gun control/safety lobbyists who frequented the halls of the legislature, as Howie quickly learned. They liked the story he had to tell and how he told it—a grieving father now devoting his life to making the changes that might have prevented his daughter's untimely and tragic death by an abusive guy with a gun. It was the kind of human-interest story the media loved, not to mention social media, and it put the public pressure on legislators to pass laws to protect the citizens of the state.

Whenever Howie appeared, looking mild-mannered but passionate as the father of a murdered child, along with Sophie and Lisette who were equally committed to make changes in Lacey's name, everyone knew the piece of legislation they were advocating for was sure to move forward. They'd get the public's attention, if not righteous indignation (read: anger), about an issue, and legislators would vote for the measure either because they wanted to do something good with their vote in the legislature or they wanted to get reelected by being on the public's side of a thorny policy issue.

Today, Howie, Sophie, and Lisette were going after the gun store owners. They had gotten legislation proposed that required gun store owners to report the sale of guns to people that seemed to indicate that they wanted to kill, hurt, or maim innocent people on college campuses; at elementary, middle, or high schools; in nursing homes; or in public housing. Other cities and states had passed similar measures, called "red flag laws," that allowed a judge in a civil hearing to temporarily take guns away from people with potentially violent behavior and possibly prevent them from purchasing guns in the future. Sophie, the attorney in the group, said that none of those red flag laws had been found unconstitutional or in violation of the Second Amendment. Sophie, of course, as Howie was to learn, took a dim view of the currently overbroad and dangerous interpretation by the Supreme Court of the Second Amendment's right to bear arms.

"The Amendment was written years ago about a militia's right to bear arms," Sophie argued, "but it is now being interpreted to allow individual citizens to bear arms. Today, the proliferation of guns and new 'open carry' laws in many states make the presence of guns more dangerous than any other threat or crime wave in our history. And the scope of the Second Amendment, like any other amendment to the Constitution, is not unlimited." Hearings like this could get boisterous, if not downright dangerous, she warned Howie, but he didn't care.

Senseless violence had already taken his daughter, one of the most precious things in his life. Then, only a few years later, his son, Jimmie, was taken from him, this time in the war in Afghanistan.

Today Howie's work with the SISTER organization was all he had left. His goal was to advocate for laws, regulations and school policies and practices that might change the course of young people's lives so they could live long and happy ones.

That was what he could do now in Lacey's name.

That was all he could do, but it still didn't feel like enough.

CHAPTER NINE

Erick's Journey

Defining Moment

Picking Up Where We Left Off

October 15, 2009

Two Days Before the Tenth Anniversary

Erick was late.

He had promised Sophie that he'd come to the lunch with the Angel Investors. These were the wealthy people who supported Sophie when she started her *Survivor Strong, Thriver Resilient* organization, and they continued to help her to do something good in the community. Sophie explained how they particularly liked hearing that she was doing things no one else was doing, and that's why they were all in town for the Tenth Anniversary Celebration Gala on Saturday. She had invited Erick to talk at the lunch about the Men's Initiative he was heading up. Sophie told him she needed him to show these investors that they were putting their money into an amazing, innovative program.

But this invitation was very last-minute on Sophie's part, and Erick was preoccupied thinking about how to describe the Initiative at the lunch as he rushed through the hotel's front door. Quickly looking for signs pointing toward the hotel dining room, he brushed past and nearly knocked over a young woman standing with her back to him near the hotel's entrance.

"I'm so sorry," he said quickly, grabbing the woman by the arm to steady her so she wouldn't fall over. "This is my fault. I didn't mean to . . ."

As she turned to look at him, he stopped talking and stared at her.

"Lisette?" he blurted out. "Is that you? I didn't realize that . . ."

She jumped in to finish his sentence. ". . . I was standing here, minding my own business, just waiting for someone to bump into me like that." Then she laughed. "Sophie did predict we might be 'running into each other' this weekend."

He laughed, too, but added rather shyly, "I thought as much, too. That I'd be seeing you, I mean. And it is great to see you. You look wonderful! Wow! And you are so successful with your Atilla the Hunny clubs and . . ." His voice trailed off. "And did I say it is great to see you?"

Lisette laughed. "Yes, you did. It's good to see you, too, and I'm impressed that you know so much about my business. And no, I won't be yelling at you a lot, like I did when we were together. Or maybe I should say when we last broke up. So not to worry about that."

"Okay, yeah," Erick said with a sigh. "That was quite a break-up ten years ago, but I survived. I'm doing well. I have my own gym now. I'm a personal trainer. Bought the place a few years ago. I love it most days. You know, somedays yes, somedays no."

Oh God, he thought. *I'm rambling.* He was so excited, so surprised to see her.

"I'm surprised to see you too," Lisette said as if she read his thoughts. "Sophie made it sound like we wouldn't be at the same events this weekend. Unless . . ."

"Yeah, unless," he began suspiciously. "She planned this, right? Don't you see? At the last minute, she asked me to come to the lunch for the Angel Investors, and she knew you'd be here as an investor. She didn't tell me that, but now I see why I'm here."

"So we could run into each other, just like we did," Lisette teased. "I think our friend Sophie is what you might call a 'matchmaker.' Trying to put us back together and see if sparks might fly again." Then Lisette added, "Do you agree?"

"What?" Erick asked with a grin. "That sparks are flying, or that Sophie is sneaky?"

"You did try to run me over just now. That counts as something, right?"

"Maybe, maybe not. It wasn't full-body contact. I'd say it was a skirmish."

As they walked and talked like that on their way to the dining room, Erick noticed how Lisette touched his arm or held his eyes. He took it as a sign that maybe they could be friends after all. But whatever might happen, he had to admit that it sure felt good being in the orbit again of this beautiful and amazing woman.

It was as though they picked up where they left off ten years ago.

Wow!

When Erick woke up next to Lisette the following morning, he wondered why he was so damn lucky to be there.

It was hard to believe that after bumping into each other at the lunch with the Angel Investors, he and Lisette had spent the afternoon together, then went out for dinner and talked some more. She told him a lot more about her life. Even when they lived together for that short period of time ten years ago, she had never really let him know what a true disaster her childhood was. Now he knew why.

Yesterday he had taken her to see his gym, which she really liked. She told him she was proud of what he had done with the place. After work, he met her at the hotel for dinner, and they ended up in her room for the night.

He rolled closer to Lisette who was sleeping soundly, and wrapped his arms around her in a soft, gentle hug. God, she was as beautiful and sexy as ever! It was an impromptu lovemaking session last night, but it was spectacular as far as Erick was concerned. So full of passion, but also so gentle and easy. As with their conversation the day before, they simply picked up where they left off with the lovemaking, and it was good.

To top off last evening's pleasure this morning, he wanted to cook Lisette a nice breakfast in the small kitchenette of her hotel suite, but he needed groceries. So he got out of bed, gathered up his clothes, and quietly left the bedroom. He walked out into the outer suite of the hotel room, where he got dressed and left her a quick note in case she woke up while he was gone. He wrote that he'd be back soon and that he had taken one of her hotel room keys so he could get back into the room. He also wrote that he'd stop at the front desk on his way back to see if there were any messages for her. She had told Erick last night that it was still her habit from days of traveling from one seedy strip joint to another to tell the front desk clerk that she was unavailable if anyone called and to take messages for her even if she was in her room.

Back in the room now with the groceries, Erick happily started making breakfast. He wanted Lisette to wake up to the inviting smells of a good, hearty meal.

It only took a few minutes before Lisette swept into the room with her long robe flowing behind her and her hair cascading down in ringlets around her face. She was gorgeous even without any makeup. She gave Erick a sultry look and one of her big, beautiful smiles.

"Good morning, Erick. Something smells good! And you

cooked just for me. Aren't you the dearest of the dears? I think I'll keep you around for a while, okay?"

His heart melted.

Lisette was back in his life, and he was happy!

WHAT'S NEXT?

Paired with a Survivor

October 2019

Erick had worked with a lot of strippers over the years when he was a bouncer, and many of them had trauma histories. He was used to their moods, bouts of depression, and irrational behavior, but Lisette was like none of the others.

First of all, she was beautiful. Stu*nning* was probably a better word for it, but she was also smart (although not book smart), and she had a wicked sense of humor. When he first met her twenty years ago, he loved everything about her, except her unexpected bursts of anger, frustration, and sheer exasperation that came from her trauma history and from working in strip joints where she was exploited, dehumanized, and degraded every night. But until Lisette, he had never met anyone who had so few people to love and take care of her. He didn't have many people around him, but at least after his parents died, his grandmother took him in and raised him like he was her son, not grandson. He was forever grateful for her. But it made him realize what a deficient life Lisette was living.

He remembered what a difficult a time it was for him when she left him so abruptly the first time, after only a few months. As hard as it was for him, he thought it must've been harder for Lisette. There had been so many challenging things in her life at that time—maybe it was too much for her to stay and try to work things out with him.

Instead, their breakup was fast and precise. She screamed at him, accused him of cheating on her—which he wasn't—and basically told him she didn't want to be with him anymore. He knew she had suffered a lot of trauma as a kid, with her mother dying so young and then having to live with her father who, from what little Erick knew, was not a very nice guy. Erick knew from the classes he had taken in psychology that such trauma can have an impact on a person's emotional life, their ability to cope, and their capacity to have healthy relationships. So, in a way Lisette's breakup with him didn't really surprise him that much. Still, it hurt. He really cared about Lisette and wanted to be in her life. He thought he could help her heal from her childhood trauma and they could have a good life together.

But now that they had been back together again for the last ten years, happily married and with two kids, it struck him that he had learned a lot in that time about having a relationship with a woman who had survived violence, trauma, and abuse in her life. He thought there must be thousands of guys out there who were also partners or soon-to-be partners with women who had suffered terrible abuse by their ex-husbands and ex-partners. Was there something Erick could do about that? Could he find these other guys who were in the same situation as he was and figure out some kind of class, program, or group to support them?

He could do that. He hadn't had a chance to finish his education and become a clinical psychologist. That would have required him to get his PhD, but he did get his bachelor's degree in exercise science, and he was interested in working with men—not only showing them how to build their bodies but also how not to use their bodies (and minds) to do harm. He had read about some programs for men who were arrested for domestic violence, teaching them not just anger management, but a whole curriculum about what domestic violence is, how witnessing it as a child can make it more likely to someday become a victim or perpetrator oneself, and what a healthy intimate partner relationship would look like.

Erick thought he could enroll in that kind of training program and get certified to provide those kinds of classes for men who had been arrested for domestic violence. By using what he learned there, he might go on to develop a curriculum for men who were involved with women who had had experienced abuse in their previous relationships. He'd consider teaching them about how trauma affects a person's body and brain, and how those impacts might show up in a relationship and need to be addressed in a compassionate, understanding way. Maybe he'd call his program something like "Living with a Survivor: How to Build a Strong, Healthy Relationship."

This kind of program would fit with the other programs he and Lisette were developing for their Living Well Centers as well as their virtual offerings—audios, videos, and podcasts.

The sky was the limit!

WHAT IF?

Working with a PhD

Erick walked into his office that morning at the clinic and noted with pride his name and credentials as a PhD on the door. No matter how many times he walked into his workspace through that door, it always surprised him to see that yes, he was a clinical psychologist, a job he dreamed of having ever since he was a kid and a mental health professional had helped him, changing his life. He wanted to do the same for other kids someday even before he knew what a clinical psychologist was. So he earned both his master's and doctorate and got a job in a place where he could work with troubled young boys and teens and help them grow up to be good men.

There were many people who took the time to help get him where he was today. It wasn't easy. His parents weren't alive to help him, and his grandmother, who raised him, didn't have money to send him to college. He took classes, but to pay for tuition, he worked full-time as a bouncer in a number of strip clubs throughout the area. The pay was good, and the hours didn't interfere with the times his classes were scheduled.

It was a brutal schedule, working to the wee hours of the night as a bouncer and taking classes during the day. He had time to study in between, but little time to sleep. It was a long journey, but he finally made it. The last few years he was able to quit his bouncer job except for special assignments. This allowed him to get a couple of jobs in the clinics, where he did laboratory scut work or anything else, including janitorial work. Eventually he got his PhD and was offered a job at one of those clinics, now as a clinician.

Erick loved what he did. He had a full caseload that day, so he didn't have time to dawdle, but he did recognize that the referrals he had been receiving lately fell into a single category. They were mostly young men, maybe fifteen to twenty-five years of age, who had been singled out at some point for their violent behavior and sent to him for help. They weren't being prosecuted yet, but they had been flagged under the new, fairly recently passed "Red Flag Laws" in a number of states around the country, including the one he worked in.

Although the laws were new, he was considered by many of his referral agencies to be an expert in the area, as he had been working for a number of years with men in those age groups, conducting some research studies himself. He was known for compiling the research around this issue and its ties to gun violence. His studies led him to conclude that since the prefrontal cortex, critical to understanding the consequences of our actions and controlling impulses, does not fully develop until about age twenty-five, granting a young man under that age easy access to a gun was not a great idea. And if possessing a gun was combined with an obsessive use of social media to broadcast his anger over real or imagined grievances, then that gun owner might proudly take the opportunity to shoot someone just to prove he was a "real man."

Two of Erick's cases today were typical referrals for him. One was from a local college. A young man, almost twenty years of age, had been flagged for buying a gun from a local gun store using his college dormitory address. While the gun store owner wasn't required legally to report the sale of the gun to a college student, he did call the college with that information and the college added a few other things together. This same student had been cited previously for being in a fight with another male student during which he put his hand through a window at the school. Also his ex-girlfriend and her roommate had notified the campus police that he had been stalking them, both on the school email server and by text, refusing to leave them alone. Finally, his friends had been concerned about him since the breakup with his girlfriend, because he sounded depressed and was saying final things—like he wouldn't have to worry anymore once it was all over. They didn't know what he meant, but they went to a school counselor about him, afraid he might hurt himself or his ex-girlfriend because he was still so mad at her for breaking up with him.

The call from the gun store owner gave the school reasonable cause to search the student's dorm room for the gun and confiscate it under the school's newly instituted zero-tolerance policy for guns and other explosives on campus. With this information, the college also referred the student to Erick for "anger management" counseling and was regularly monitoring the student's progress with Erick.

The other referral was from a lawyer. His son had been displaying some questionable behavior, particularly having an obsession with guns and wanting his father to buy him an assault weapon for his eighteenth birthday, thereby getting around the law that only those over twenty-one years of age could buy such a weapon. This father was concerned about his son, and he didn't want to get a phone call from the police that his son had just used a gun to kill multiple people in a shopping mall on a Saturday afternoon.

That was a nightmare no parent wanted, and Erick had his work cut out for him.

He was ready to help.

CHAPTER TEN

Jenny's Journey

Defining Moment

Out of Work

Early December 2014

"Jenny Jablonski—our one and only 'Girl Governor,'" Dorothea Wiggens exclaimed as she walked into her old friend's office in the State Capitol on a cold, blustery day in mid-December.

Jenny rose from her desk and walked toward the woman.

"Dorothea, it's wonderful to see you, " Jenny said, breaking into a warm smile.

Dorothea grabbed Jenny's hand extended in welcome but then threw her arms around her for a full body hug. She enveloped Jenny in the soft girth of her body. For a moment, the two women held each other tightly.

When Dorothea broke the embrace, she held Jenny by the shoulders at arm's length, and continued jokingly, "My gracious! Look at us. Who would've thought that two sassy old broads like us would've gone so far?"

Then her voice got quieter and more sincere as she added, "I am so sorry you didn't make it through this last election. It's never easy losing, but this one . . . it was so mean-spirited. My gosh, they brought up everything against you since the beginning of time. Mall shootings, an ex-husband, an estranged daughter, a new stepdaughter who used to be a stripper, and . . . now two

---

grandchildren." Then she laughed and teased Jenny. "But are they really your grandchildren? Or just kids you brought in to make yourself look like a more kindly, sympathetic and approachable governor? Oh my! What you went through!"

Jenny joined in on the laughter for a moment, then added more soberly. "Some part of it must have stuck because my poll ratings had been going down for a while before I lost the election. I guess 2014 was not my lucky year."

"No matter what, you didn't deserve it. You've served so brilliantly. I should know. I've watched your career since we first met years ago both newly elected legislators who were assigned desks next to each other on the House floor. You worked your way up to lieutenant governor and then the governor and I was elected the first female African American secretary of state until I retired a few years ago. We actually got pretty close to some real power, didn't we?"

"Maybe the boys should've kept a closer watch on us," Jenny said, laughing. "Hell, they should've known I was trouble after they asked me why I didn't change my name when I got married." She added with glee, "Either time."

"Why didn't you?" Dorothea asked impulsively, as if she suddenly realized she didn't know the answer herself.

"Why should I? That's what I told them," Jenny said brazenly, with a wide grin on her face.

"Absolutely!" Dorothea broke into a big laugh and shook her head in delight as she released Jenny from her grip.

"Please sit down," Jenny said, recovering from the laughter they shared. She guided Dorothea to an armchair, and as Dorothea eased herself into the chair, Jenny moved around to sit back at her desk.

Settled in her seat now, Dorothea eyed her surroundings. "My, this room looks great, Jenny. It has a few of your touches. I like it."

"Thanks," Jenny said, sitting down in the leather executive chair. "I've tried to roust out the arrogant, condescending ghosts of my exclusively male predecessors in this high office every chance I get."

Dorothea laughed.

Then Jenny added, "I really did want to get rid of that dark wood paneling," pointing with a forlorn look to the walls behind and to her left. "But since I campaigned on bringing austerity to state government, I *had* to keep resisting my urges for interior decorating. I finally did manage to banish those awful dark velvet drapes on the windows, though. Thank God! They blocked the incredible view of the front lawn."

Dorothea turned to look with Jenny at the view, notable even in mid-December when neither the historic spreading oak trees nor multicolored flowerbeds were in bloom. Both framed the walkway that intersected the lawn from the statehouse steps down to Capitol Avenue and led across the street to the State Supreme Court building.

"I agree with you, Jenny. Those light floral curtains definitely brightened up this room. But I would've gone for something a little bolder than pastel myself," Dorothea said, snickering as she looked down at the large red polka dots on her white dress trimmed in black. She wore a wide-brimmed hat in red, white, and black to match.

Jenny laughed. "You know me, Dorothea. I like those *muted* tones. Like the colors I chose over there."

Jenny pointed to a cluster of furniture to her right. Three rose-colored upholstered chairs were positioned facing a long, plush couch with slipcovers of rose-and-ivory stripes. A spray of peach-and-white silk roses intermixed with baby's breath was arranged in a narrow, low flower dish on the coffee table. The wall behind the couch, the only space on the walls of the room not covered with wood paneling, was painted a pale peach.

Dorothea eyed her friend. "Okay, let me have it. Why did you drag me to your office on a December morning? Surely I'm not here to admire how you gave this room 'a woman's touch' for the first time in state history. You're moving on here, Jenny. What are your plans?"

"That's exactly the question I wanted to talk to you about. I need your help. As you know, my political aspirations to rise from this job as governor to something bigger on the national scene, perhaps as the first female vice president or president of the United States have not been realized. So I need a job—and not just any job. God knows, I've had many jobs in and out of government, but as I come to this defining moment in my life, I realize that maybe I only have one or maybe two more jobs to add to the list before I get put out to pasture. We still call it 're-tirement' in our generation, right?"

Dorothea chuckled. "I'm not the one to ask about that! I swear I'm never going to stop doing something, right? We don't retire! We just move on to the next best thing and put our heart and soul into that."

Jenny smiled. "Yes, I can see that you've done that. Since you left as secretary of state, you've settled into a few volunteer and philanthropic activities that I admire greatly. I'm particularly interested in your position as a member of the board of one of our local colleges. You know that Brad and I have been interest-ed and involved in that college ever since that young woman, Lacey Lockhart, was shot and killed there by her ex-boyfriend about fifteen years ago. It was a sad day for us here in the state, and as it was one of the early school shooting cases—with the Columbine High School incident only a few months earlier—it was a real shocker."

Jenny watched Dorothea, waiting for her reaction. Noticing none, Jenny went on.

"I'm sure that as a member of the board of that college, you've heard rumors that its current president—who is a White man like everyone one of his predecessors since the college's founding—will be leaving his position soon. I suspect you might even know the exact timing of that resignation."

Again, Dorothea had no response.

"So," Jenny continued, "I invited you here while I was still in this auspicious but somewhat toned-down office to impress you perhaps, but mostly to command your presence before the governorship of this state is unceremoniously taken from me and to let you know that I'd like to have a chance at being the next president of the college."

Dorothea opened her mouth for a moment, then closed it, as if she wasn't ready to speak yet.

So Jenny went on. "But I really wanted to ask you is if I can rely on our long-standing friendship and ask your advice. Do you think I should go for this? I really think I could be good at it and make a difference. I think our colleges have had their heads in the sand on the issue of violence against women, particularly with Lacey's death. I think there is an opportunity to do something visionary around that issue and so many others that impinge on the ability of colleges today to really prepare these kids for the future they are going to face. This could be done, of course, completely within the parameters of maintaining the high academic and scholarly reputation of the school and further . . ."

Suddenly Dorothea had something to say.

"Let me just stop you here, Governor." She cleared her throat. "As a member of the board of the college, I can't disclose any information about a possible vacancy at the college. But I can tell you that in not discussing this further with you, it's not that I don't appreciate your interest in such a position if one were available, but it's better that I don't discuss it with you right now." Dorothea took a breath and sighed. "You know what I mean, right?"

"Okay, okay. I'm getting a vibration here that maybe an old friend of mine just came to see me at my office, wanting to know how I was doing, and while she would be happy to see me move on to other work, it's best that we don't discuss any particular job openings right now. Did I get that right?"

Jenny waited for Dorothea to nod her head in agreement. Neither of them wanted to create a "conflict of interest" situation in which a potential job offer to Jenny as president of the college would be tainted in the pre-application/interview stage. As an applicant, Jenny could be seen as having made a questionable decision to ask the Chair of the Hiring Committee to come chat with her in her office as an old friend.

"Yes, I agree" was Dorothea's only response. Then she paused for a moment and pointed to something on the table behind Jenny. "Is that a recent photo of your grandkids, Jenny? I'd love to see it and hear more about how they are doing these days. They are so cute, getting so big. As I recall, their names are Sasha and Jeremy, right?"

Jenny looked at the table behind her and reached for the photo. "Yes, I'd love to fill you in more. That would be a great thing for us to discuss. I'll remember that in this discussion, we talked about our grandkids—and oh, the fact that I'm also looking for a charitable institution interested in receiving the muted tone curtains that have officially hung in the governor's office, which I plan to donate once my term is done."

Dorothea looked at her, dumbfounded.

"Yes," Jenny continued. "Did you know that the drapes are actually mine to take with me? I paid for them myself since the state budget only included a 'redecoration' allowance for my first term in office. I decided not to redecorate the office during my first term. I didn't want to shake up too many things as the first woman governor, and I didn't know how long I was going to last. But now, after three terms, I think I can give them away with an assurance that perhaps there are job opportunities for me elsewhere.

"Exactly," Dorothea said, a short and sweet response.

"Over the next few weeks, I'm going to be meeting with a number of other agencies to see if they might take the drapes. Let me call my secretary in now so he can take a few notes on this meeting and document that it was the first of a number of meetings that I'll conduct to find a home for the drapes. Just for the record."

Jenny smiled as she hit a button on her phone, then said as an aside with a giggle. "Don't you love that I have a man as my secretary? Actually I think his title is executive assistant. Very politically correct!"

As her secretary opened the door to the governor's office, Jenny was asking Dorothea, "And how are your grandkids doing? You've such a head start on me on this. One of them at least is finishing high school this year, right?"

"Actually two of them."

"How wonderful!"

WHAT IF...

Maryssa, Jenny, and Francesca, a Grandchild

In the Unrealized Future

By early on Christmas Eve, Jenny had already rummaged through the boxes of ornaments and holiday trimmings that had been transported from the storage area to the sitting room of the upstairs living space she called home. Jenny sat in a stuffed chair admiring the tree to be decorated—a spruce pine, real, not artificial, and larger, she noted, than most of the trees she had decorated in her lifetime. This particular room was spacious enough to show off this tree in all its splendor.

Jenny had pulled the tree lights out of one of the boxes yesterday afternoon so they could be put on ahead of time by her staff. That was a task that neither she nor Maryssa cherished, and they had banished it from their ritual as soon as Maryssa's father, who was Jenny's first husband, disappeared following the divorce. It was annoying to Jenny's feminist sensibilities that putting lights on a Christmas tree was designated as "men's work," but she had to admit that George did it well, and after he left, no one wanted to do it.

Sipping her sherry, Jenny mused that she'd never imagined this family ritual being played out in such a grand room. The ritual had been passed from generation to generation. She remembered trimming her grandparents' tree as a child. She had watched her grandmother string "angel hair" through the branches, mesmerized by the white lights twinkling on the boughs. Jenny, the granddaughter of Polish immigrants, treasured the few ornaments she had from her grandmother's tree.

A jumble of noise arose suddenly from outside the living quarters. The door flew open, and a child burst into the room carrying a package in her arms that was wider than her four-year-old body. Francesca, known as Frankie, peered around the box and spotted her grandmother.

"Busia, Busia! We have a present for you," the child shouted, calling Jenny by the Polish word for grandmother. She raced over to her and plopped the package into Jenny's lap. "It's for the top of the tree."

"Oh, Frankie, I told you not to tell Busia that much. You'll spoil the surprise," said Maryssa, coming in behind Frankie.

"Oh, what a big package!" said Jenny, looking into her granddaughter's face. "This is all for me?"

"Yes! We have other presents too. Do you have some presents for me?"

"Frankie, don't be so fresh," warned Maryssa, grabbing her daughter by the hand and bending down to take off her bright red wool coat. "Let's take off your coat before we get into all that talk about presents."

Frankie took off her hat in one sweeping motion and threw it on the floor.

"No, no, Frankie. Don't throw your hat on the floor," said Maryssa in a motherly tone as she reached out with her other hand. "Please give it to me."

"I want to see the tree," Frankie said as she tried to squirm away from her mother's grasp without retrieving the hat first. "Busia, I want to see the tree."

"Frankie! Pick up the hat first. Then we can see the tree," said Jenny in a conciliatory tone, rising up from her chair and extending her hand to Frankie. "Pick up your hat and give it to your mother. Then you and I can go see the tree."

Frankie wrinkled up her face for a moment, as if she was still contemplating disobedience, then swooped down to grab the hat, stuffed it in her mother's hand, and grasped for her grandmother's outstretched hand in front of her, all in one grand, totally focused movement. Jenny and Frankie approached the tree together, its width far greater than the two of them combined.

"Busia, can we turn on the lights now?" begged Frankie, tugging at Jenny's hand. "I want to see the twinkle, twinkles."

Maryssa came over after stashing the coats in the other room and stood next to her mother. "We have been singing that song all afternoon," she whispered to Jenny. "Every time we saw Christmas tree lights. *Twinkle, twinkle, little star.*" Maryssa began to sing to Frankie. Then she said to Jenny, "It was so cute."

Frankie raised her voice an octave. "The twinkle, twinkles, Busia. Please."

"But, Frankie, you know the ritual. The lights don't go on until all the ornaments are up, and the ornaments don't get turned on before the roping is on the tree. So, ladies, let's get started."

The boxes of ornaments were flung open and the layers of tissue paper pushed aside. One by one, the ornaments were laid out and made ready for hanging. The Christmas music was cued with secular music to start, including "Jingle Bells" and "Rudolph, the Red-Nosed Reindeer," some of Frankie's favorites that kept the four-year-old focused while the tree was being prepared for hanging the ornaments.

Maryssa stood on a small ladder and placed the popcorn roping carefully on the limbs of the Christmas tree. Although Jenny and Maryssa usually popped the popcorn the night before, this year the task was done by the cook and her staff. Jenny had to go down and instruct them in advance as to how to do it. Oddly, none of them had ever used popcorn strung with cranberries on their own Christmas trees. Jenny wasn't quite sure where that ritual came from in the Jablonski family, but she liked it because it was more natural and better than garish, plastic tinsel.

Jenny and Frankie kept busy taking the ornaments out of the boxes. Maryssa and Jenny had learned last year to put the less delicate ornaments in one box for Frankie to open. Her hands, at four years old, were a bit bigger this year, but her excitement was even more exuberant.

"These toys," said Frankie to her grandmother, pointing to the hobby horse, teddy bears, and Mickey Mouse ornaments, "go on the bottom so I can play with them whenever I want."

"Yes, Frankie, that's the way we do it. And Momma and I will put these ornaments higher on the tree." Those ornaments ranged from preserved, hand-blown glass ornaments that Jenny had collected through the years to the ornament she had bought Maryssa each year as a child. When Frankie, the first grandchild for Jenny was born, the tradition continued, and Jenny had an ornament ready for both Maryssa and Frankie this year. They'd be, according to tradition, the last ornaments to be added to the tree. With Maryssa now off the ladder and placing the roping of popcorn and berries at eye level on the tree, Jenny began hanging ornaments higher up where Maryssa had already placed the roping until Jenny heard Frankie scream behind her.

"No, Busia," the little girl shrieked. "You can't put the ornaments on until all the popcorn is on. That's the ritual." She pronounced the word slowly and carefully, standing with her hands on her hips and glaring at her grandmother.

Jenny let out a laugh, and Maryssa peered around from the back of the tree. "She's been at it for less time than we have, but she's got it down," said Maryssa with a twinkle in her eye. "She must be a Jablonski."

"All right, sweetie," said Jenny to Frankie. "You are right. I shouldn't be putting up the ornaments until the roping is done. I'm sorry."

"All done," declared Maryssa, as she rounded the tree for the last time and tucked the end of the roping into the tree, out of sight. "Now we are ready for the ornaments." This part of the ritual required different music. Maryssa put in a tape of traditional Christmas music with more religious themes, such as "Silent Night." The two women began to sing along as they decorated.

One by one, the ornaments filled the tree. Each one was a memory for Maryssa and Jenny, especially as Maryssa placed her special ornaments on the tree, one marking each year of her life. Frankie busied herself placing her box of ornaments at the base of the tree. Soon they stood back to admire their work.

The final part of the ritual also had special music: Polish *kole-dies*, or carols. They reminded Jenny of her parents, both dead now, who played them at Christmastime and sang along in Polish.

Jenny had never learned the language, but she came to love the melodies and tried some of the words. Maryssa knew as much after all her years of hearing them. The Polish carols signaled that it was time for the giving of the ornaments for the year followed by placing the final ornament on the top of the tree. Jenny had a star for the top that was packed away in its own separate box.

As she walked over to get it, Maryssa stopped her and said, "Mom, why don't you wait with that until after we open our ornaments?"

"But isn't it for the top of the tree?"

"Yes, Mom, but can't it wait until last?"

Jenny gave in and put the box back on the floor. She handed her presents to Frankie and Maryssa. Frankie tore open her package and found an animated Mickey Mouse ornament that danced to music when the key was turned. Frankie cranked the key and watched the show.

Maryssa opened hers and smiled when she saw the delicate figurine of a mother and child hand in hand, Christmas packages in tow. Maryssa's name was engraved on the mother figurine and Frankie's on the girl. Below that it said, "Love from Mom, Merry Christmas." Maryssa leaned over to kiss her mother on the cheek. "It's lovely, Mom. Thank you."

"You're welcome. Merry Christmas." She turned to her granddaughter, drawing her attention away from her Mickey Mouse ornament. "Now, Frankie. I should open up that big package you brought."

At Jenny's invitation, Frankie got up and ran to the other side of the room where Jenny had left the package Frankie had brought in with her earlier.

"Don't run with that, Frankie. You'll drop it," cautioned Maryssa.

Frankie careened toward to her grandmother, now seated in a chair before the tree. As Jenny took the box from Frankie, Maryssa pulled out her phone and began to snap pictures of the two of them.

"Oh, I'm so glad you remembered to take photos. They wanted to send up the official White House photographer, but I didn't want to have an intrusion on our ritual," said Jenny. She opened the package carefully. It had come from a Georgetown shop and was beautifully wrapped in elegant foil paper with a large red ribbon. Frankie bubbled over, grabbing the side of the box in her excitement.

"Careful, Frankie. Let Busia get it out of the box first," said Maryssa as she stood back to take a picture.

"Let me see. My, my, there is a lot of tissue paper here," said Jenny to Frankie. "I wonder what this could be. Oh, I think I have it now."

Jenny lifted an object out of the box, still wrapped in tissue. Slowly, as she peeled the paper away, Jenny could see it was an angel.

"Oh, Maryssa," Jenny exclaimed. "I have always wanted an angel for the top of the tree. I just never had time to shop for one."

"This is a very special angel, Mother," Maryssa responded.

As Jenny pulled the last piece of tissue from the ornament, she saw a large angel with flowing robes, trimmed in gold with silver tassels. The angel had a banner across its chest that bore an inscription and a seal.

Through her tears, Jenny read the inscription and gathered her family into her arms. "To Our Mother and Grandmother, the First Woman President of the United States, Christmas 2000."

WHAT'S NEXT?

Being the First Woman

I never thought I'd be happy doing what I'm doing today. Some people would think of it as just an administrative job, which in my mind translates as boring, but this job has it all. Sure, the job of governor was more ceremonial than being a college president, but here I get to work with young people every day and learn from them in such profound ways.

One of my favorite things to do, particularly on difficult administrative days, is to sit in the back of a classroom and just listen. Not only to what is being taught by the instructor, but also—and more importantly—to hear what the students are talking about. I love their excitement for learning, the insights they share, and how they see the world.

They have even allowed me to run my own seminars with select students, particularly the women, and they are eager to know more from me about how I made it to the high levels of government. What did it feel like? What did I like about it? What was the worst part? Somehow all of this fascinates them. But what fascinates me is that this is a generation of women who could actually imagine themselves, without any constraints, going for and achieving that level of participation—and higher!— in the government of this country . . . and internationally too.

What was that quote that I love from Justice Ruth Bader Ginsburg? "Women belong in all places where decisions are being made."

I believe that today, but I grew up in the 1950s, a decade where women were subjugated to being "just" wives and mothers, and as a girl, there was no way that I saw myself in high places where decisions were being made in any sector of our society. Today these young women have that dream, and they have role models to follow. Some see me as their role model. That is so great.

I like to remind them that, as women, we are here today standing on the shoulders of so many other women who fought and died for our rights to be equal and full members of this society.

After all, my mother was born in 1919, the year women got the right to vote in this country. That's how "young" our liberation is, how hard-fought and fragile the victories have been. I encourage them to study hard, dream big, and take risks—because they will direct the future of this world and make it a better place for us all.

So this I know. I'll never have biological grandchildren of my own, but I have my dear, dear ones, Sasha and Jeremy. I'll never be president or vice president of the United States, certainly not the first female to hold those offices, but I was the first woman governor of our state and served for three terms in that office. I have also been a lawyer and a judge. All these are positions and career goals that most women only a generation before me didn't have access to. I am the first woman president of a college, and when I leave this job, my portrait will hang with those of all the White men who served before me. I hope that when the next generations of women students hit this college, there will be many, many more women and people of color whose portraits hang in the President's Gallery. No one can hold us back when right is on our side.

I am changing the lives of young men and women every day.

I am blessed.

CHAPTER ELEVEN

Sophie's Journey

Defining Moment

The Danger Signs

April 1999, on Campus

"I don't get it," Sophie called out to Lacey as the two of them stood shivering in the cool April night in the parking lot outside their dorm. "Tell me again, why do we have to wait for Ari to drive us to The Keg? It's freezing out here!"

Sophie was so cold that her body trembled underneath a skimpy, hip-length coat that barely covered her body.

Lacey turned around and frowned at Sophie. "I told you to wear something warmer," Lacey admonished her, purposefully changing the subject. "It's not August anymore."

Lacey had already told Sophie why Ari was driving them tonight, but Sophie thought there was something more she could do about it. Lacey wasn't about to let Sophie make her feel stupid for letting Ari have his way, but now she gave Sophie another sour look and added, "Why don't you wait inside the building with Laura and the rest of the girls? It's warmer in there. I'll let you know when Ari comes."

"But you said he'd be here twenty minutes ago," Sophie said, barely able to stop her teeth from chattering.

"He'll be here when he gets here," Lacey said. Sophie could hear the irritation creeping into her voice. "Go inside. You don't have to wait here with me."

"But that's what I don't get," Sophie insisted. "We're standing out here in the cold when my car is right over there. We could be at The Keg already. Why are we waiting for Ari?"

"Because it's complicated! That's why."

"What's so complicated about saying no to this guy?" Sophie shot back. "You say, 'No, Ari! You don't need to drive me and my girlfriends to The Keg tonight. We can get there all by ourselves. That's what women in this country do. Go places by themselves and have fun.' That's it, Lacey. Sound pretty simple to me."

"That's enough, Sophie. I thought you, of all people, would understand."

"Oh, I understand. This guy has got his hooks into you, and you don't even know how deep."

Lacey glared at Sophie.

"You don't believe the story he gave you about going to fill up Scott's van with gas before we can leave, do you?" Sophie continued. "Don't you see that he's doing everything in his power so that we never get to The Keg tonight?"

"But the van does need gas," Lacey protested. "And it's only nine o'clock," she added, looking at her watch. "We still have plenty of time to party tonight."

Sophie eyed her carefully. "I think he's making us stand out in the cold so you'll just give up and stay home. Jesus, can't you see how he's trying to keep you away from your friends?"

"He is not," Lacey insisted.

"I hate to be the one to tell you this," Sophie continued solemnly, "but I think he's crazy."

"Sure, he's crazy," Lacey said with a laugh. "He's crazy about me."

"No," Sophie went on. "It's crazy how he needs to have you with him or know where you are every minute of the day. Like he doesn't trust you. Like you can't have a life of your own. That's not right. There's something wrong with him."

"You're wrong, so wrong, about this, Sophie." Lacey's face flushed with anger, and Sophie could feel Lacey's eyes burning into hers. "You talk like Ari's evil or something, and he's not."

"How do you know he's not? How else can you explain his obsession with you?"

"He's not obsessed with me. He loves me."

Before Sophie could reply, a squeal went up as Laura and the other girls came running out of the building behind them. Sophie and Lacey looked up to see that Ari had arrived, stopping in front of them in the parking lot.

"See, he's here," Lacey said in triumph, standing back with Sophie as the other girls opened the back door and piled into the van. "Look, I know what I'm doing here. Everything's cool with Ari. Honest it is."

Sophie gave her a look as though she wasn't so sure about that, but Ari's voice interrupted them, calling out from inside the van. "Are you girls coming or not?"

"Yeah, get inside, will you?" Laura cried out from the back seat. "You're letting all the hot air out. Ari's got it all nice and cozy inside here for us."

Sophie sighed resignedly, then climbed up into the van and closed the door. Lacey got into the front seat next to Ari and acted, for Sophie's sake at least, like she was upset with him. As he rolled out of the parking lot and mumbled something about being sorry for taking so long, Lacey looked at him but didn't respond. Sophie could see from Lacey's behavior that she was trying to show her that Ari didn't control her every thought and action. That's why, Sophie thought, Lacey was ignoring him now and focusing all her attention on what was going on in the backseat where everyone except Sophie was in pretty high spirits.

Jennifer was teasing Laura, the drop-dead gorgeous one of the group. "I can't believe you cut off all of your hair this afternoon.

What were you thinking?"

Sophie could imagine Lacey in that moment picturing Laura's long, frizzy black hair and how she looked like a pixie now, cute but not so beautiful. As if Ari were reading her thoughts, he said in a low voice that he thought only Lacey could hear, "I love your hair long, baby. Don't ever cut it, okay? You're so beautiful."

But Sophie caught it all, including how he reached over and squeezed her hand. At any other time Sophie knew Lacey might have squeezed it back, but her words must have penetrated into Lacey's thick skull when it came to Ari.

Lacey turned around and yelled into the back seat as if showing Sophie she could stand up to Ari. "I've thought of cutting my hair. I'd do it in a minute, but I know I would feel so naked without it!"

As soon as those words were out of her mouth, Sophie could see Ari jerk his hand away from Lacey's, and he scowled, both hands gripped tightly on the steering wheel.

Laura chirped from the back seat. "That's what I always said. But you can't believe how freeing it is to not have all that hair on your back all the time." Then she giggled. "My boyfriend, Ray, likes it clipped short. He says it's like my pubic hair now!"

A howl went up from the van, and Lacey turned around and let out a whoop with the rest of the girls. Sophie heard Ari groan in disapproval, but this time Lacey didn't even look at him. Sophie knew that in Ari's world women were demure and invisible and never talked dirty. Well, not here in this country, she wanted to shout at him. Women are free here, and so were they.

But Sophie wasn't sure that Lacey was making all those connections about Ari, and she worried that her friend wasn't getting the message she was getting tonight about Ari loud and clear.

The red flags were going off. It was clearer tonight than it had ever been in this tumultuous relationship between Lacy and Ari.

Ari was controlling, possessive, and manipulative. He wanted Lacey all to himself, and he would bend her to his needs no matter what.

What scared Sophie the most that night was that Ari was obsessed with Lacey and would never let her go.

The only question that remained was what Sophie was going to do about it. How was she going to save her best friend from this monster, or could she?

But Sophie knew one thing for sure: If she wasn't successful, the kind of power and control Ari was wielding in this relationship might come down to a matter of life and death for Lacey.

That realization was like a slap in the face to Sophie. But what was she to do about it now?

WHAT IF . . .

A Life Saved

Night of October 17, 1999

Neal really didn't want to check on Ari that night. He was his suite mate in an adjoining dorm room with a shared bathroom in-between. Neal knew that Ari was agitated ever since what happened at The Keg a few months ago, and he was trying to get Lacey back.

The agitation seemed to have subsided a bit earlier that afternoon when Neal walked with his suite mate to get a late lunch off campus. But by then it was more of a sadness, like Ari was depressed about his breakup with Lacey.

Neal had learned that lecturing Ari about letting Lacey go over the last few months didn't work, so they talked about other stuff. They had computer science classes in common, so they talked about how when they got out of school, they were going to make video games for kids like them.

"Yeah," Ari said. "I'm going to do one about blowing people's heads off. That would be cool."

Neal thought that was an odd thing for Ari to say, but he was used to hearing Ari pop off at whomever he was mad at in any given week and then threaten—all in a fantasy, of course, Neal thought—that he was going to shoot someone.

By the time they had finished off a pizza at a place just off campus, it had begun to get dark on that Sunday night in October as they walked back to the dorm. Neal had homework to do for one of his classes, and Ari was talking about working on a paper that night too.

"Yeah," Ari said quickly. "Lacey is coming over to read it for me. She said she would when I talked to her yesterday."

"She's coming to see you?" Neal was surprised. "I thought the two of you had broken it off. That's what we talked about last night. You need to let her go. She's seeing someone else. She can do that, you know. Break up with you and move on to another relationship."

"Yeah, but we can still be friends, right?" Ari said with some clarity in his voice. "That's what she wants, and that's what I want. Besides, she really knows how to fix English papers really well. With her help, I'm getting better grades now, and that always pleases my father."

Ari said that sarcastically, of course, Neal noted. He knew that Ari had nothing but disdain for his father. And his father was never pleased with him or anything he did. Not ever.

So, Neal didn't even go there with Ari. But he did wonder why Lacey was coming over that night. Was she trying to dick around with Ari? Hadn't she been clear she was done with their relationship? Did she really believe that she and Ari could be just friends? Neal didn't get it, but then maybe Lacey was coming to tell him one more time to leave her alone.

Good luck with that, he thought. *Not going to happen.*

At about 11:20 p.m. something else prompted Neal to check on his suite mate. Not realizing that Lacey was still there, he went through the bathroom and knocked on the door. He didn't wait for a response and stuck his head in.

First, he saw Lacey sitting on Ari's roommate's bed right next to the bathroom door. Her face was red from crying, but there was something more. She looked at him. She definitely looked at him, and that look haunted Neal. Like she wanted something from him—like she needed something, but what?

Then Ari rose up from his computer across the room, waving some papers in his hand.

"Hey man, you are interrupting us here," he said, gesturing to include Lacey. "We're kind of talking right now. I told you she's helping me with my paper." Then Ari continued, rambling now. "Lots more to do. No time to waste. You know what I mean."

Ari stared at Neal, his eyes cloudy and threatening. Threatening toward him, for interrupting him while working on a school paper, Neal thought at first. Or was it toward Lacey, whom Ari had told him repeatedly had broken his heart?

Neal eyed Lacey again. When he did, she held his eyes and stirred in her seat. He knew Ari was trying to get him out of the room, but then another thought came to him, and he went for it as if by instinct.

He reached out, grabbed Lacey's hand and with one quick movement pulled her off the bed and on her feet. She felt light and airy as her body came up close to his. He pushed her around him and into the bathroom.

Speaking rapidly now, Neal said to Ari, "Hey, I need to borrow Lacey for a minute. Be right back."

Before Ari could react, Neal dove into the bathroom himself right behind Lacey and slammed the door between the two rooms. As he locked it from his side, he yelled to Lacey.

"Get into my room quick—and lock the door to the hallway."

With some kind of instinct as sure as Neal's, Lacey moved swiftly, doing what she was told. As Neal came through the bathroom, he closed and locked the door leading into his room. Then he went to the window, the only one in his dorm room. It overlooked the yard between the dorm buildings.

As he unlocked it and threw it open, he yelled to Lacey.

"Come on. We're going out the window. You first!"

In that moment, a noise came from the bathroom that sounded like a bomb going off. Lacey reacted, but Neal didn't flinch.

"It's a ways down there," he continued. "We're on the second floor. You need to jump. Quick."

Lacey didn't hesitate for a moment. She grabbed the windowsill and leapt out, falling into the bushes down below.

Neal did the same, jumping out of the window just as he heard a second blast go off. He knew that sound. He had been hunting with his dad since he was a kid. It was a little distorted and exaggerated, but then he had never heard a rifle blowing through wooden doors inside a brick building like their dorm.

Suddenly he knew what had unsettled him from the moment he entered his suitemate's room.

Ari had a gun and he meant to kill someone tonight. With any luck, it wouldn't be him or Lacey. They'd just have to run for their lives.

WHAT'S NEXT?

A Grand Introduction

Ladies and gentlemen, I'd like to introduce to you Sophie Stafford, our congresswoman representing the Fifth District of our state.

While she is an attorney and former college professor, she is also a survivor of homicide. Lacey Lockhart, her roommate and best friend in college, was shot and killed in October 1999 by her ex-boyfriend on a college campus.

Since then, Representative Stafford had dedicated her life and career to that cause. Now in Congress, she has been a vigorous and vocal advocate for victims of violence against women. She believes that a full spectrum of services from victim to survivor to thriver should be available that not only provide safety and stability to victims, but also set survivors on a healing journey to reclaim their lives after abuse.

To that end, Representative Stafford has fought for services and protections for victims of domestic violence, sexual assault, child abuse, and human trafficking as well as gun safety, racial justice, and the right to privacy for all. A main focus of her work has been not only to increase services to victims of violence against women, but also to make a stronger commitment to connect and intersect programs for those who have harmed others with services for those who have been harmed. She believes that healing should be a priority in our nation, while recognizing and addressing how historic, institutional, and intergenerational trauma has affected all of our lives and curtailed our ability to move forward after such trauma.

Today Representative Stafford is going to address how the federal government could and should partner and collaborate more with local nonprofit organizations and programs like the one she formed and ran for many years, SISTER *Survivor Strong, Thriver Resilient.* These non-profit programs can provide valuable information and input to a number of federal programs including SNAP (formerly known as Food Stamps), assistance to the homeless, and WIC (Women, Infants, and Children). For example, many of those served by WIC, which offers nutrition, breastfeeding support, health education, and other services free of charge to pregnant women, mothers, infants, and children up to the age of five, are also likely to be clients of non-profit agencies across the country.

Representative Stafford sees that these issues intersect with services in the private sector for victims of violence against women, as those victims show up in disproportionately higher percentages as homeless, impoverished, and unable to adequately feed, educate, and prepare their children to have success in the future. A renewed effort to coordinate services and collaborate among providers means that there is a possibility that victimization, homelessness, and poverty may not be transmitted to the next generation of children today. But if we fail to adequately address the needs of these trauma victims, future generations will work at a disadvantage to catch up and live the promise of America.

Please give a warm welcome today to Representative Sophie Stafford, a champion for us all. Thank you so much for speaking to us today and sharing your inspiring story and amazing work.

Epilogue

It was the first Saturday in December, and Jenny was attending the holiday party SISTER was throwing for the women and their children in the Archangel Community of Sophie's *My Avenging Angel Workshops*™ program.

As a community volunteer, Jenny was having fun, although somehow she got relegated to working at the face-painting booth. She assumed it wasn't because of her artistic ability but more that Lisette and her astute staff recognized that she, as former governor, would be good at keeping order and directing people.

While there were many holiday facepainting images to pick from—snowflakes, holly, snowmen, and even a Santa face—by far the favorite seemed to be the fairy princess. This presented a problem, Jenny quickly discovered, because only one of the face painters could actually do that image. So Jenny quickly found a sign-up sheet sitting on the table, currently not being used, and made that her first order of business.

"Okay, everyone put their name on this sheet if you want to get your face painted," she announced. "It's only fair to wait your turn!"

There was some grumbling at first, but gradually and proficiently Jenny got order established, and the happy kids, one by one, got their faces painted. When things settled down, Jenny had a chance to look around at all the other activities going on for the kids and moms to enjoy at the party.

She was impressed. Lisette and her crew had this event very well organized and well thought through. Jenny remembered how Sophie, the founder of the program, explained at the first meeting of the Holiday Party Planning Committee that the holiday party had always been on the first Saturday of December for a reason.

In the early years of the parties, when the numbers were small, Sophie explained, "We'd go to someone's house and bring potluck items to share. As the group got larger, I'd rent a small hall and roast a large turkey with everyone bringing the trimmings for a feast. Then we moved the event into larger rooms at community centers and churches to accommodate not only the women, but also their kids, making it a time for everyone to enjoy. Next we added free chair massages, reiki energy sessions, and makeup lessons for women as well as arts and crafts and face-painting for both women and kids. Now a downtown hotel has donated ballroom space for the party, and we've raised enough funds to pay for a huge buffet lunch as well as have door prizes for the women and gifts for the kids. We even have a Santa who shows up in person to everyone's delight."

Sophie went on to add that as the Holiday Party got larger and more celebratory each year, it occurred to her, and now Lisette, that the party wasn't so much about celebrating the holidays together. It was more about getting these women and children ready for the holidays, a tough time of the year for all of them.

Jenny knew that these families didn't look like the ones in the usual preholiday advertising in which a "perfect" family celebrates the season in style. These families were more likely to have been torn apart by domestic violence, sexual assault, child abuse, and past trauma histories. Money wasn't plentiful, so the kids couldn't expect an abundance of gifts, sumptuous meals, or fun activities. Moreover, memories of past violence and family disruption, even at the holidays, weren't easy to forget.

But being here, Jenny could see that the party made the women and their kids feel special, loved, and surrounded with happiness. They were pampered and celebrated on a Saturday afternoon, experiencing the holiday spirit as "thrivers," not just survivors of all that had ever happened to them. Jenny could see today that this thriver spirit was infused in the way the whole party was organized and coordinated. Lisette herself was a natural at this. She seemed to know the moms and kids really well, knew what they were good at, and knew how to encourage them to really enjoy themselves and not hold back. Jenny was impressed.

Jenny's thoughts were interrupted by a voice that greeted her. She looked up to see Howie, Lacey's father. She grasped his outstretched hand and patted it lightly.

"How are you doing, Mr. Lockhart?"

"Oh, please! Call me Howie. We've shared so much over the years with Lisette and Sophie. We can be less formal. You're not governor anymore, or should I call you Judge?"

Jenny smiled. "I've answered to a lot of titles over the years." Then she laughed. "Call me Jenny. Here at the fairy princess face-painting booth, I'm just Jenny."

Howie laughed. "Yes, there are a lot of fairy princesses here today. How's your husband, Brad, doing? We had a great time planning Lisette and Erick's wedding a few years ago. I feel like we bonded for life."

Jenny giggled. "Yes, you both were the nervous fathers of the bride walking her down the aisle. It was so sweet and wonderful that both of you could do that for her."

"Oh no. Lisette insisted on it. She asked me to walk her down the aisle, and Brad was gracious enough to let me share that honor with him. It was very special for me!"

Howie's voice shook with emotion for a moment, and Jenny could imagine him thinking he'd never walk his own daughter,

Lacey, down the aisle. She let him take a breath and then added, "It was such a happy day for all of us."

"Yes. Erick is such a great guy. So perfect for Lisette. It's so amazing to see them with their kids too. Particularly Erick. He's such a natural with them, isn't he?"

By then, they had both turned to look at Erick across the room in the kids' arts and crafts area with Sasha and Jeremy, managing both of them with ease.

"In my day, you'd never see a father so engaged day-to-day in taking care of his kids," Howie said with a tightness in his voice. "That was 'women's work.' We men were the providers." Then he added with a sigh, "I wish I would've had more time with my kids when they were growing up."

Noticing the regret in Howie's voice, Jenny changed the subject. "I heard Erick is doing a program for young boys—marital arts, gym work, and communication skills. You're going to be a part of that, right?"

"Yes," Howie responded enthusiastically. "It's something new, something experimental, but I wish I'd had that training when I was growing up. Would've made a difference in my life."

Jenny watched Howie's face twitch again, perhaps feeling more regret for the mistakes in his life. Changing the subject again, she went on. "I also heard you're the top fundraiser for this party. You even got the lunch donated by the hotel. We have a lot to thank you for."

"I guess so," he said modestly. "I was a salesman for many years. Now that I'm retired, I can't turn it off, and this program sells itself. Everyone I talked to knew about SISTER and what it is doing for these women, their kids, and now for men and boys." Then he smiled broadly. "Volunteering with SISTER is my focus now in retirement. Lisette and I are talking in the new year about what I can do next."

"If you ask me, keep up your work in the legislature. I've heard you're a formidable foe for the gun nuts there and a strong advocate for more services for victims. Good job, Howie!"

"Like I said, I'm a salesman at heart, and those lawmakers need to hear the real-life consequences of gun violence, domestic violence, and the impact on families. We need changes, some things that could have saved Lacey or made other lives easier. I'm all for that." Then he paused, shaking his head, "Still need to get a ban on assault weapons—or at least no sales to kids under twenty-one, if not twenty-five. We tried after the mall shooting by that twenty-year-old, but it didn't happen. However, we'll keep at it."

Just then, Jenny saw someone coming toward her across the room at top speed. "Hold on a second, Howie. I need to deal with this."

Howie must have seen the man approaching, too, and for a moment, he reacted as though Jenny were in danger.

"No, that's my security guy," she said quickly. "Brad and I still have hired protection even though I'm no longer governor. It's more for Brad's business. People are upset about the shooting at the mall where his company was working. Some blame him."

"Yeah," Howie said. "I'm surprised Brad's not here today."

"He wasn't feeling well. Just a bad cold, I think. Maybe the flu." By then, Jenny was walking toward the security guy, but she turned back to add, "Nice talking to you, Howie. Can you watch the face-painting booth while I see what this is about?"

It wasn't until she got to the hospital that afternoon that Jenny texted Lisette. She tried to call first, but neither Lisette nor Erick were picking up.

Jenny's text read, "I'm at the hospital. Brad has gotten worse.

Docs don't know. Concerned he was just in Wuhan, China. Some strange illness there?"

A second text came right after that one.

"Sending my security guy back to pick you up. Meet him out front of hotel."

Then one final text. "Come see your dad. Come right now, Lisette. He needs you!"

THE END

DISCUSSION QUESTIONS
A Reader's Guide
For Individuals and Groups

◇ ◇ ◇

The Best Revenge Series™ is a trilogy of novels about the two young women, Lacey and Lisette, who are on a healing journey from victim to survivor to "thriver." In the first book, *Awaken,* when Lacey is killed by her ex-boyfriend and trapped inside the body of Lisette, the two women work together so Lacey can cross over and be at peace. In the second book, *Emerge,* Lisette joins with Sophie, Lacey's best friend, to have something good come out of Lacey's death, including Lisette finding and connecting with her real father, to give her unconditional love and support. This third book, *Thrive,* completes the series and explores how the power of Lacey's legacy helps all who love her to find a life of purpose, a way to forgive, and a path to move forward and thrive.

All three of these books are available in print, e-book, and audio.

1. In what ways has Lisette worked to heal herself and move forward with her life? How did going to Sophie's workshop help Lisette on this journey?

2. What did you learn about the healing process in this book that was most helpful to you? Can you see your life in the stages of victim to survivor to thriver?

3. How do you rate Lisette as a mother? Do you see her overcoming her own childhood and becoming a great mom? Who is a good role model as a mom for Lisette in this book – Marie, her own mother, Radiance who raised Sophie or Jenny? Why?

4. What couples in this story (e.g. Brad and Jenny, Erick and Lisette) show signs of having a healthy, non-abusive

relationship? What issues have they had to work through and resolve in this book? How did they do that?

5.   Has anything ever happened to you in a relationship that might be described as unhealthy or abusive? How did you deal with it? (See Warnings Signs of Abuse and Resources later in this book to get help if you need them.)

6.   What advice would you give Sophie and Lisette as they continue to take on issues of violence against women and the healing process? Who are their friends, allies?

7.   How does the work of Sophie and Lisette on violence against women give Lacey a lasting legacy? What can a community do to prevent dating violence and domestic violence?

8.   How have the political aspirations of women changed in recent years? How would Jenny have fared if she ran for President or Vice-President of the United States?

9.   Who was your favorite character in this and previous novels in the trilogy? Why?

10. Which character would you have liked to have had a different ending in this story?

WARNING SIGNS OF AN UNHEALTHY, ABUSIVE RELATIONSHIP

He is controlling, possessive and overly demanding of her time and attention. He appears at times to be two different people: one, charming, loving, and kind; the other, abusive, vicious, and mean. He has what is called a "Dr. Jekyll and Mr. Hyde" dual personality. He keeps her on edge, not knowing who he'll be at any moment. He manipulates what she feels for him and makes her feel bad about herself.

He will at times be sorry for what he has said and done and will promise never to do it again, but he will also deny, minimize, or blame others for his behavior. She will feel it is her fault, that if only she had done something else, pleased him more, been more compliant, she would not be treated this way by him.

EMOTIONAL

- He insults her, calls her names, and belittles her in private and in public with her family and friends.
- He isolates her from family and friends, forbidding her to see them or limiting her access to them.
- He is jealous of her contact with others, particularly with other men. He exaggerates her relationships with other men, accusing her unfairly of having affairs outside of their relationship.
- He wants to know where she is at all times, calling or texting her to find out who she is with. He invades her privacy by checking her cell phone, viewing her email, or monitoring her Web pages.
- He refuses to accept when she ends the relationship and may stalk her long afterward.

PHYSICAL
- He yells, screams, and loses his temper easily, sometimes disproportionately over unimportant things.
- He destroys her things, kicks or breaks other property, making her fear that he could hurt her, too.
- He intimidates her, making her afraid of him by his looks, actions, and gestures.
- He grabs her, kicks her, slaps her, punches her, strangles her, draws a gun or weapon, and threatens to kill her. He harms her pets or threatens to hurt or harm her family or friends.
- He stalks her with unwanted phone calls, visits to her house or job, and secretly monitors her actions.

ECONOMIC
- He controls her access to money, even her own money or money she has earned herself.
- He refuses to pay bills or let her know about family income, investments, or property.
- He keeps her from getting or keeping a job, and he refuses to support their family or children.
- He makes all the big decisions, using male privilege to get his way and insisting on rigid gender roles.

PSYCHOLOGICAL
- She feels like she is going crazy, that his view of the world is not reasonable, but she will have little chance of convincing him otherwise, and he demands her absolute loyalty to his way of thinking.
- He says he can't live without her or will kill himself if she leaves, so she fears ending the relationship.
- He pushes the relationship too far, too fast, and is obsessed with her and wants her for himself.

- He has unrealistic expectations and demands, and she feels it is her fault he's not happy.

SEXUAL
- He demands to have sex forcibly without her consent with him or with others.
- He withdraws sex from her or makes it conditional on her compliance to his demands.
- He calls her crude names, implying she is promiscuous and unfaithful sexually to him.

Signs of a Healthy Relationship

In a healthy relationship, two people are on an equal footing, and they respect, trust, and support each other. They are honest with each other and take responsibility for their actions. They are good parents, sharing responsibility in raising their kids. They have an economic partnership in which the best interests of both are considered, and they communicate, negotiate, and treat each other fairly.

Reprinted from

Entering the Thriver Zone: A Seven-Step Guide to Thriving After Abuse

by Susan M. Omilian, JD

For more information on Susan and her work, visit *ThriverZone.com.*

RESOURCES

Crisis Intervention

For immediate crisis intervention services in your local community, contact:

- The National Domestic Violence Hotline 1-800-799-SAFE (7233) **www.thehotline.org**

- National Sexual Assault Hotline at 1-800-656-HOPE (4673) **www.rainn.org**

- National Center for Victims of Crime **www.victimsofcrime.org/help-for-crime-victims**

- Office for Victims of Crime, U.S. Department of Justice. **www.ovc.gov**

Dating Violence and Stalking

- Break the Cycle: Empowering Youth To End Dating Violence **www.breakthecycle.org**

- Love Is Respect—National Teen Dating Abuse Help Line 1-866-331-9474 **www.loveisrespect.org**

- End Stalking in America **www.esia.net** provides information and assistance to potential victims and those currently being harassed, including a list of state laws against stalking.

- Women's Law.org **www.womenslaw.org** is a project of the National Network to End Domestic Violence, providing legal information and support to victims of domestic violence, stalking and sexual assault.

Domestic Violence

- National Network to End Domestic Violence (NNEDV)

> www.nnedv.org offers support to victims of domestic violence who are escaping abusive relationships and empowers survivors to build new lives.

- National Coalition Against Domestic Violence (NCADV) **www.ncadv.org** works closely with battered women's advocates around the country to identify the issues and develop a legislative agenda.

- **www.domesticshelters.org** Free, online, searchable database of domestic violence shelter programs nationally.

- National Resource Center on Domestic Violence (NRCDV) **www.nrcdv.org** is a source of information for those wanting to educate themselves and help others on the many issues related to domestic violence.

Sexual Assault

- RAINN—Rape Abuse & Incest National Network **www.rainn.org** operates the National Sexual Assault Hotline and has programs to prevent sexual assault, help Victims, and ensure they receive justice.

- National Sexual Violence Resource Center **www.nsvrc.org** provides leadership in preventing and responding to sexual violence through creating resources and promoting research.

- The Victim Rights Law Center **www.victimrights.org** is dedicated solely to serving the legal needs of sexual assault victims. It provides training, technical assistance, and in some cases, free legal assistance in civil cases to sexual assault victims in certain parts of the country.

Child Abuse

- Childhelp USA National Child Abuse **www.childhelp.org** directly serves abused and neglected children through the National Child Abuse Hotline, 1-800-4-A-CHILD® and other programs.

Post-Traumatic Stress

See information listed at National Institute of Mental Health website, **www.nimh.nih.gov**.

BOOKS BY SUSAN M. OMILIAN, JD

THE THRIVER ZONE SERIES™

Entering the Thriver Zone

A Seven-Step Guide to Thriving After Abuse

Staying in the Thriver Zone

A Road Map to Manifest a Life of Power and Purpose

Living in the Thriver Zone

A Celebration of Living Well as the Best Revenge

THE BEST REVENGE SERIES™

Awaken

The Awakening of the Human Spirit on a Healing Journey

Emerge

The Opening of the Human Heart to the Power of Love

Thrive

The Journey of the Human Soul to Discover a Life of Purpose

To purchase autographed copies of Susan's Books visit www.ThriverZone.com/books.

ABOUT THE AUTHOR

An attorney, author, and motivational speaker, Susan Omilian has worked extensively as an advocate to end violence against women for the past four decades. In the 1970s, she founded a rape crisis center and represented battered women in divorce proceedings in the early 1980s. She also litigated sex discrimination cases including helping to articulate the legal concept that made sexual harassment illegal in the 1990s.

Since her nineteen-year-old niece Maggie was shot and killed by her ex-boyfriend in 1999, Susan has worked extensively with hundreds of women who have experienced abuse helping them take the journey from victim to survivor to "thriver."

A recognized national expert on the process of recovery after violence and abuse, Susan is the author of two book series, *The Thriver Zone* and *The Best Revenge*.

For more about Susan, her books and further resources, visit thriverzone.com.

www.ingramcontent.com/pod-product-compliance
Lightning Source LLC
Chambersburg PA
CBHW061032120726
47910CB00006B/2205